VIRGINIA WOOLF

A Centenary Perspective

MACMILLAN STUDIES IN TWENTIETH-CENTURY LITERATURE

Further titles in preparation

Also by Eric Warner

VIRGINIA WOOLF

A Centenary Perspective

Edited by
Eric Warner

MACMILLAN

Introduction and editorial matter © Eric D. Warner 1984
Foreword © Quentin Bell 1984
Chapter 1 © Hermione Lee 1984
Chapter 2 © Allen McLaurin 1984
Chapter 3 © Ian Gregor 1984
Chapter 4 © Lyndall Gordon 1984
Chapter 5 © John Bayley 1984
Chapter 6 © T. E. Apter 1984
Chapter 7 © Gillian Beer 1984
Text of panel discussions © the individual contributors 1984

First published 1984
Reprinted 1985

Published by
THE MACMILLAN PRESS LTD
London and Basingstoke
Companies and representatives
throughout the world

ISBN 0-333-35316-1

Printed in Great Britain by
Antony Rowe Ltd
Chippenham, Wiltshire

Contents

Acknowledgements

The co-operation of many people made the Virginia Woolf Centenary Conference possible. The first and largest debt is the easiest to state: without the Master and Fellows of Fitzwilliam College the event would not have taken place. Their sympathy with the project in its early stages was heartening to the organiser; but their logistical, financial and moral support at subsequent points was crucial to the Conference, and the success of the occasion owes everything to them. In particular, I would like to express my gratitude to the Master, Professor J. C. Holt, the Bursar, Dr David E. Bowyer, the Steward, Dr John R. A. Cleaver, and my colleague in English, Miss Rivkah Zim, for the time and effort they gave in the early moments of planning the event.

I must likewise thank all the speakers and panellists who agreed to participate in the Conference. Their willingness to come at short notice and with scant reward indicates an affection for the subject which goes beyond professional obligation. As this volume testifies, the enthusiasm of these men and women effectively gave the celebration of Virginia Woolf's centenary in her own country the shape and substance it has, and for this contribution I am grateful. Here too, I must extend my thanks to Quentin and Olivier Bell, who agreed to come as special guests of the Conference, and who presided over an affair which must be regarded as an outcome of their own labours with characteristic grace and charm.

There is a substantial debt to the Conference Secretary, Mrs Sheila Green, which must be recorded. She helped at every stage to co-ordinate the administrative work of the event and her calm composure often proved the necessary antidote to my frazzled haste. The Conference benefited accordingly from her efforts.

I must similarly thank my two Conference Assistants, Ms Caroline Murphy and Ms Joan Scanlon, who coped with the actual running of the Conference with an undemonstrative efficiency and aplomb. Throughout the two and a half days of the Conference, they provided reassuring support for an anxious organiser's nerves.

I should also like to express my thanks to the Catering Manager, Mr Howe, and the College Chef, Mr Stosieck, for their superb work in arranging the menus for the Conference. The College Butler, Mrs Audrey Cann, and her staff saw to the dining arrangements with a thorough and unruffled competence that Virginia Woolf herself might have predicted from the first woman butler in Cambridge, and to them as well thanks are due.

I am also extremely grateful to John Mantle, feature producer of 'The Arts Round-Up', and to Tim Lloyd, Engineer-in-charge of BBC Radio Cambridgeshire, for their considerable help in taping the panel discussions, and for featuring the Conference on the air.

Finally, I offer my thanks to my wife, Ann, who planted the seed of suggestion for this Conference in the first place, and who then gave it all the support and encouragement in her power to see it come to fruition.

Fitzwilliam College
Cambridge   E. W.

I am grateful to the following for permission to reproduce copyright material: Quentin Bell, the Author's Literary Estate, the Hogarth Press and Harcourt Brace Jovanovich for the extracts from 'A Sketch of the Past' in *Moments of Being* by Virginia Woolf, edited by Jeanne Schulkind; Martin Secker & Warburg and Harcourt Brace Jovanovich for the extract from *If on a Winter's Night a Traveller* by Italo Calvino.

Notes on the Contributors

T. E. Apter is the author of three novels as well as critical studies of Virginia Woolf and Thomas Mann. Her most recent book is a study of fantasy literature. She is currently living and working in Washington DC.

John Bayley is Warton Professor of English Literature at St Catherine's College, Oxford. His numerous critical works include studies of Pushkin, Tolstoy, Shakespeare and Hardy. He is currently working on Henry James.

Gillian Beer is a University Lecturer in English and Fellow of Girton College, Cambridge. She has published widely on nineteenth- and twentieth-century fiction. Her latest book is on topics related to her contributions here, and is entitled *Darwin's Plots: Evolutionary Narrative in Darwin, George Eliot and 19th Century Fiction* (1983).

Bernard Bergonzi has been Professor of English at Warwick University since 1971. He is the author of several books on modern literature, including *The Situation of the Novel* (1970) and *Reading the Thirties* (1981). He has also published a novel, *The Roman Persuasion* (1981).

Elaine Feinstein has written several novels, of which the last was *The Survivors* (1982). She has also published many volumes of poetry, including *Some Unease and Angels* (1982), and has translated Marina Tsvetayeva's poems. An extended second edition of these translations appeared in 1981.

Lyndall Gordon was born in South Africa and studied at Columbia University. She is currently a Senior Research Fellow at Jesus College, Oxford. Her biography, *Eliot's Early Years* (1977),

won the Rose Mary Crawshay Prize in 1978. She is now writing a
critical biography of Virginia Woolf.

Ian Gregor has been Professor of Modern English Literature at the
University of Kent since 1969. A prolific writer on nineteenth- and
twentieth-century fiction, his publications include (with Mark
Kinkead-Weekes) *William Golding: A Critical Study* (1967) and *The
Great Web: A Study of Hardy's Novels* (1973). He is at present working
on a critical study of Virginia Woolf's novels.

John Harvey is a University Lecturer in English and Fellow of
Emmanuel College, Cambridge. His critical writings include a
study of Victorian novelists and their illustrators. His novel, *The
Plate Shop* (1979), was awarded the David Higham Prize for fiction.
He has recently completed a second novel on Greek politics.

Frank Kermode was, until 1982, King Edward VIIth Professor of
English Literature at the University of Cambridge. His numerous
critical works include *Romantic Image* (1957), *The Sense of an Ending*
(1967) and *The Genesis of Secrecy* (1979).

Hermione Lee is a Lecturer in English at York University. In
addition to reviewing fiction regularly for The *Observer* and *The
Times Literary Supplement*, her critical studies include *The Novels of
Virginia Woolf* (1977), *Elizabeth Bowen: An Estimation* (1981) and
Philip Roth (1982). Her most recent work is a selection from the
writings of Stevie Smith.

Allen McLaurin has taught at universities in England and Japan,
and is currently Senior Lecturer at Humberside College of Higher
Education. He has published extensively on modern literature, and
edited (with R. Majumdar) the *Critical Heritage* volume on
Virginia Woolf. He is presently working on a study of some themes
in the history of ideas touched on in the essay included here.

Iris Murdoch, formerly lecturer in Philosophy at St Anne's
College, Oxford, has published critical studies of Sartre and Plato. In
1982 she delivered the Gifford Lectures in Edinburgh on *The Idea of
the Good*. One of the most distinguished and prolific novelists in
England today, her most recent novel is *The Philosopher's Pupil*
(1983).

Eric Warner is a Lecturer in English at Fitzwilliam College, Cambridge. He is the editor, with Graham Hough, of *Strangeness and Beauty* (1983), a two-volume anthology of nineteenth century aesthetic criticism. He is currently preparing a study of Virginia Woolf's romanticism for publication.

Foreword

There were reports from Belgrade, lecture theatres were packed to capacity with Jugoslav admirers of Virginia Woolf. I myself can bear witness to the enthusiasm in Rome, Venice, Florence, Bologna and Paris, and I was told of a surge of interest amongst the younger writers in Peking. As for the excitement in North America, one must attempt to imagine it as best one may.

The Times (of London), its supplement, the media of the air and the vast majority of the other voices of opinion were silent. The Virginia Woolf Centenary was a non-event in Great Britain; if in other lands it had been noticed, here it should be disregarded – or so it seemed. Whether our masters, the people who I suppose organise public commemorations, were simply forgetful or ignorant, or had some policy one cannot tell; but they might certainly claim that their inactivities were sanctioned by public acquiescence. It seemed the whole business would pass off without a word said.

Then there came a summons – no, 'summons' is too harsh a term with which to describe the kindly, sensible, well-reasoned letter addressed to my wife and myself from Fitzwilliam College. The writer wondered why nothing was happening and, since nothing had happened, he wondered further whether he should not make it happen. In short, he himself was organising a Virginia Woolf Centenary Conference and he hoped that we would attend. He was, obviously, an engaging, an intelligent, indeed an irresistible young man. It should be added, for this makes the comedy of the situation complete, that he hailed in fact from Vermont. If it had been left to the public spirit and activity of our countrymen and women, there would, I suppose, have been no centenary celebration in Virginia's native land.

Still, when once the idea had been put into our slow heads we responded very nicely. The Conference became a very splendid and impressive reality. I can say this because my own contribution consisted almost entirely in eating, drinking and listening. On the gastronomic side there was a memorable *Boeuf en Daube*. The spiritual refreshment consisted of some very brilliant interventions by some very distinguished people; of these I need say nothing for they lie before you in these pages.

All that I can do is to thank Dr Eric Warner for having startled a dozing nation from its slumbers, for having worked incredibly hard with very little time at his disposal, and for having invited us to the fine entertainment of which this book is the record.

QUENTIN BELL

Introduction

Eric Warner

This volume presents the proceedings of the Virginia Woolf Centenary Conference which took place on 20-22 September 1982 at Fitzwilliam College, Cambridge. Perhaps it is worth saying at the outset how this event came about. For a long while Virginia Woolf's centenary threatened to pass without notice in England; as far as I am aware, no formal public ceremony took place on the centenary day itself (25 January 1982) and the advancing year brought no sign of any organised memorial. This absence was puzzling, and in marked contrast to the many centenary observances abroad. Whatever the reasons for this peculiar state of affairs, it was consequently late in the year when I began to think of rectifying the situation – less out of an exaggerated notion of my own competence than a simple desire to see justice done. The disadvantages of my undertaking such a project were too numerous and considerable to dwell upon; but there were two recommendations for the idea. The first of these was Cambridge itself. E. M. Forster had long since recognised that, for all her reservations, this was the university closest to her heart, and it would be uniquely appropriate to hold her centenary here.[1] Secondly, it seemed to me that my own College, Fitzwilliam, would also be fitting to house such an event, as its striking modern architecture would be in harmony with the spirit of much of her work. Fortunately, I speedily received support from both quarters. Mrs Gillian Beer, doyenne of Woolf studies at Cambridge, instantly and eagerly agreed to help with the project, and the Master and Fellows of Fitzwilliam readily consented to have the College host the occasion.

With the fragile conception thus far secure, I set about collecting a suitable group of invited speakers. I anticipated a great deal of difficulty with this stage. It was already late in the year and calendars were doubtless filling up; moreover, I had little means of offering the honorariums and related expenses which usually attract distinguished speakers to such occasions. Here, however, I was to be surprised. Those persons whom I contacted were as puzzled about the absence of a proper centenary as I was, and their desire to help honour Virginia Woolf came with a spontaneous and heartening generosity. In a short time I had a full programme, and with the acceptance of Professor and Mrs Quentin Bell to come as special guests of the Conference, the event was firmly launched. There followed a gratifying, steady response from the public, dispelling in its obvious display of affection for Virginia Woolf any lingering suspicion of indifference. A centenary celebration in Britain thus passed swiftly from a prospect to a reality.

How would Virginia Woolf have greeted her centenary? The question is an unavoidable temptation to anyone who has studied her, since she herself was given to constant speculation about how things would appear to her ten or twenty years hence, and particularly to how her own work would be regarded and received. About the latter point, at least, she would have been reassured: all of Virginia Woolf's novels are available in paperback, as are most of her essays, and she is in great demand in bookshops and university classrooms throughout the world. (Lately, indeed, her books have begun to be made into films; nearly the contemporary form of canonisation.) In addition, her life has sparked a fascination that reaches well beyond the academy, so that her press has undertaken the immense task of publishing her complete letters and diaries in handsome, carefully-edited editions. She has even been the subject of a popular West End play, suggesting that on approaching one hundred Virginia Woolf has become, in every sense of the word, notorious. No doubt she wouldn't have been entirely happy about this; the irony has often been noted that, shy and reclusive with strangers herself, she is now renowned largely because of an intimate knowledge of her life. Still, one suspects that her dominant feeling today would have been one of pleasure, even relief. The one fact which emerges clearly a century after her birth is that Virginia Woolf is among the most highly regarded and appreciated of modern authors, something which no writer could help but find gratifying.

As to any particular celebrations in honour of her centenary, however, she might well have been puzzled as to what all the fuss was about. Throughout her work she displays a strain of plain good sense which adds ballast to the enchanting, extravagant flights of fantasy, and she might well have applied this to any notion of a specific centenary occasion. 'What is there to celebrate? My books are there; let people read them,' it is easy to imagine her saying. Most of the official organs of the media in Britain would have apparently agreed, since in instructive contrast to the widely publicised hurrah for James Joyce in this country, there was little mention of the fact that he shared a centenary with one of England's finest modern authors. Such neglect persisted through the occasion of the centenary celebrations recorded here. The BBC carried lavish productions, both on television and radio, in honour of the creator of *The Dubliners*, but was unable to give similar treatment to the writer of *Mrs Dalloway*.[2] *The Times* published a report on the Virginia Woolf centennial celebrations in New York, but could not find space for the one in Cambridge. *The TLS*, that venerable organ to which she contributed so much at its inception, failed to carry any notice of the event. While such official indifference may have been consoling to a certain sensible aspect in Mrs Woolf, it seems more likely, judging from her dampened spirits when her own books passed without notice, that it would have had the reverse effect.

No such response, at any rate, was apparent among the people who assembled in the mild autumn weather at Fitzwilliam. Here indeed I think Virginia Woolf would have felt at ease and content, for the most immediate and most prevalent emotion was simply one of celebration. Centenaries are complex affairs with strangely mixed motives; but perhaps the first and strongest impulse we feel is to mark the occasion of a great artist's birth as a way of honouring a presence which has given us great pleasure, or joy. The 120–odd people who attended the Conference were a diverse group, both culturally and professionally. Participants came from England, Japan, Canada, France, Germany, Holland, Australia, New Zealand and the United States; they were schoolteachers, university lecturers, housewives, husbands, librarians, musicians, gallery owners, and students. Yet they all had an interest in, or a love of, Virginia Woolf, and this common bond instantly made itself felt. Throughout the strenuous two and a half days of Conference activities, there was always perceptible this sense of fellowship and good spirits, even an air of exhilaration in the joint enterprise, as if 'looking together united them', to borrow a phrase, and 'they were all conscious of making a party together'. The brightness of this celebratory spirit was never greater, perhaps, than at dinner on the second night of the Conference, when the Fitzwilliam chef outdid himself in producing a superb version of *Boeuf en Daube*, followed by a veritably Woolfian 'moment' when Olivier and Quentin Bell rose to speak and expressed their own gratitude for the occasion which their own work had done so much to bring about.

Yet the honorific impulse, however essential, is only part of the occasion of a centenary. Equally present is the urge to take stock, to examine and measure the achievement, in an attempt to clarify it both for ourselves and our successors. This desire, indeed, may be said to have been the foundation of this Centenary Conference, since the seven papers and two panel discussions printed here were all initiated with the express purpose of attempting to see Virginia Woolf in a centenary perspective, exploring how she appears to us now. Here, it becomes impossible to ignore the fact that centenary celebrations have a way of rebounding on their organisers. Northrop Frye once remarked that such anniversaries call attention not only to our great figures, but to what we do with them;[3] as the focus of current perception is sharpened, so the critical blindnesses of the moment are more tellingly exposed. There is thus a constant danger of turning such an occasion into a celebration of our own partial perspective rather than of the subject's continuing presence. Nowhere is this danger more threatening than in the case of Virginia Woolf. Her current notoriety stems in part from her being used for all manner of partisan purposes, many of which would probably have alarmed and dismayed her, and which have only an adventitious connection with the profounder, more enduring part of her work.

This peril was, I think, largely avoided in the series of proceedings collected here. To begin with, the focus was firmly and steadily upon the subject – on the work of Virginia Woolf, particularly the novels wherein her permanent reputation is likely to rest. Secondly, despite this concurrence of focus, the papers printed here are all extremely diverse in both subject and treatment. While such a limited survey can in no sense be called comprehensive, the papers range over the entire corpus of Woolf's fiction, with a variety of opinion and approach, an eclecticism which evades any single or partisan perspective. The collective view of this Conference (if it can be called that) thus chimes with Woolf's famous observation that 'nothing was simply one thing', a point to which we will return. Lastly, I might note that all seven papers read at the Conference

were of a high standard – thoughtful, well-researched and impec-
cably presented. Each speaker took his or her task seriously and paid
Virginia Woolf the compliment of a searching regard, a careful
analysis. This combination of high seriousness and independence is
liable to make this centenary assessment a lasting and fruitful
contribution to the study of Virginia Woolf.

The Conference got off to a fine start with Hermione Lee, author of
an excellent book on Virginia Woolf, reading what many people
considered among the most stimulating papers of the two days.
With great thoroughness and care, taking examples from all areas of
Woolf's *oeuvre*, Ms Lee revealed how images of reflection and
'burning glass' become almost habitual in her writing, as she
struggled to represent consciousness at its most inspired moments.
Indeed, the paper itself became intensely illuminating as this
difficult ground was covered with dexterity and skill, to develop a
surprising linkage between Virginia Woolf and the Romantic poets
whom she read with such attention. A just placement of Woolf on
the curve from the Romantics to modernism was one of the paper's
most telling insights, which remained lighting the mind of many
who heard it.

A focus on represented patterns of consciousness was also the
subject of the following paper, though seen from quite a different
angle. Allen McLaurin plunged into the turbulent waters of the
stream of consciousness which has been part of the ongoing debate
about Virginia Woolf since her death. His subtle paper attempts to
throw some needed clarity on the topic, a clarity of exacting
discrimination between the phenomenon described and the method
employed in the fiction. Through this approach, Dr McLaurin is
able to highlight the tentative but steady thrust towards a group
mind, or collective consciousness, in Virginia Woolf's work. Here
too, the success of this paper owes much to an ability to relate his
thesis to important currents of thought prevalent in her own time.

Professor Ian Gregor's paper the following morning was another
stimulating performance. His concern with the description of
consciousness in Virginia Woolf's fiction took the form of focussing
upon procedures of reading, displayed as a process, in her work.
Concentrating on passages from *To the Lighthouse* which depict
various styles and strategies of reading, Professor Gregor elucidates
what Woolf, in her essay on Hardy, termed 'the margins of the

unexpressed' present in each case, which force us as readers to take part in the process and complete the meaning of her art. In a penetrating analysis of such passages, he brings out 'the shifting relationship with the reader, a relationship which eludes the traditional categories of subject and object', and describes the extraordinary mobility between event and feeling in her work. Following in the tradition of Erich Auerbach's great essay, this paper seems set to become a new classic in the study of Virginia Woolf's mixing and mediation of reader and writer.

In the panel discussion of the day before he read his paper, Professor Gregor pleaded for a fresh comparison between the two archetypal figures of modernism, Virginia Woolf and T. S. Eliot. In the paper succeeding his, he received that for which he had asked. Lyndall Gordon's sensitive study of Eliot's early years turned biographic resource to critical purpose with great resource and skill. She is presently engaged on a similar study of Virginia Woolf and the Conference was privileged indeed to hear a portion from that work in progress. The paper begins by sketching the points of contact between Woolf and Eliot in their shared conception of the few essential points or 'moments' in a writer's life which initiate, shape and develop the work. It was these that the literary biographer must search out, with tactful but persistent regard, learning to interpret those 'margins of the unexpressed', or as Dr Gordon puts it, the 'zone of silence' in the artist's work. With a detailed knowledge of both published and manuscript sources, and a sensitive grasp of Virginia Woolf's own conception of biography, Dr Gordon pursues this task, giving an account of Woolf's imaginative life that complements and extends the record of her actual existence. Many who heard this deeply suggestive paper will be waiting eagerly for the finished book.

It was a great personal pleasure to introduce the succeeding speaker, Professor John Bayley, who supervised the present writer's doctoral thesis on Virginia Woolf. I doubt, however, whether I or anyone else was quite prepared for the talk we heard him deliver. It was by any standard a superb performance – easily the most amusing and engagingly delivered at the Conference. Yet Professor Bayley's humour masked a remarkable, one might almost say subversive, intent, namely to make a claim for Virginia Woolf's first novel, *The Voyage Out*, as her greatest. This book is often regarded as apprentice work by Woolf scholars, as indeed it came to be by the author herself. But it is precisely this quality which draws John

Bayley to the work, as here Woolf most fully and painfully engages the great tradition of fiction which she knew so well. He goes on to point out how certain elements in her late work revert back to the school of Naturalism. The argument remains an excentric one, which perhaps few devoted readers of Woolf's works will share. Yet Professor Bayley's lively intelligence is well known for overturning conventional viewpoints and valuations, and the case presented here is easier to dissent from than dismiss. Perhaps this fetching diversion from the main road may yet come to have its impact on Virginia Woolf studies.

The second day of the Conference was brought to a close by two deeply considered and distinguished papers. The first of these, read by T. E. Apter, was a probing inquiry into the various psychological strategies employed by Virginia Woolf's characters. Drawing examples from a wide range of Woolf's fiction, Ms Apter dwelt upon 'the paradoxes and conflicts surrounding the secrecy of self-knowledge, and the necessity of a shared identity'. She begins by illustrating the contraction of the ego in vanity, as a form of protection and self-defence, in some of Woolf's main characters, notably Jacob in *Jacob's Room*. Following this, Ms Apter reveals the corresponding movement of expansion, moving out of the prison of isolated selfhood into the deeper satisfactions of friendship. Here the examples are drawn principally from *The Waves*, that most challenging of Virginia Woolf's works where these issues are most fully explored. In contrast to Bernard's effort to describe 'the world seen without a self', Ms Apter's paper provides a rigorous analysis of versions of the world seen through the self, thus mapping out Virginia Woolf's deep, persistent interest in the process of self-realisation.

Finally, Gillian Beer's paper, read with great exuberance and panache, brought the formal proceedings of the Conference to an inspired close. She was concerned with Woolf's fascination with pre-history, seen as an attempt to mediate the influence of that seminal figure in the history of ideas, Charles Darwin. In a lucid analysis, Mrs Beer demonstrated how ideas of transformation and development as set forth by Darwin were engaged by Virginia Woolf at a very deep level, connecting crucially with her struggles to escape, or rather, transform, her Victorian past in both personal and literary senses. Carrying her erudition lightly, moving deftly through the language and concepts of contemporary critical theory, Mrs Beer shows how the weight and resonance of this heritage is most crucially present in Virginia Woolf's last novel, *Between the Acts*. The reading Mrs Beer provides of that novel, Virginia Woolf's deepest meditation on the process and meaning of history, will surely change how it is read and regarded in the future.

The seven formal papers of the Conference were punctuated by two very different exercises. These were the two panel discussions, in which four main speakers discussed a variety of topics before confronting the audience directly; a more open forum which sought to mingle the views of specialist scholars, creative writers and common readers. The first of these, on the Monday afternoon, was under the able chairmanship of Gillian Beer; steering the discussion expertly, she managed to introduce many of the points which would be dealt with at greater length in her paper the following day. The rest of the panel, interestingly enough, consisted of three practising novelists, Iris Murdoch, Bernard Bergonzi and John Harvey, who proved extremely reluctant to discuss their own creative work in relation to Virginia Woolf. Instead, discussion centred on such topics as Woolf's feminism, her relation to modernism generally, and her attitude towards history. Bernard Bergonzi sparked off considerable discussion on this last point by questioning her openness to the facts of her time, particularly the First World War – though the thrust of his remark was to observe her increasing engagement with political facts culminating in *Between the Acts*. On a different tack, John Harvey admired her ability to re-interpret family experience in *To the Lighthouse*. He too initiated considerable discussion when, in commenting on Woolf's 'negotiation' of the daimon of her father in Mr Ramsay, he criticised the handling of Mrs Ramsay in the book. This was a point on which Iris Murdoch was in agreement, but which many of the audience were not. Though in the following panel discussion Frank Kermode was to question the lasting influence of a feminist viewpoint on Virginia Woolf's stature, many of the women at the Conference clearly felt that Woolf had something particular to say to them – and they said so. Iris Murdoch, however, remained sceptical about any excessive insistence upon a distinctive feminine consciousness; rather, she focussed on the matters of art and invention which Woolf's writing always throws into prominence, and dwelt upon its relation to reality, or truth. A question from the floor highlighting Virginia Woolf's crucial use of the term 'reality' drew the discussion on to the issues of mysticism and humour, on which point the discussion, which can only be reproduced in part here, came to a close.

The second such discussion, chaired by the present writer, consisted of Hermione Lee, Frank Kermode and Elaine Feinstein. Here, a more concerted and deliberate attempt was made to examine the question of a centenary perspective, by focussing on the questions of her literary influence and what a canon of her works might contain. Hermione Lee inaugurated this discussion with a phenomenally informed account of the women's novel in England since the death of Virginia Woolf. She observed that there was no very detectable *stylistic* influence in the manner of Joyce, but that there were other definite, sometimes surprising areas in which Woolf's impact has been felt. Professor Kermode concurred that Virginia Woolf had had little literary influence, but argued that this paradoxically raised her stature, since she reached peaks of achievement, particularly in her last novel, which few writers since her day had the capacity to detect, let alone emulate. This prompted a speculation on my own part as to whether, in that case, it was not richer to see Virginia Woolf as the culmination of a tradition which passed to her from Henry James rather than as an originator of 'modernism'. Opinions about this were varied in the lively discussion which ensued. Elaine Feinstein then traced her own shifting attitudes and responses to Virginia Woolf's work, in such a way as largely to agree with the point about the lack of a literary influence. Such agreement, however, brought a vigorous protest from Roger Poole of Nottingham University, who politely but eloquently made a critique of this trend, and by extension, of the Conference as a whole. His phenomenological view of Woolf as 'a precious resource' of subjectivity in the face of current critical and cultural trends toward the dissolution of the subject brought a warm response from the audience, and injected a new note into the discussion which carried on in the spirited debate which followed.

This represents all the proceedings of the Conference which can be published here. No account of the occasion could be complete, however, without some mention of the single activity of the third day, an exhibition of material from the archives of King's College Library. Arranged and presented by Dr Michael Halls, the Modern Archivist of King's College, this exhibition consisted of a number of hitherto unpublished letters from Virginia Woolf to Julian Bell, the typescript of one of her short stories, 'Nurse Lugton's curtain', and a long letter from Woolf to Roger Fry written in October 1921, which has been published. Also exhibited were documents from related members of the Bloomsbury Group, including the manuscript of a lecture by Roger Fry, entitled 'Aestheticism and Symbolism', and the autographed manuscript of E. M. Forster's 'Bloomsbury Memoir'. Finally, an intriguing item on display was Jane Austen's copy of *Orlando Furioso*, presented by Virginia Woolf to Maynard Keynes for Christmas of 1936. Many of the participants felt they had derived considerable profit from this exhibition, as well as from Dr Halls' expertise and engaging manner. The relaxed, slow-paced morning was in marked contrast to the programme of the previous two days, and brought the Virginia Woolf Centenary Conference to a gentle conclusion.

' "Now to sum up," said Bernard.' This was always recognised as a difficult undertaking, and here it is one which brings us back to the question of what was achieved in this Conference. Is there, in the end, a 'Centenary Perspective'? It is not an easy question to answer. The Conference was not encyclopedic or exhaustive – it was not meant to be, given the constraints of time and opportunity. Nor was there any effort to conduct an elaborate investigation in the history of taste with respect to Virginia Woolf, a task which may be safely left to the *Critical Heritage* volume.[4] Rather, the attempt was through a number of individual voices and views to observe how the subject is seen today. 'So much depends upon distance: whether people are near us or far from us.' Virginia Woolf's shrewd analysis of the problem of perspective is perhaps apposite. Each of the speakers here took up a different emotional and critical position in relation to their subject, as indeed did those others who attended the Conference. Perhaps all felt that their relation had been changed as a result of the experience. In any case, what emerges most clearly is that, as we have already observed, Virginia Woolf herself is not 'simply one thing', but a manifold presence, that there is or can be no single view of her work. Paradoxically, this is a measure of her success, since only those figures who continue to give rise to new impulses and interpretations, new possibilities and prospects, become most firmly fixed in the canon. Perhaps, after all, this note of refreshment and renewal is the best legacy a centenary event could leave; after a century, Virginia Woolf is still capable of giving rise to quite different responses and satisfactions. Of the Virginia Woolf Centenary Conference itself, what is left both in this volume and more intensely in the minds of those who participated, is merely the fact that a writer who is warmly admired was remembered, writing which is cherished was honoured. Like one of her own 'moments of being', Mrs Ramsay's party or Lily's exhausted vision,

Jacob's mysteriously absent presence or Bernard's final soliloquy, what remains is the remaining. Virginia Woolf, one hopes, would have understood this as a fitting tribute.

Notes

1. E.M. Forster, *Virginia Woolf*, The Rede Lecture (Cambridge University Press, 1942)
2. I must here make a mention of the fact that BBC Radio Cambridgeshire did carry a brief report on the Conference in its 'Arts Round Up' programme, for which I am very grateful.
3. Northrop Frye, 'Blake After Two Centuries', *English Romantic Poets: Modern Essays in Criticism*, ed. M. H. Abrams (New York: Oxford University Press, 1960) p. 55.
4. Cf. *Virginia Woolf: The Critical Heritage*, eds Robin Majumdar and Allen McLaurin (London: Routledge & Kegan Paul, 1975).

1 A Burning Glass: Reflection in Virginia Woolf

Hermione Lee

I

... and so I was taken in cab with George and Nessa to meet
Thoby at Paddington. It was sunset, and the great glass dome at
the end of the station was blazing with light. It was glowing
yellow and red and the iron girders made a pattern across it. I
walked along the platform gazing with rapture at this magnificent blaze of colour, and the train slowly steamed into the
station. It impressed and exalted me. It was so vast and so fiery
red. The contrast of that blaze of magnificent light with the
shrouded and curtained rooms at Hyde Park Gate was so intense.
Also it was partly that my mother's death unveiled and
intensified; made me suddenly develop perceptions, as if a
burning glass had been laid over what was shaded and dormant.
Of course this quickening was spasmodic. But it was surprising –
as if something were becoming visible without any effort. To take
another instance – I remember going into Kensington Gardens
about that time. It was a hot spring evening, and we lay down –
Nessa and I – in the long grass behind the Flower Walk. I had
taken *The Golden Treasury* with me. I opened it and began to read
some poem. And instantly and for the first time I understood the
poem (which it was I forget). It was as if it became altogether
intelligible; I had a feeling of transparency in words when they
cease to be words and become so intensified that one seems to
experience them; to foretell them as if they developed what one is
already feeling. I was so astonished that I tried to explain the
feeling. 'One seems to understand what it's about', I said

awkwardly. I suppose Nessa has forgotten; no one could have understood from what I said the queer feeling I had in the hot grass, that poetry was coming true. Nor does that give the feeling. It matches what I have sometimes felt when I write. The pen gets on the scent.

But though I remember so distinctly those two moments – the arch of glass burning at the end of Paddington Station and the poem I read in Kensington Gardens, those two clear moments are almost the only clear moments in the muffled dulness that then closed over us.[1]

Written between 1939 and 1940 of the year 1895 – reaching back, that is, over a distance of about forty-five years – this passage perfectly demonstrates the nature of perception in Virginia Woolf, and is a fine example of 'what makes her a writer'. Earlier in the essay, 'A Sketch of the Past', she describes her creative process as the experiencing of a shock, followed at once by 'the desire to explain it'. The shock, she says, is 'a token of some real thing behind appearances; and I make it real by putting it into words'.[2] The apprehension of such shocks are the 'moments of being' which are embedded in the 'many more moments of non-being' – writing orders to Mabel, or seeing to the broken vacuum cleaner. In this case the shock is her mother's death, but that is not the subject of the passage. As with the deaths in the novels (Mrs Ramsay's, or Percival's) the death, paradoxically, feeds into the intensified moments, which are thus salvaged from non-being: 'death is the mother of beauty'.

The passage consists of two connected memories: a great glass dome blazing with light, or 'arch of glass burning', and a sudden feeling of 'transparency in words' on reading out a poem to Vanessa in 'the hot grass'. These two moments are followed by a double attempt to explain them, once at the time, and now, in the retrospective essay. Neither attempt is felt to be entirely successful, and each is made with some effort or awkwardness. But the moments themselves happen 'without any effort', as though an alchemical conversion were taking place of its own volition. Something solid or opaque or impenetrable is changed into something 'transparent': something shadowed or dormant is 'quick-ened' or 'intensified'. Conventionally evaluative words like 'rap-ture' or 'understand' are used, but these words do not sufficiently explain the activity of the mind, which, like the 'androgynous' minds of Coleridge or Shakespeare, becomes 'porous' and 'incandescent'.[3]

The mind, that is, becomes a 'reflector'. The crucial image for this, which links the blazing dome of the station and the poem read in the hot grass, but is itself a figure for, not an ingredient of, the occasion, is the image of 'a burning glass': a magnifying glass, presumably, laid on hot grass, through which the sun shines and makes fire. This image does not permit a distinction to be made between the thing perceived and the state of mind. The thirteen-year-old Virginia Stephen, already in a strange state because of Julia's death and the 'melodramatic' scenes of lamentation at Hyde Park Gate, finds that the station roof at sunset and the poem read in Kensington Gardens reflect, give back to her, 'what she is already feeling'. The mirroring, self-echoing language of the passage (which repeats 'blazing', 'intensified', 'feeling'), turns the arch of glass into a burning glass laid on the mind, and the words of the poem into the reader's perceptions. What is perceived, by a kind of magic, turns into the perceiver. Coleridge's quotation from Sir John Davies, cited by Abrams in *The Mirror and the Lamp* in describing Coleridge's images for the imagination, is apt: 'As fire converts to fire the thing it burns'.[4] Mrs Ramsay, hearing 'Luriana lurilee' recited by her husband after dinner and finding that 'the words seemed to be spoken by her own voice', or looking at the lighthouse beam 'until she became the thing she looked at', is involved in the same sort of process as the one in this passage, where the mind is glass and grass, light and reflection, colour and shadow.

The passage is not merely about the 'moment of being' at which the mind becomes a reflector, but also a reflection on the past, and, as throughout 'A Sketch of the Past', on how such moments can be translated into language without losing their transparency and intensity. Avrom Fleishman ends his book on Virginia Woolf (much concerned with the process of repetition in her work) by reminding us of her affinities with Wordsworth's, and Proust's, re-finding of 'spots of time' which link the past and the present. 'These writers are her proper company', he concludes. 'She takes her place in the tradition – still alive, although Romantic art has passed – that tells us not only how it feels to be but how it feels *to have been*'.[5] I will return to the comparison with Wordsworth, and to the relationship between 'A Sketch of the Past' and this reflection in the Diary for 1925:

The past is beautiful because one never realizes an emotion at the time. It expands later, & thus we don't have complete emotions about the present, only about the past.[6]

But in the passage under discussion, Virginia Woolf finds considerable difficulty in telling us 'how it feels to have been'. Virginia Stephen's awkward failure to tell Vanessa what she is feeling, which takes the form, even at thirteen, of a self-conscious upper-class idiom ('One seems to understand what it's about') is like the inadequate clichés and inexact phrases to which her characters constantly resort, especially in *Between the Acts* and *The Years*. The use of 'one' is characteristically evasive and ambivalent. And the retrospective attempt to put the moment into words is also inadequate. A sense of strain is felt in the repeated use of 'as if': '*as if* a burning glass had been laid', '*as if* something were becoming visible', '*as if* it became altogether intelligible', '*as if* they developed what one is already feeling'. Intensity has to be rendered by approximation, by a piling-up of similitudes none of which will quite 'do'. Abrams on Coleridge is again apposite:

As Coleridge said, 'No simile runs on all four legs'; analogues are by their nature only partial parallels, and the very sharpness of focus afforded by a happily chosen archetype makes marginal and elusive those qualities of an object which fall outside its primitive categories.[7]

Abrams is talking about the way in which the Romantics took possession of, and transmuted, the traditional image of art as a mirror. Virginia Woolf, as she is writing it down, finds that her images of a 'burning glass', of 'something' becoming suddenly visible or intelligible, leave the sensation still 'marginal and elusive'. The feeling can only be rendered vaguely: almost every sentence begins 'It was'. 'It' has to 'do' for everything, as in 'It impressed and exalted me' (the train, the whole station, or the light?) or 'One seems to understand what it's about' (the poem, or the meaning of life?). 'Nor does that give the feeling', she has to say, ending with a vague last try – 'the queer feeling' – and with a casual, colloquial metaphor, 'the pen gets on the scent', which, as so often in her work, has to do justice to a complex experience.[8] There follows the return to 'muffled dulness', a Shakespearean synaesthesia which gives us deafness, blindness, being shadowed or covered up (the curtains drawn, as in all her Victorian homes) and being shrouded, as in death.

II

The threefold process in this retrospective autobiographical passage – moments of incandescence, the memory of such moments, and the attempt to put them into words – will be extremely familiar to readers of Virginia Woolf, and so will the combination of elements – burning domes, glass on grass – used for the process. Harvena Richter's book on Virginia Woolf, *The Inward Voyage*, was the first to pay attention to the use of 'mirror modes'. She notes, for example, that Virginia Woolf calls a landscape in a Meredith novel (which begins 'The sky was bronze, a vast furnace dome') 'the description of a state of mind'.[9] There is a fuller and subtler account of Virginia Woolf's mirror-images in Allen McLaurin's *The Echoes Enslaved*. He, like Fleishman, is especially interested in her use of repetition, and in the devices of framing, which, he suggests, she owes to Roger Fry.[10] My own interest in Virginia Woolf's mirror-images suggested to me three related areas for consideration, which can only be dealt with briefly here: the habitual, almost involuntary yoking together in her work of glass, reflectors, and fire, as terms for the mind in its moments of creative intensity; the re-working of such terms in different kinds of writings; and the extent to which such terms can be used to place Virginia Woolf on the curve extending from the Romantic to the contemporary imagination. Four illustrations follow, in support of the example from 'A Sketch of the Past', of Virginia Woolf's use of these terms. They are taken from a non-fictional work, an essay, a Diary entry, and a novel.

> To the right and left bushes of some sort, golden and crimson, glowed with the colour, even it seemed burnt with the heat, of fire. On the further bank the willows wept in perpetual lamentation, their hair about their shoulders. The river reflected whatever it chose of sky and bridge and burning tree, and when the undergraduate had oared his boat through the reflections they closed again, completely, as if he had never been. There one might have sat the clock round lost in thought. Thought – to call it by a prouder name than it deserved – had let its line down into the stream. It swayed . . . hither and thither among the

reflections and the weeds, letting the water lift it and sink it, until – you know the little tug – the sudden conglomeration of an idea at the end of one's line: and then the cautious hauling of it in, and the careful laying of it out? Alas, laid on the grass how small, how insignificant this thought of mine looked . . .[11]

The feminine, lamenting willows and the burning bushes – biblical images – are reflected in the river, which thus becomes a burning glass, an analogue for the narrator's random, profound process of reflection. The reflections of river and writer are momentarily interrupted by a blithely unconscious young phallic oarsman, whose undergraduate privileges spark off the subject of the essay's reflections – which take the shape of fishing in the depths rather than oaring through the surfaces. The shape of her thought, though mockingly held up as inadequate at this point, turns out to be the argument of the book: that only in being released from sexual bias can the mind become incandescent and creative.

Yet what composed the present moment? If you are young, the future lies upon the present, like a piece of glass, making it tremble and quiver. If you are old, the past lies upon the present, like a thick glass, making it waver, distorting it. All the same, everybody believes that the present is something, seeks out the different elements in this situation in order to compose the truth of it, the whole of it.
    To begin with: it is largely composed of visual and of sense impressions. The day was very hot. After heat, the surface of the body is opened, as if all the pores were open and everything lay exposed, not sealed and contracted, as in cold weather.[12]

As 'reflection' is given its physical analogue in the previous passage, so 'composition' is translated into physical terms in this essay. The body's 'porous' receptivity to heat is like the 'moment's' susceptibility to the pressure of time. The thick glass (whether of retrospection or anticipation) acts like heat on the skin. As in the 'burning glass' passage, the paradox of the moment is explored: it must be fixed, composed, framed, but it cannot be taken in isolation: it belongs to the rest of one's life. The moment is both in and out of time and it is registered passively, but must be formally 'composed'.

And I begin this sentence on a grey noisy evening might be mid September in Chartres, determined to let a long slide of time pass before I go motoring again. The pane of glass that is pressed firm over the mind in these travels – there I am vitreated on my seat . . . makes the 2 last days as intolerable as the first two are rapturous.

. . .

And, putting down my pen, I fetched L. & we went to the Cathedral which was almost dark & melodramatic – I mean surprising, there only the arches & shadows showing, we all alone, & the blue windows blazing in the cold grey night. In fact it was like seeing the skeleton & eyes of the cathedral glowing there. Mere bones, & the blue red eyes . . . the glass varied from gloomy to transcendent.

. . .

The usual tremor & restlessness after coming back, & nothing to settle to, & some good German woman sends me a pamphlet on me, into which I couldnt resist looking, though nothing so upsets & demoralises as this looking at ones face in the glass. And a German glass produces an extreme diffuseness & complexity so that I cant get either praise or blame but must begin twisting among long words.[13]

The extracts, from two consecutive days in 1935, show the involuntary way in which the image of glass comes to her mind. The pressure of being 'vitreated', literally and imaginatively, in the long car journey, leads to the liberating blaze of the stained glass at Chartres (which seems to have escaped from the flesh of the cathedral building), and then home to the 'distorting glass' of a German critique of her work.

It was a summer evening; the sun was setting; the sky was blue still, but tinged with gold, as if a thin veil of gauze hung over it, and here and there in the gold-blue amplitude an island of cloud lay suspended. In the fields the trees stood majestically caparisoned, with their innumerable leaves gilt. Sheep and cows, pearl white and particoloured, lay recumbent or munched their way through the half transparent grass. An edge of light surrounded everything. A red-gold fume rose from the dust on the roads. Even the little red brick villas on the high roads had become porous, incandescent with light, and the flowers in the cottage gardens, lilac and pink like cotton dresses, shone veined as if lit from within. Faces of people standing at cottage doors or padding along pavements showed the same red glow as they fronted the slowly sinking sun.[14]

In this rather ordinary piece of Woolfian descriptive writing, a setting sun irresistibly gives rise to the familiar terms – incandescence, transparency, porousness – so that the landscape may be felt to take the hot light into itself and reflect it back.

In all these different, and differently occasioned passages, a burning glass is in some form suggested as a term for the moment and for the perception. Similar terms are found everywhere in Virginia Woolf, often in quite conventional versions, such as the simple use of the word 'reflection' to mean process of thought,[15] or the use of a glass or lens to describe a writer's point of view. Thoreau sees life 'through a very powerful magnifying glass', Macaulay's version of Boswell is like 'a twisted mirror in the fair', Sir Thomas Browne's 'magic glasses' are full of 'emerald lights and blue mystery', and Jane Austen's eyes are as glittering and impenetrable as 'a glass, a mirror, a silver spoon held up in the sun'.[16]

But the traditional figure of the work of art as looking-glass is travestied and altered by Virginia Woolf, as by the Romantics. She makes play startlingly with the tradition by asking the reader to think of it with closed eyes:

If one shuts one's eyes and thinks of the novel as a whole, it would seem to be a creation owning a certain looking-glass likeness to life, though of course with simplifications and distortions innumerable.[17]

Later in *A Room of One's Own*, she yokes 'reflection' to 'fire' in her discussion of art. The action of a great work of art (such as *Lear* or *Emma* or *À la Recherche*) is cauterising:

the reading of these books seems to perform a curious couching operation on the senses; one sees more intensely afterwards; the world seems bared of its covering and given an intenser life.[18]

As in the 'burning glass' passage, these phrases refer at the same time to an inner, visionary sight (the sort one gets by 'shutting one's eyes' to the muffled everyday reality) and to an actual seeing. The word 'intense' is transferred, by the alchemical agency of the work of art, from the perceiver ('one sees more intensely') to the perceived ('the world . . . given an intenser life').

Any account of the imagination in Virginia Woolf is also a description of landscape; any description of landscape is also an account of the way the mind works. She is a great writer of light: you can see her in the Diaries continually trying to find new ways of getting it down on paper, as in this entry:

> That fading & rising of the light which so enraptures me in the downs: which I am always comparing to the light beneath an alabaster bowl &c.[19]

What look to be purple passages about the action of light on place are always attempts to write about ways of seeing: hence the insistence on transparency. Virginia Woolf's railway stations (like Monet's) have luminous haloes: in *The Years*, 'the glass roofs of the great railway stations were globes incandescent with light'; Mrs Brown gets off at Waterloo and goes off into 'the vast blazing station'.[20]

Sunshine is always 'making the grass semi-transparent', or the 'leaves of the plant in the window . . . transparent with light'; a flame burning in sunlight will make 'the air waver like a faulty sheet of glass'.[21] In *Mrs Dalloway*, the grass of Green Park is lit up 'as if a yellow lamp were moved beneath'; in *The Waves*, this image, frequently used of landscape, is more ominously applied to Louis's inner life: 'I go beneath ground tortuously, as if a warder carried a lamp from cell to cell'.[22] That transferring of the figure of speech from place to person is characteristic of the overlap between perceiver and perceived in all her images for the imagination and its climaxes: the match in the crocus, the shower of atoms, the semi-transparent envelope, the lighthouse beam, the luminous halo, the searchlight, and the dome of fire. In *The Waves* the limitations of this process are, I think, acutely felt: the formal analogues between landscape and personality, the need to write up imaginative life as though it were scenery is an effortful, even awkward process at its most extended and formalised.

III

'As fire converts to fire the thing it burns'. In *The Mirror and the Lamp*, Abrams describes the transformation by the Romantic writers, in their definitions of the imagination, of Renaissance, Platonic mirrors as formal analogues for the work of art, into '*reversed reflectors*'. In Coleridge's phrase:

> To make the external internal, the internal external, to make nature thought, and thought nature – this is the mystery of genius in the Fine Arts.[23]

'The mirror held up to nature becomes transparent and yields the reader insights into the mind and heart of the poet himself'. Coleridge combines mirror and lamp in his first response to the *Prelude*: 'Thy soul received/ The light reflected, as a light bestowed'. Shelley, in Abrams' terms, 'reverses the aesthetic mirror in order to make it reflect the lamp of the mind'; incandescence and intensity (or, in Hazlitt's favourite word, 'gusto') become the highest critical criteria for poetry.[24]

That Virginia Woolf was deeply and consciously affected by the patterns of thought and by the language of the Romantic writers is everywhere apparent in her constant references to, and work on, Hazlitt, Byron, Shelley, Leigh Hunt, De Quincey, Wordsworth, and Coleridge. I have only space for three examples relevant to my subject. First, there is her experience of 'dejection'. In the Diary for September 1927 she appropriates Shelley's line: 'Rarely, rarely comest thou, spirit of delight' to describe her own feelings of 'profound gloom, depression, boredom, whatever it is';[25] moments when:

> I may not hope from outward forms to win
> The passion and the life, whose fountains are within.

Second, there is her veneration for Shakespeare as the perfection of the incandescent, porous, androgynous mind. 'The pliancy of his mind was so complete'; 'Shakespeare must have had this [the power to make images] to an extent which makes my normal state the state of a person blind, deaf, dumb, stone-stockish and fish-blooded'.[26] This is very close to the Romantic writers' idea of Shakespeare: 'As to the poetical character itself . . . it is not itself – it has no self – it is every thing and nothing – It has no character – it enjoys light and shade; it lives in gusto, be it foul or fair, high or low, rich or poor, mean or elevated – It has as much delight in conceiving an Iago as an Imogen'. [His was] no twisted, poor, convex-concave mirror . . . a perfectly level mirror.'[27]

Thirdly, there is her preoccupation with the re-finding of the past, which is explicitly, not merely vaguely, Wordsworthian. The Diary for 22 August 1929 quotes this passage from the *Prelude* (which Virginia Woolf would have read in de Selincourt's 1926 Oxford edition of the 1850 text):

> The matter that detains us now may seem,
> To many, neither dignified enough
> Nor arduous, yet will not be scorned by them,
> Who, looking inward, have observed the ties
> That bind the perishable hours of life
> Each to the other, & the curious props
> By which the world of memory & thought
> Exists & is sustained.[28]

My central passage about the 'burning glass' is a good example of her 'observation' of such 'curious props'. In the 'spots of time' of this passage, Paddington Station (which might seem to many 'not dignified enough') is transformed into the equivalent of Kubla Khan's pleasure dome, and the poem read out loud becomes a moment of 'splendour in the grass'. It is tempting to think that the poem was, indeed, Wordsworth's 'Immortality Ode', the penultimate poem in *The Golden Treasury* (followed by Shelley's 'Music when soft voices die'), of which Wordsworth wrote:

> The poem rests upon two recollections of childhood; on that of a splendour in the objects of sense which is passed away, and the other an indisposition to bend to the law of death, as applying to our own particular case. A reader who has not had a vivid recollection of these feelings having existed in his mind in childhood cannot understand that poem.[29]

The Romantic poet's fear that such 'splendour in the objects of sense' may fail – that the sources of joy, delight, inner vision, may absent themselves, and not be obtainable from 'outward forms', which in that case exercise an oppressive tyranny (a tyranny opposed by Wordsworth, as Geoffrey Hartman says, by 'subduing the eyes' to an inner identity 'which is not less real . . . no less indestructible than the object of its perceptions'[30]) – that 'dejection' becomes, in the post-Paterian, post-Symbolist writer, a less soluble anxiety about the imagination and its objects. Virginia Woolf resembles Pater in presenting the alchemical action of the mind on external objects as a making transparent:

> When reflection begins to play upon those objects they are dissipated under its influence; the cohesive force seems suspended like some trick of magic; each object is loosed into a group of impressions - colour, odour, texture - in the mind of the observer.[31]

But what is the value of such impressions if they can only be locked in the mind, 'each mind' (as Pater continues) 'keeping as a solitary prisoner its own dream of a world'; if, as Mary Datchet imagines it in *Night and Day*, life is a process of being 'immured . . . the same feelings living for ever, neither dwindling nor changing, within the ring of a thick stone wall?'[32] The modernist's fear that one's impressions are incommunicable, solipsistic (as in 'One seems to understand what it's about') is matched by the fear that the outside world is a 'natural chaos inhospitable to humans', mere 'blankness and indifference'.[33]

The reciprocal fusion between the perceiver and the perceived is still intensely desired and felt as possible; the modern artist's imagination exercises itself to order an inhospitable reality into 'a superhuman, mirror-resembling dream'. As in Yeats, or in another way in Wallace Stevens, the modern artist very often projects himself as a magician, an alchemist, a conjurer, a prestidigitator, a speculator. This passage from Italo Calvino's *If On a Winter's Night a Traveller*, the narrative of a business 'speculator' who collects kaleidoscopes, playfully sums up the modern artist's aspirations:

> At this point the story could mention that among the virtues of mirrors that the ancient books discuss there is also that of revealing distant and hidden things. The Arab geographers of the Middle Ages, in their descriptions of the harbor of Alexandria, recall the column that stood on the island of Pharos, surmounted by a steel mirror in which, from an immense distance, the ships proceeding off Cyprus and Constantinople and all the lands of

the Romans can be seen. Concentrating the rays, curved mirrors can catch an image of the whole. 'God Himself, who cannot be seen either by the body or by the soul,' Porphyry writes, 'allows himself to be contemplated in a mirror.' Together with the centrifugal radiation that projects my image along all the dimensions of space, I would like these pages also to render the opposite movement, through which I receive from the mirrors images that direct sight cannot embrace. From mirror to mirror – this is what I happen to dream of – the totality of things, the whole, the entire universe, divine wisdom could concentrate their luminous rays into a single mirror. Or perhaps the knowledge of everything is buried in the soul, and a system of mirrors that would multiply my image to infinity and reflect its essence in a single image would then reveal to me the soul of the universe, which is hidden in mine.[34]

'Perhaps'. Calvino's narrator cannot be as sure of God as Porphyry was, nor of the harmonious relation between the universe and the soul. In Virginia Woolf, that mirroring harmony, which ought to be the basis for her persistent analogies between landscape and imagination, is in doubt. The anxiety is most eloquently expressed in the 'Time Passes' section of *To the Lighthouse*:

Did Nature supplement what man advanced? Did she complete what he began? With equal complacence she saw his misery, condoned his meanness, and acquiesced in his torture. That dream, then, of sharing, completing, finding in solitude on the beach an answer, was but a reflection in a mirror, and the mirror itself was but the surface glassiness which forms in quiescence when the nobler powers sleep beneath? Impatient, despairing yet loth to go (for beauty offers her lures, has her consolations), to pace the beach was impossible; contemplation was unendurable; the mirror was broken.[35]

The broken mirror, which reflects an alien, fragmented, mocking universe, is, according to Allen McLaurin, the necessary mirror for the modern writer. He points out that at the time of writing *Between the Acts*, in which the pageant audience is mocked by mirrors held up to represent 'present-time reality', Virginia Woolf was reading Coleridge's *Letters*, and reminiscences of him in *Coleridge the Talker*: 'It is the only way of getting at the truth'; she comments of this book, 'to have it broken into many splinters by many mirrors and so select'.[36] The mocking, distorted mirror, the cracked glass – Buck Mulligan's shaving mirror? – are at the end of a tradition which began with the public use of the mirror as satire or exemplum: mirrors of fools and mirrors for magistrates. A broken mirror can still have satirical, social powers, as the audience finds in *Between The Acts*. But that power is always at risk.

Virginia Woolf's personal, physical embarrassment at seeing herself caught in the glass ('the looking-glass shame'[37]), painfully expressed by Rachel in *The Voyage Out* and by Rhoda in *The Waves*, is partly social and sexual, but is also a feature of the modern writer's anxiety about the imagination. What if no self is reflected back from the glass? What if an inner eclipse takes place, like the eclipse of the sun which Virginia Woolf 'wrote up' so often, and no light 'miraculously' returns?[38] What if the tyranny of the eye disallows composition or reflection: things simply are, in all their vacancy and chaos, and nothing happens when they are looked at? Bernard's experience at the end of *The Waves* of being like the world without a sun, 'without a self, weightless and visionless', unable to 'conjure' up any opposition, is foreshadowed by Peter Walsh's experience in *Mrs Dalloway* ('the cold stream of visual impressions failed him now as if the eye were a cup that overflowed and let the rest run down its china walls unrecorded'[39], and by a couple in an early short story:

> Over them both came instantly that paralysing blankness of feeling, when nothing bursts from the mind, when its walls appear like slate; when vacancy almost hurts, and the eyes petrified and fixed see the same spot – a pattern, a coal scuttle – with an exactness which is terrifying, since no emotion, no idea, no impression of any kind comes to change it, to modify it, to embellish it, since the fountains of feeling seem sealed and as the mind turns rigid, so does the body . . .[40]

Without a reflector, nature becomes its own pointless mirror, as in 'Time Passes', where, in the absence of people, 'light reflected itself'. Virginia Woolf's burning glass, so effortfully recaptured in 'A Sketch of the Past', is the image for an exceptional moment surrounded by muffled dulness. The whole of her work is a process of strenuously fixing such moments and trying to turn them into narrative.

Notes

1. Virginia Woolf, 'A Sketch of the Past', *Moments of Being*, ed. J. Schulkind (University of Sussex Press, 1976) p. 93.
2. Ibid, p. 72.
3. Virginia Woolf, *A Room of One's Own* (1929; rpt. London: Hogarth Press, 1931) Ch. 6, p. 148.
4. M. H. Abrams, *The Mirror and the Lamp* (Oxford University Press, 1953) p. 175.
5. Avrom Fleishman, *Virginia Woolf: A Critical Reading* (Baltimore: Johns Hopkins University Press, 1975) p. 227.
6. Virginia Woolf, diary entry dated 18 March 1925, *The Diary of Virginia Woolf*, eds Anne Olivier Bell and Andrew McNeillie (London: Hogarth Press, 1980) Vol. III, p. 5.
7. Abrams, *Mirror and Lamp*, p. 35.
8. 'A Sketch of the Past' was not revised for publication; had it been so, some of its tentative quality might have gone.
9. Harvena Richter, *Virginia Woolf: The Inward Voyage* (Princeton University Press, 1970) p. 108.
10. Allen McLaurin, *Virginia Woolf: The Echoes Enslaved* (Cambridge University Press, 1973).
11. Woolf, *A Room of One's Own*, Ch. 1, pp. 8–9.
12. Virginia Woolf, 'The Moment; Summer's Night', *Collected Essays*, ed. L. Woolf (London: Chatto & Windus, 1966) Vol. II, p. 293.
13. Woolf, diary entries dated 29 and 31 May 1935, *Diary*, Vol. IV, pp. 316–17.
14. Virginia Woolf, *The Years* (London: Hogarth Press, 1937) p. 329.
15. For example, in *A Room of One's Own*, Ch. 6; and *Diary*, Vol. III, pp. 219, 253, 255.
16. Virginia Woolf, 'Thoreau', *Books and Portraits*, ed. Mary Lyon (London: Hogarth Press, 1977) p. 75; 'The Genius of Boswell', Ibid., p. 149; 'The Elizabethan Lumber Room', *Collected Essays*, Vol. I, p. 53; 'Personalities', *Collected Essays*, Vol. II, p. 275.
17. Woolf, *A Room of One's Own*, Ch. 4, pp. 106–7.
18. Ibid., Ch. 6, p. 166.
19. Woolf, diary entry dated 31 Aug. 1928, *Diary*, Vol. III, p. 192.
20. Woolf, *The Years*, p. 206; 'Mr Bennett and Mrs Brown', *Collected Essays*, Vol. I, p. 324. Virginia Woolf's railway stations are post-Impressionist in their light and dazzle; as in the fictions of Forster, Elizabeth Bowen and Henry Green, they strike the modern novelists' imagination as twentieth century cathedrals.
21. Woolf, diary entries dated 28 May and 27 Dec. 1931, *Diary*, Vol. IV, pp. 27, 56; Virginia Woolf, *The Voyage Out* (1915; rpt. London: Hogarth Press, 1929) Ch. 19, p. 316.
22. Virginia Woolf, *Mrs Dalloway* (1925; rpt. London: Hogarth Press, 1947) p. 128; Virginia Woolf, *The Waves* (1931; rpt. London: Hogarth Press, 1946) p. 144.
23. Abrams, *Mirror and Lamp*, p. 53.
24. Ibid., pp. 23, 60, 130.
25. Woolf, diary entries dated 30 Sept. 1926 and 4 Sept. 1927, *Diary*, Vol. III, pp. 113, 153.
26. Woolf, diary entries dated 13 April 1930 and Aug. 1926, ibid., pp. 300–1, 104.

27. John Keats, letter to Richard Woodhouse, dated 27 Oct. 1818, *The Letters of John Keats*, ed. H. Rollins (Cambridge University Press, 1958) Vol. I, pp. 386–7; Thomas Carlyle, 'The Hero as Poet', *Heroes and Hero-Worship*, *The Works of Thomas Carlyle* (London: Chapman & Hall, 1904) Vol. V, p. 104.
28. Woolf, diary entry dated 22 Aug. 1929, *Diary*, Vol. III, pp. 247–8.
29. William Wordsworth, letter to Catherine Clarkson dated Dec. 1814, *The Letters of William & Dorothy Wordsworth: The Middle Years Vol. II 1811–1820*, ed. Ernest de Selincourt (Oxford: Clarendon Press, 1937) p. 619.
30. Geoffrey Hartman, 'Pure Representation', *The Unmediated Vision* (New Haven: Yale University Press, 1954) p. 132.
31. Walter Pater, 'Conclusion', *The Renaissance* (1873; rpt. London: Macmillan Press, 1910) p. 234.
32. Virginia Woolf, *Night and Day* (1919; rpt. London: Hogarth Press, 1930) p. 289.
33. Frank Kermode, 'The Modern', *Modern Essays* (London: Fontana, 1971) pp. 54; 51.
34. Italo Calvino, *If On A Winter's Night A Traveller*, trans. Wm. Weaver (London: Picador, 1982) pp. 131–2.
35. Virginia Woolf, *To the Lighthouse* (1927; rpt. London: Hogarth Press, 1930) Sect. II, Ch. 6, pp. 207–8.
36. Cf. Allen McLaurin, *Virginia Woolf: The Echoes Enslaved*, p. 55.
37. Woolf, 'A Sketch of the Past', p. 68.
38. See Woolf, *Diary*, Vol III, pp. 142ff; 'The Sun and the Fish', *Collected Essays*, Vol. IV, pp. 178–83; and *The Waves*, pp. 310ff.
39. Woolf, *Mrs Dalloway*, p. 181.
40. Virginia Woolf, 'Together and Apart', *A Haunted House* (London: Hogarth Press, 1944; rpt. 1967) p. 136.

2 Consciousness and Group Consciousness in Virginia Woolf

Allen McLaurin

In a letter written in 1919, George Eliot's centenary year, Virginia Woolf confessed to her correspondent: 'I am reading through the whole of George Eliot, in order to sum her up, once and for all, upon her anniversary'[1] – a typically extravagant and irreverent statement, mocking the centenary convention. Despite the tongue-in-cheek attitude evident here, Virginia Woolf is touching upon a natural desire, which a centenary prompts, to gain some firm perspective on a writer's work. I hope that the following consideration of consciousness and group consciousness in Virginia Woolf will allow me to trace a current of thought and feeling which runs throughout her writing, and to suggest a placing of Virginia Woolf's work in the kind of historical perspective which a centenary celebration might encourage us to consider. I intend to explore an idea which links Virginia Woolf clearly to a current of thinking which was of great importance in her lifetime, but which has since been somewhat neglected, or obscured, or treated in only a fragmentary way. As the discussion will be of an aspect of her work which her contemporaries, her first reviewers, seized upon, then perhaps my argument should be seen as an effort of recovery; an attempt to look afresh at one aspect of the wave of critical commentary which has accompanied Virginia Woolf's work from the very beginning of her career as an imaginative writer. We are here to celebrate a writer who offered a unique vision of the world, but it was part of Virginia Woolf's distinction that she was extraordinarily receptive to the major currents of thought in her time.

One web of interrelated ideas which she presents, not as lumpy doctrine, but as a network of images and suggestions, is the notion of a group mind. And because Virginia Woolf's imagination progressed characteristically by contraries we will need to consider a drama of opposites in her treatment of the theme, which often presents itself as a doubt or a question rather than a statement or a belief. Typically, as with Clarissa Dalloway, the idea is fuelled by an overwhelming need to understand the meaning of death:

> Odd affinities she had with people she had never spoken to, some woman in the street, some man behind a counter – even trees, or barns. It ended in a transcendental theory which, with her horror of death, allowed her to believe, or say that she believed (for all her scepticism), that since our apparitions, the part of us which appears, are so momentary compared with the other, the unseen part of us, which spreads wide, the unseen might survive, be recovered somehow attached to this person or that, or even haunting certain places, after death. Perhaps – perhaps.[2]

Clarissa's speculation is hedged around with qualifications, and is in any case presented as only a theory which she entertained in her youth. Yet the very memory of that belief serves to connect her, through idea and imagery, with Septimus Smith, so creating that 'odd affinity' which seems to be undermined by reason. In order to explore the questions raised by passages of this kind I will certainly not be attempting, in Virginia Woolf's mocking phrase, to sum up her work 'once and for all', my aim is the more modest one of mapping out some work in progress.

Critics have discussed extensively the treatment of individual consciousness in Virginia Woolf's work, and have naturally emphasised the idea of the 'stream of consciousness'. These discussions are often helpful and interesting, but we need to consider why analyses of the individual stream in most discussions of Virginia Woolf's work have been given a disproportionate emphasis. One of the reasons for the imbalance in past discussions possibly stems from the belief that one can make an easy step from stream of consciousness as a subject to stream of consciousness as a method or technique. This, I suggest, is a mistaken assumption. In other words, I will be arguing that the failure to understand the relevance of group feeling in Virginia Woolf's work stems in part from confusion about the depiction of the stream of consciousness in literature.

In its relation to literature the term 'stream of consciousness' has been used in two basic ways. First of all, to describe the phenomenon itself, and naturally reference is made here to William James, and to the chapter in *The Principles of Psychology* in which the idea was first discussed:

> Consciousness, then, does not appear to itself chopped up in bits. Such words as 'chain' or 'train' do not describe it fitly as it presents itself in the first instance. It is nothing jointed; it flows. A 'river' or a 'stream' are the metaphors by which it is most naturally described. In talking of it hereafter, let us call it the stream of thought, of consciousness, or of subjective life.[3]

The depiction of this stream in literature, that is to say the stream of consciousness as subject matter in fiction, is simply an extension of this basic meaning. But there has developed a second and confusing usage of the term; to designate a method or technique, and as this confusion may have played its part in obscuring Virginia Woolf's portrayal of group consciousness, it needs some further discussion. This preliminary argument might also help in the analysis of formal correlatives of the portrayal of group minds in Virginia Woolf's work – but that leads beyond the scope of my present paper. We can avoid the confusion caused by the two uses of the term 'stream of consciousness' by refraining from using it to refer to a method or technique. In making this suggestion I am following the recommendations of a growing number of scholars who have plunged into, and successfully re-emerged from, the rather turbid waters surrounding the debate about the stream of consciousness novel.

Of those who would speak of the stream of consciousness *method*, we might ask whether they are referring to a variety of methods which writers have developed to indicate the flow of inner speech or consciousness. If so, surely these methods can be identified and separately named, and in fact some very fine work has been done in this area of formal analysis, avoiding the use of the 'stream of consciousness' label. The alternative to this blanket use of the term would be to use 'stream of consciousness method or technique' to designate a specific mode of writing, and the usual choice here has been either direct or indirect interior monologue. Restriction of the term to cover direct interior monologue, with its characteristic dislocation of grammar and syntax would mean that we would have to limit the stream of consciousness to cover very few passages in very few novels, and be forced into the contradiction of saying that Virginia Woolf is a stream of consciousness writer who does not use the stream of consciousness technique. Using the phrase 'stream of consciousness method' to refer to indirect interior monologue leads to an even greater absurdity. Indirect interior monologue, though a favourite device of stream of consciousness writers, is also used, not only by those who are not particularly interested in the stream of consciousness but also, and characteristically, by Lawrence, a writer who was explicitly opposed to the stream of consciousness idea. For Lawrence it was, in his own words 'the stream of hell which undermined my adolescence'. To call indirect interior monologue the 'stream of consciousness method' would therefore put us in the position of saying that a writer who hated and detested the stream of consciousness idea used a stream of consciousness technique. I do not think that that degree of contradiction should be ascribed even to Lawrence. We can avoid this confusion quite simply by reserving the term 'stream of consciousness' to refer to the phenomenon itself, or for its appearance as the subject matter of certain works of literature. We can then proceed to examine with greater clarity the relationship between the portrayal of individual consciousness and the way it is related to group consciousness in Virginia Woolf's work.

A natural beginning for such an investigation is the original source of the stream metaphor, and what might strike us on re-reading William James, coming to his work with an eye to elucidating Virginia Woolf's novels, are the close correspondences which are revealed. James describes the way in which inner life contains 'sensations of our bodies and of the objects around us, memories of past experiences and thoughts of distant things, feelings of satisfaction and dissatisfaction, desires and aversions, and other emotional conditions, together with determinations of the will, in every variety of permutation and combination.'[4] All these aspects, he argues, are simultaneously present, but the focus and margin of attention are constantly changing. The depiction of that changing focus of attention is central to Virginia Woolf's art: her characters are surrounded by a halo of consciousness and their acts of attention emphasise now this amalgam of present feelings and memories, now another. In addition, Virginia Woolf simulates those little shocks described in *The Principles of Psychology* which change the focus of attention without ever interrupting the continuity of the stream of consciousness. Both Virginia Woolf and Joyce present a phenomenon common to everyone's experience; the feeling of having something on the tip of the tongue but not quite being able to bring it to mind.

These detailed similarities are of course less important than the general conception which they share about the nature and importance of the stream of consciousness. But it is precisely this overall agreement which has obscured a crucial difference between James and Virginia Woolf. If we are to trace the idea of group consciousness in Virginia Woolf's work we must look closely at a major divergence from James, which comes at the point in his discussion where he considers the possibility of contact between the streams which constitute the inner lives of individuals:

> Neither contemporaneity, nor proximity in space, nor similarity of quality and content are able to fuse thoughts together which are sundered by this barrier of belonging to different personal minds. The breaches between such thoughts are the most absolute breaches in nature.[5]

For William James, this partition between consciousnesses is a self-evident assumption; common sense tells him it is the case, and he is emotionally neutral about the matter. But for the stream of consciousness writers this isolation presents itself as an intellectual and emotional problem.

James's assumption about the privacy of each individual's inner life has had its influence on critics of stream of consciousness writing. Surely, their argument runs, by emphasising unduly these inherently private states of mind, streams which, by James's definition, cannot be shared, are not these writers stressing an aspect of human experience which cuts off one human being from another, making each of us, to adapt a phrase of one of the most notable of these critics, Wyndham Lewis, 'hermits in our own head'? It is part of my argument that for the stream of consciousness writers of the early twentieth century, including Virginia Woolf, the isolation of the individual consciousness is not simply a given, a matter of fact, as it is for James. The sundering of mind from mind which he asserts is questioned; it raises conflicting emotions and therefore becomes part of the drama of the work rather than a given fact. In Virginia

Woolf's work there is a tension between the idea of privacy and the notion of a group feeling or consciousness, and it is this aspect of her work which I would now like to explore.

It would not be true to say that the depiction of group feeling has been completely neglected in discussions of Virginia Woolf's work. One critic states that 'her books are full of scenes where whole groups of people share thoughts and become like a single organism',[6] and another speaks of 'collective images drawn from a larger community of mind', and relates a passage in *Jacob's Room* to what he calls 'then-current notions of a collective mental being'.[7] But apart from a passing reference to Hardy's *Dynasts* these notions remain unspecified. In other words, in comparison with the enormous amount of discussion of stream of consciousness ideas, there has been little systematic exploration of the idea of the group mind in Virginia Woolf's work. Why are there so many scattered references and so few extended discussions? As I suggested earlier, one of the reasons for the imbalance might well stem from the idea that one can make an easy step from stream of consciousness as subject to stream of consciousness as a method – a belief which I hope I have established is a mistaken one. Another explanation for the ascendancy of the stream of consciousness idea is that it is relatively easy to key the literary expression of the individual consciousness into the powerful tradition of speculation which has that most persuasive of writers, William James, as one of its leading lights. My strategy here, in promoting a recognition of the importance of the 'group' in Virginia Woolf's work, will be to suggest that it too belongs to a current of speculation which was of considerable importance during Virginia Woolf's lifetime and of which she was very much aware. By relating her work to this tradition, I hope to indicate that the depiction of group feeling which we find in her work is not simply an idiosyncrasy or an eccentric flourish added to the fundamental business of simulating individual streams of consciousness. In other words, what I am suggesting is that there was a current of speculation which paralleled, and in some respects ran counter to, the stream of consciousness ideas expounded by William James. By concentrating on the idea of group consciousness I hope, naturally, to illuminate some details of Virginia Woolf's work, but I am also suggesting a new context for that work in the history of ideas.

Ideas about a 'group mind', about 'crowds' – in other words, notions about group psychology – were very much in vogue at the time when Virginia Woolf began her writing career, and continued throughout the early decades of the century. Members of the Bloomsbury Group, including Virginia Woolf, were very conscious of this current of thought. Perhaps the most accessible part of this speculation, for those of us interested in literature, is in the work of the Unanimist writer Jules Romains because he embodied some of these ideas about the group mind in literary form. Virginia Woolf herself summarised Romains' ideas in a review written in 1913:

> What really interests him is the feelings of persons, not as individual characters, but as members of groups; what he delights and excels in doing is to trace the mysterious growth, where two or three are gathered together, of a kind of consciousness of the group in addition to that of each individual of the group. It is probable that M. Romains intended *Les Copains* to be the farce of Unanimisme; but it is important, as showing where his powers and his future lie, that the best things in the book are to be found, not where he is laughing at anything, even his own doctrines, but where he makes us feel in subtle language those kinds of feelings which particularly interest him.[8]

It is at this point that a glance at contemporary reviews of Virginia Woolf's novels can be revealing. For her contemporaries, the comparison between Virginia Woolf's work and that of the Unanimists seemed a natural and obvious one. E. M. Forster commented, in a review of her very first novel, that he found in *The Voyage Out* 'an atmosphere unknown in English literature, the atmosphere of Jules Romains' *Mort de Quelqu'un*'.[9] It is significant that Romains' novel, first published in 1911, was translated by Virginia Woolf's friends, Sydney Waterlow and Desmond MacCarthy, who published their translation in 1914 with the title *The Death of a Nobody*. (We might note here, glancing ahead, that MacCarthy was to become the model for Bernard, the spokesman for the collective consciousness portrayed in *The Waves*.) Forster's comment was perceptive, and the similarity he notes is further confirmed by the early drafts of *The Voyage Out*. But it was also prophetic because the similarities between Romains and Virginia Woolf are very much clearer in her later work. *The Death of a Nobody*, with its powerful evocation of a group feeling which is triggered by the death of the central character, continued to echo in Virginia Woolf's mind long afterwards. A couple of brief quotations will I think be enough to establish the similarity in image and feeling between the translation of Romains' work and *Mrs Dalloway*, for example. When the news of the death of the central character of Romains' novel reaches his home village, the houses, which had previously been like separate lumps, become 'linked together by a mesh of fine elastic nerves that throbbed beneath the strokes of the midday chimes'.[10] Here, the way in which the chimes of the clock spatialise the mesh of nerves is of course very close to the whole conception of space and group feeling which we experience in *Mrs Dalloway*. Towards the end of Romains' novel, the last person to remember the dead man has his memory stirred by the passing of a vehicle, from which, to quote the MacCarthy translation, 'he caught . . . a little vibration which brushed the surface of his mind, and a deeper, less conscious disturbance',[11] inevitably reminding us of the passing car in Virginia Woolf's novel: 'For the surface agitation of the passing car as it sunk grazed something very profound'.[12]

This idea about the affinity between Virginia Woolf's notion of a group mind and the Unanimist ideas of Romains has recently been given some corroboration by the discovery of that review by Virginia Woolf from which I quoted earlier. The review was discovered because of a note found in Virginia Woolf's papers from Romains himself thanking the anonymous reviewer, through the editor of *The Times Literary Supplement*, for the understanding review. In her article, Virginia Woolf suggested that Romains' work belonged to a type of writing of which there was scarcely the equivalent in England, the novel in which there are 'no characters, no humour, no plot . . . '. That comment is bound to bring to our minds, as readers of Virginia Woolf, her comment in the famous essay entitled 'Modern Fiction': 'if a writer were a free man and not a slave', she writes, 'if he could write what he chose, not what he must, if he could base his work upon his own feeling and not upon convention, there would be no plot, no comedy, no tragedy, no love interest or catastrophe in the accepted style . . . '.[13] (Full emphasis must be given to that final phrase – nobody would want to suggest that her work is lacking in comedy, for example.) 'Modern Fiction' has of course become a standard reference point for many discussions, not only of Virginia Woolf but also more generally of the stream of consciousness novel. It is surely of some considerable significance that one of its leading ideas (even down to the phrasing) is prefigured in an article which deals, not with the stream of consciousness, but with group consciousness.

I am sure that by this stage in my argument you will have brought to mind innumerable instances in Virginia Woolf which can be seen in this context of an exploration of group feeling. *The Waves* is obviously relevant to our discussion, being a novel that clearly attempts to express the idea of a group mind. The early drafts show in a very interesting way how Virginia Woolf searched around for a way to express what she calls in her review of Romains the 'mysterious growth' of a 'kind of consciousness of the group'.[14] But speculation about the group was not confined to Unanimist writers, nor to literary explorations of the idea. Virginia Woolf was aware of other works on group psychology and crowd theory which were written in the first decades of the century, and which were discussed with great interest by members of the Bloomsbury Group.

In a review written in January 1916 Leonard Woolf spoke of the huge upsurge of interest which had taken place in the study of group psychology, an interest which had become, he said, much more pronounced, for obvious reasons, since the outbreak of the War. At this point in time, early 1916, Woolf was extremely sceptical about the possibility of an adequate theory of crowd psychology. In view of the fact that one of the books which he had been reading claimed that leadership of a crowd depended upon the body weight of the leader, his scepticism is not surprising. The author of this heavyweight theory had discovered that the average weight of an American bishop was 176.4 lb, whereas preachers in small towns had an average weight of 159.4 lb (a nice touch, the '.4s'). So proving, I suppose, that Julius Caesar's preference for fat men was ill-advised. But Leonard Woolf's attitude was to change significantly in the following months.

We find in the *Catalogue of Books from the Library of Leonard and Virginia Woolf* that the Woolfs owned a copy of a book by Wilfred Trotter called *Instincts of the Herd in Peace and War*, published in 1916. Despite the use that is sometimes made of this catalogue, I do not think that we should place too much weight on it as evidence of anything. Luckily, we have more substantial proof of the great effect which Trotter's book had on Leonard Woolf. From an article published by Woolf in July 1916, we can gather that Trotter had achieved the almost impossible task of dispelling the scepticism about group psychology which had been established a few months earlier by the man who weighed bishops. Leonard obviously found the book convincing, and it is clear that it altered the direction of his thinking, for he began to see the crowd in terms of its non-rational or instinctive motivation.

From her biography of Roger Fry we can see that Virginia Woolf was involved in discussions about Trotter's theory in the early twenties. But as her diaries reveal she was aware of his herd theory much earlier. She was at first sceptical about Trotter's analysis of the herd-like quality of human collective behaviour, but she began to see group behaviour from Trotter's point of view. (It should be pointed out that she and other members of the Group interpreted the herd theory in a much more pessimistic sense than Trotter intended.) Writing in her Diary in November 1917 she recorded a relevant conversation with Roger Fry:

> Old Roger takes a gloomy view, not of our life, but of the world's future; but I think I detected the influence of Trotter & the herd, & so I distrusted him. Still, stepping out into Charlotte Street, where the Bloomsbury murder took place a week or two ago, & seeing a crowd swarming in the road & hearing women abuse each other & at the noise others come running with delight–all this sordidity made me think him rather likely to be right.[15]

Years later, we find Virginia Woolf still using images and ideas arising from these discussions of Trotter's work. We can see then, when we consider Virginia Woolf's close knowledge of Trotter and of the Unanimist Romains, that she could draw on a powerful body of thought which explored the nature of group consciousness. It is significant, though, that in terms of *feeling* these ideas pulled in opposite directions; the Unanimists being patently optimistic, whereas Trotter was understood by Virginia Woolf as conveying a pessimistic message (whether this was a true understanding is of course another matter). In the pull of these contraries Virginia Woolf could find a pattern which was very familiar in her own emotional life, of elation and depression, of expansiveness and withdrawal.

This interest in group consciousness remained with Virginia Woolf throughout her writing career. As Leonard Woolf says, the advent of the First World War greatly stimulated interest in explorations of the group idea, and we have seen that Virginia Woolf's own observations of 'herd behaviour', as Trotter called it, were especially active in the War, and in the peace celebrations which followed. It is quite natural then, that with the threat of another war, in the late thirties, her thoughts should turn in that direction again, and in this perspective her final novel, *Between the Acts*, can be seen as the culmination of Virginia Woolf's exploration of group consciousness. The background which I have been sketching in helps to explain why she should have been so fascinated by Freud's 'Group Psychology and the Analysis of the Ego' whilst writing *Between the Acts*. The influence of Freud's essay on Virginia Woolf has been noted,[16] but never in this larger context which I have been trying to establish. That context can help to explain Miss La Trobe's relief when a herd of cattle joins in her pageant, and why they are visited by Eros, but these local matters of explication are much less important for my purpose in this argument than the recovery of an important and powerful stream of speculation of which Virginia Woolf is a part. Virginia Woolf was certainly an idiosyncratic writer; I am suggesting that her interest in the group mind is not one of her idiosyncrasies.

William James chose the stream metaphor from amongst a number of possibilities, as we can see in his general description of the stream of consciousness in the book called *Talks to Teachers* (was this the book which poisoned Lawrence's adolescence?): 'There is a stream', says James, 'a succession of states, or waves, or fields (or whatever you please to call them), of knowledge, of feeling, of desire, of deliberation etc., that constantly pass and repass, and that constitute our inner life. The existence of this stream is the primal fact, the nature and origin of it form the essential problem, of our science'.[17] James's favoured metaphor, the stream, has been taken up by subsequent generations. For the artist, and perhaps ultimately for the scientist as well, the choice of metaphor is not such a matter of indifference as James seems to suggest. The incidence of wave and sea imagery in Virginia Woolf's work is an obvious feature which has been extensively documented. What does this imagery tell us when we look at it, not as a kind of abstract pattern, or part of her personal 'handwriting', as it were, but to ask what its implications are for our perception of consciousness as it is conveyed in Virginia Woolf's novels?

Certainly the ebb and flow of waves is a better image for the texture of Virginia Woolf's portrayal of moments of reverie than 'stream' would be, but much more important for my immediate argument is the continuity which is established in Virginia Woolf's sea imagery between the individual and the group. I was tempted to suggest that the wave and sea metaphors are easier to elaborate in the direction of group consciousness than the image of a stream, but my suspicion that this is not the case is confirmed by an interesting recent study of the crowd, Elias Canetti's *Crowds and Power*, (I would like to thank my colleague Ms Sheelagh Strawbridge for drawing my attention to this work) in which he elaborates both river and sea metaphors as symbols of the crowd (or rather of crowds having different degrees of openness). What we can say is that Virginia Woolf certainly did use the sea metaphor to create a continuity between individual and group consciousness, as we can see explicitly in her *Diary*. Writing in 1925 she commented, 'I sometimes think humanity is a vast wave, undulating: the same, I mean: the same emotions'.[18] And of course *The Waves* is her most thoroughgoing attempt to establish a continuity between the individual and group consciousness through the elaboration of the image of the title. As one critic has succinctly put it, the sea in Virginia Woolf is never completely estranging.[19]

I do not expect that the terms 'wave of consciousness' or 'sea of consciousness' will ever gain the currency of 'stream of consciousness', even in discussions of Virginia Woolf's work, but I think that if we occasionally consider the alternative metaphor we will have a truer notion of the relationship which I hope I have established was a significant one for Virginia Woolf; that between individual and group consciousness.

Notes

1. Virginia Woolf, *The Question of Things Happening: The Letters of Virginia Woolf*, eds Nigel Nicolson and Joanne Trautmann (London: Hogarth Press, 1976) Vol II, p. 321.
2. Virginia Woolf, *Mrs Dalloway* (1925; rpt. London: Hogarth Press, 1947) p.168.
3. William James, *The Principles of Psychology* (1890; rpt. New York: Dover, 1950) Vol I, p. 239.
4. William James, *Talks to Teachers on Psychology* (1899; rpt. London: Longman, 1910) p. 17.
5. William James, *Principles*, p. 226.
6. James Naremore, *The World Without a Self* (New Haven: Yale University Press, 1973) p. 73.
7. Avrom Fleishman, *Virginia Woolf: A Critical Reading* (Baltimore: Johns Hopkins University Press, 1975) pp. 84; 59.
8. 'Les Copains', review of Jules Romains, *Les Copains*, *Times Literary Supplement*, 7 Aug. 1913, p. 330.

9. E. M. Forster, review of *The Voyage Out*, *Daily News and Leader*, 8 April 1915, p. 7.
10. Jules Romains, *The Death of a Nobody*, trans. Desmond MacCarthy and Sydney Waterlow (London: Howard Latimer, 1914) p. 37.
11. Ibid, p. 145.
12. Woolf, *Mrs Dalloway*, p. 21.
13. Virginia Woolf, 'Modern Fiction', *Collected Essays*, ed. Leonard Woolf (London: Chatto & Windus, 1966) Vol II, p. 106.
14. See my 'Virginia Woolf and Unanism', *The Journal of Modern Literature*, vol. 9, no. 1 (1981-2).
15. Virginia Woolf, *The Diary of Virginia Woolf*, ed. Anne Olivier Bell (London: Hogarth Press, 1977) Vol. I, p. 80.
16. See Hermione Lee, *The Novels of Virginia Woolf* (London: Methuen, 1977) p. 218.
17. William James, *Talks to Teachers*, p. 15.
18. Virginia Woolf, *The Diary of Virginia Woolf*, eds Anne Olivier Bell and Andrew McNeillie (London: Hogarth Press, 1980) Vol. II, p. 22.
19. Carl Woodring, *Virginia Woolf* (New York: Columbia University Press, 1966).

3 Virginia Woolf and her Reader

Ian Gregor

I

Let me begin by striking a personal note. Some weeks ago I was listening to a radio programme called 'Pleasures' in which the actress Siǎn Phillips was describing some of the pleasures she derived from literature. In the course of the programme she talked about the pleasure to be obtained from the description of food and she instanced the dinner party in *To The Lighthouse* and Mrs Ramsay's celebratory serving of the 'Boeuf en Daube'. Before the actual passage was read, she remarked that she had gone to her copy of the novel with the expectation that the passage was much longer than, in fact, it is and that it had the kind of detail which could provide the basis, at least, of a recipe. Instead of which she found a comparatively few lines, but lines which had glowed in her memory for years, so whenever the novel was mentioned it was that scene which came vividly before her.

Siǎn Phillips' experience, her expectation, and her subsequent surprise, is not an unfamiliar one to readers of Virginia Woolf's novels – we could all, I think, provide our own short list of such occasions, but what is interesting is that they are not a series of striking dramatic moments (such as we recall from many other novels), rather they are a sudden crystallisation of mood, caught often in a seemingly arbitrary detail, which then fuses with the mood of the reader, as he is reading, and begins to expand in the memory. It is that process of absorption, concentration and expansion that interests me in these remarks about the role of the reader in Woolf's novels.

To continue the personal note for a moment. Some years ago I became interested in the way in which reading as a process, rather than 'reading' as a completed action ('a reading', so to speak) affected the critical accounts we could give of certain novels. My interests at the time were largely in the novels of Hardy and it seemed that his fiction could be illuminated by an emphasis on sequence, pace, anticipation, recollection. The famous phrase, 'a series of seemings', suggested the appropriateness of such an emphasis, and in turn, the approach seemed to re-vivify the phrase.

From one point of view, Hardy and Woolf seemed to have little in common as novelists, but from the point of view of their 'moments of vision' (to borrow a title from a late collection of Hardy's poems), and their concern with 'impressions', they had much more in common than we might, at first, suspect. In both writers we have a constant stress on shifting perspectives, flickering intimations, continually evolving movement – these apprehensions seem central to their mutual act of imagining the human consciousness. My present concern is the way in which this centrality of impression, of movement, of consciousness, affects our reading response, and in turn, our understanding of the novels.

It was no doubt Woolf's feeling for Hardy that enabled her to write one of her best critical essays, in the course of which she made a remark which seems to me to be felicitous both about Hardy and herself. She is talking about the inequalities of Hardy's novels and she continues:

> there is always about them a little blur of unconsciousness . . . [a] margin of the unexpressed which often produces the most profound sense of satisfaction. It is as if . . . [Hardy's conscious-ness] held more than he could produce and he left it for his readers to make out his full meaning and to supplement it from their own experience.[1]

'The margin of the unexpressed', 'he left it for his readers to make out his full meaning' – these phrases serve to mark out that aspect of Virginia Woolf's work which I would like to try and describe. For the sake of economy, and hopefully clarity, I am going to confine my discussion largely to a single novel. I have chosen *To The Lighthouse* – but I will conclude by indicating the drift my remarks would seem to have for Woolf's novels in general.

II

Like one of those pictures which contains a picture of itself, *To The Lighthouse* contains an episode which suggests how it should be read. There is in fact a good deal of reading done in the novel; Mrs Ramsay reads a fairy tale to her son, Mr Carmichael reads Virgil, Mr Ramsay takes a 'little shiny book with covers mottled like a plover's egg' with him on his trip to the lighthouse, but there is one moment in the novel where the interest is not on *what* is being read, but on *how* it is being read, and when this episode marks the fullest expression of the dominant human relationship in the novel, then the connection between the nature of reading and the substance of that reading needs no further stress.

The scene occurs in the final part of the first section of the novel. A day has been described in the summer house of the Ramsay family, a day recalling the summer days spent by the Stephen family some thirty years earlier at St Ives. It is late evening and for the first time Mr and Mrs Ramsay find themselves alone. Mr Ramsay is reading Scott's *The Antiquary:*

> Don't interrupt me, he seemed to be saying, don't say anything, just sit there. And he went on reading. His lips twitched. It filled him. It fortified him. He clean forgot all the little rubs and digs of the evening . . . . This man's strength and sanity, his feeling for straight-forward simple things, these fishermen, the poor old crazed creature in Mucklebackit's cottage made him feel so vigorous, so relieved of something that he felt roused and triumphant and could not choke back his tears. Raising the book a little to hide his face he let them fall and shook his head from side to side and forgot himself completely . . . forgot his own bothers and failures completely in poor Steenie's drowning and Mucklebackit's sorrow (that was Scott at his best) and the astonishing delight and feeling of vigour that it gave him.[2]

For Mr Ramsay, Scott's novel has ordered, extended, given definition to human experience. The feelings aroused by Steenie's drowning are so immediate that he has 'to raise the book to hide his face', but the book has made Mucklebackit's sorrow so transparent to him that he has become oblivious to his own 'bothers and failures'. Scott's art has been so complete in its communication that he closes the book in triumph and delight.

Mrs Ramsay is also reading, but her text, Shakespeare's sonnet 82, is being read in a very different way:

> Mrs Ramsay raised her head and like a person in a light sleep seemed to say that if he wanted her to wake she would, she really would, but otherwise, might she go on sleeping, just a little longer, just a little longer? She was climbing up those branches, this way and that, laying hands on one flower and then another.
> Nor praise the deep vermilion in the rose, she read, and so reading she was ascending, she felt, on to the top, on to the summit. How satisfying! How restful! All the odds and ends of the day stuck to this magnet; her mind felt swept, felt clean. And then there it was, suddenly entire shaped in her hands, beautiful and reasonable, clear and complete, the essence sucked out of life and held rounded here – the sonnet.[3]

For Mrs Ramsay reading is an anodyne, the words are withdrawn from her attention; rhythm predominates, so that the poem exerts an incantatory spell, with 'the essence sucked out of life and held rounded here'.

Two ways of reading, presented sequentially, setting each other off in a marked contrast. For Mr Ramsay his reading is an encounter with a world other than his own – 'he felt he had been arguing with somebody' – Scott's novel has unquestioned objectivity, whether it affords insight into Mucklebackit's grief or Steenie's drowning or simply as a piece of writing, 'that was Scott at his best'. This is reading as dialogue. For Mrs Ramsay, the world is patterned into language, its shape is that of the sonnet. It is reading as self-communion.

Woolf is using contrasted styles of reading as a prefiguration of a more inclusive 'reading', the author's exploration of the relationship *between* the Ramsays themselves. Up to this point it has been a relationship which is tense and uncompromising. On Ramsay's side it has been characterised by acerbity, by the demands he has made on his wife. On his wife's side there has been sympathy but remoteness, conciliation but resistance. And now as they conclude their reading, their dialogue is sparse, commonplace, intermittent:

'They're engaged . . . . Paul and Minta.'
'So I guessed.'

'How nice it would be to marry a man with a wash-leather bag for his watch.'

Behind these bare exchanges, there is a powerful ebb and flow of feeling. That self-communing which characterised Mrs Ramsay's reading of the Shakespeare sonnet begins to turn into an unfocussed melancholy, so that she is gratified by the sharp rebuke of her husband, 'you won't finish that stocking tonight', hearing in his tone a sharp reminder of a world outside her reverie. Mr Ramsay also has need of a reminder but, conversely, it is to bring reassurance to his inner world, to feel that his wife loves him. Aware of his need, aware of her love for him, she cannot grant him the comfort of its formal expression. She turns away, then looks at him, and smiles. It is enough, 'though she had not said a word, he knew, of course he knew, that she loved him'. Perfect harmony between them has been established, 'thinking to herself, Nothing on earth can equal this happiness . . . . . . She had not said it, but he knew it. And she looked at him smiling. For she had triumphed again'.

A scene which begins with the silence of separation, with the Ramsays enclosed in their reading, ends with separation transformed into mutual understanding and love. The awareness that Mr Ramsay has of Scott's feeling for his characters modulates into his awareness of his wife's need; the intensity of feeling which Mrs Ramsay responds to in the sonnet modulates into making her love for her husband known and accessible to him. But not a word has been said; it is the reader who makes the silence eloquent. When we read the final sentence, 'For she had triumphed again', we feel it detaches itself gently from the narrative and moves into a space where it can be 'spoken' simultaneously by Mrs Ramsay, by the author about her, and by the reader about the dramatic impact made by the whole scene which has led up to it. This scene between the Ramsays is an instance where the triumph of the characters and the triumph of the author's art converge in a way that releases in the reader a mood of quiet elation which makes him happy to be caught up in the emotional pattern of the scene and to complete its meaning. Expressed in this way, we can see the reader 'filling in' the gaps, so to speak, but if that was a dominant pattern in the novel, it would become much too predictable, and predictable in a way that would not account for the distinctive role that Woolf assigns to the reader in her novels.

What is distinctive about this role is that it is constantly varying and 'the meaning' of certain episodes emerges out of their variation. The scene with the Ramsays which I described reminds us of our *own* activity as readers, it provokes us to comparison, to interpretation, above all to a keen awareness of 'the margin of the unexpressed'. But the flow of this particular scene is all in one direction; there are no counter-currents. In the scenes I want to look at now the direction is continually changing, so that 'meaning' emerges out of the interplay between the substance of the text and the turbulence of its transmission.

I am going to instance three scenes which I hope will illustrate what I mean; three scenes which, when taken together, suggest *the complexity of movement* that is embodied in *To The Lighthouse*. We talk of 'the process' of reading as if it was a steady unfolding; it is much more a matter of check and counter-check, pause and acceleration, intensification and distancing.

The first of these scenes occurs just after the dinner party. Mrs Ramsay goes up to the bedroom to find Cam and James awake and quarrelling. The dispute is about a boar's head which has been nailed to the wall as a decoration. 'Cam couldn't go to sleep with it in the room and James screamed if she touched it'. Mrs Ramsay proceeds to soothe each child in turn. For Cam, she covers the head with her shawl so that 'it was like a mountain, a bird's nest, a garden . . . she could see the words echoing as she spoke them rhythmically', and soon Cam is asleep. Then she turns to James. She assures him the skull was still there under the shawl. And he too, is calmed.

The skull and the shawl – the scene offers itself riskily as a theme for a shoal of critical essays; a too easy meditation on Death and Beauty, on Time and the Moment. But it is only in retrospect that that danger becomes apparent. In the process of reading, our attention is not upon the skull or the shawl, or upon the children, it is on Mrs Ramsay and her instinctive empathy for the needs now of one child, now of the other. It is human movement, literally so in this instance, that effectively takes the harm out of the threatening abstractions. The whole episode is suffused with Mrs Ramsay's gentle understanding, conveyed more in the rhythm of her speech, direct and crisp to James, leisurely and repetitive to Cam – than in any overt content. The effect on the reader is to withdraw the details of the episode from our attention and make us overwhelmingly aware of movement and mood.

My second instance works in a different way. It is the scene earlier in the book when Lily finds herself questioned by William Bankes about 'the meaning' of her painting. 'Taking out a penknife, Mr Bankes tapped the canvas with the bone handle. What did she wish to indicate by the triangular purple shape, "just there?" he asked.' At one level the discussion that follows is familiar enough – the rival claims to truth of realist and abstract art. For Bankes, painting is representative, autobiographical, what he valued most in his drawing-room was the picture of 'the cherry trees in blossom on the banks of the Kennet'. For Lily, a painting was a question of 'the relation of masses, of lights and shadows'. It is a version of Woolf's debate with Arnold Bennett. Unlike the skull and the shawl, we are made aware when reading the scene of 'a debate', but it is a debate conducted not in the service of adjudicating between the rival claims of art, but of enabling Lily to recognise William Bankes's regard for her and her consequent response of grateful pleasure.

Woolf here is deliberately seeking to capture the isolated moment, so that unlike the episode with Mrs Ramsay and the children, there *is* a sense in which the exchange between Lily and Bankes *does* detach itself from the text as we read it, just as Lily is suddenly made to feel a sudden enclosure of mutual feeling between Bankes and herself. It is not the beginning of a relationship, it is simply a moment when Lily feels a delighted sense of mutual recognition.

> . . . thanking Mr Ramsay for it and Mrs Ramsay for it and the hour and the place, crediting the world with a power which she had not suspected, that one could walk away down that long gallery not alone any more but arm in arm with somebody – the strangest feeling in the world, and the most exhilarating – she nicked the catch of her paint-box to, more firmly than was necessary, and the nick seemed to surround in a circle for ever the paint-box, the lawn, Mr Bankes, and that wild villain, Cam, dashing past.[4]

This long sentence which brings the episode to its conclusion dramatises in miniature the way in which Woolf seeks deliberately to arrest her narrative, so that the whole episode between Lily and Bankes is held within parentheses. That 'nick' of the paint-box catches the whole scene and 'freezes' it 'in a circle for ever – the paint-box, the lawn, Mr Bankes and that wild villain, Cam, dashing past'. A motion film is made into 'a still'.

My third instance has the capacity to provoke the reader into a

variety of responses in the very process of reading. It is an episode
which brings together the Ramsays and Lily and William Bankes in
an interesting way. Lily and William, out for a walk, come across
Mr and Mrs Ramsay looking at two of their children, Prue and
Jasper, throwing catches to one another. At first we watch through
the eyes of Lily, watching the Ramsays watching their children:

> So that is marriage, Lily thought, a man and a woman looking at
> a girl throwing a ball. . . . And suddenly the meaning which, for
> no reason at all . . . descends on people, making them symbolical,
> making them representative, came upon them, and made them
> in the dusk standing, looking the symbols of marriage, husband
> and wife.[5]

Watching the scene through Lily's eyes the reader is made to feel a
slightly histrionic detachment, a deliberate framing of the Ramsays
so that they become isolated figures in a narrative picture which
might be called 'Family Pleasures'. Then, quite suddenly, a static
picture is transformed into motion. The Ramsays, Lily, Bankes, see
the ball curving through the sky and 'Prue ran full tilt into them and
caught the ball brilliantly high up in her left hand'. Detachment
dissolves immediately, the symbolical outlines vanish and Prue is
taken back 'into the alliance of family life again, from which she had
escaped, throwing catches . . .'.

In its range of effects this is more complex than the two earlier
scenes which I have discussed. There is an air of self-conscious
dramatisation about it, so that the reader is kept hovering – feeling
that if Lily's instant symbolic portraiture of the Ramsays as
'Marriage' won't quite do, neither will the swift domestication
of the scene into 'throwing catches'. The gap between the two
makes us sense the unobtrusive presence of the novelist, less self-
consciously interpretive than Lily, but more sensitive to a range of
encompassing feelings than the actual situation – 'throwing
catches' – would seem to warrant.

With passages like these in mind I hope to have suggested that
when we talk of movement and process in relation to *To The
Lighthouse,* we are talking of a whole variety of effects – sometimes
emphasising pace, sometimes the reverse, sometimes a fusion of
both. Granted this description of local effects, and granted that what
I have been describing as 'movement' plays a large part in the
memorability of Woolf's novels, the question can now be put, what

significance has this for our understanding of Woolf's achievement as a whole?

III

For the remainder of this paper I would like to reverse the perspective, turning from a consideration of the detail to the whole, while retaining the emphasis on reading as performance.

In considering these three passages from *To The Lighthouse* I have tried to bring out the shifting relationship they have with the reader, a relationship which eludes the traditional categorisation into subject and object. When the 'Boeuf en Daube' is recalled at Mrs Ramsay's dinner party, it seems to exist for us as a discrete item, making its impact because of its vivid imagining. But when confronted with the actual brevity of the description, we are made to realise that the dish is a condensation of a whole range of feeling which has been building up throughout the dinner party, inducing within the reader a contemplative intensity. To recall the dish is to recreate the encompassing mood.

Let me try and clarify, in more general terms, what I have in mind, by quoting a passage from Bradley which Eliot cites with approval in his thesis, *Knowledge and Experience in the Philosophy of F. H. Bradley:*

> In describing immediate experience we must use terms which offer a surreptitious suggestion of subject or object. If we say presentation, we think of a subject to which the presentation is present as an object. And if we say *feeling*, we think of it as the feeling of a subject about an object . . . It may accordingly be said that the real situation is an experience which can never be wholly defined as an object nor wholly enjoyed as a feeling, but in which any of the observed constituents may take on the one or the other aspect.[6]

'*May take on the one or the other aspect*'; it is that potentiality, that mobility, which is crucial in Bradley's account. There is no suggestion of a fusion or a merger, in which the tension between subject and object would be resolved. On the other hand, the reciprocity between object and feeling is so strong, so constant, that to conceive of them as distinct is to misrepresent the relationship.

I would like to bring this notion closer to Woolf by putting beside the passage from Bradley a passage from Leonard Woolf's autobiography in which he describes an exchange between his wife and Eliot:

> Virginia one evening tackled him about his poetry and told him that 'he wilfully concealed his transitions'. He admitted this, but said that it was unnecessary to explain, explanation diluted facts . . . What he wanted to was to 'disturb externals'.[7]

There the transition is conceived not as setting an 'inner' against an 'outer' world, but where an 'inner' world, a feeling, exists as a tremor, a disturbance in our apprehension of 'externals'.

> Do I dare
> Disturb the universe?

Prufrock's question expresses, simultaneously, both his feelings and the feelings which have led to his creation.

With these reflections in mind I believe it is possible to offer a way of looking at Woolf's work as a whole and to see it in terms of a changing relationship with her reader. She once remarked that she saw the reader as 'an accomplice, a fellow-worker', and I believe that in looking at the varying role the reader is called upon to play, we are also looking at the imaginative congruence she achieves in her fiction. That congruence, in her case, like Eliot's, was intimately related to the success with which she could 'disturb externals' and find, in transitions, a creative reciprocity between 'feeling' and 'the object'.

In her first novel *The Voyage Out* (1915) the reader is cast very much in the role of a witness. Woolf's remark to Clive Bell about the novel, 'You have no notion how pale and transparent it reads to me sometimes – though I wrote it with heat enough',[8] catches very exactly the reader's response also. That is to say, there is a chill about the surface of the novel, so that it seems drained of narrative energy. At the same time we are aware that there is an intensity of concern with exploring an inner life. It is as if the author found herself trapped in the conventions of one novel, while seeking to write another; *A Room with a View* uneasily over-looking *Heart of Darkness*. Only in the episode of Rachel's fatal illness do the perspectives converge. The dominant effect made upon the reader is not of people or places or things – but talk; talk about love, about education, about death, about reading done and reading yet to be done, talk carried on ceaselessly in rooms, or walks, on expeditions. The reader is there simply as auditor. 'We want to find out what's behind things'; Hewet's remark to Rachel is all too revealing of Woolf's own difficulty not only of 'finding a way', but in recognising that the polarity between 'inner' and 'outer' is not to be 'her way' at all. There is a passage early in the novel which illustrates in a rather comic manner both Woolf's vague awareness of what she wants to do and her inability to achieve it. It occurs on the outward voyage when Mrs Ambrose is doing some embroidery:

> . . . she had her embroidery frame set up on deck, with a little table by her side on which lay open a black volume of philosophy. She chose a thread from the vari-coloured tangle that lay in her lap, and sewed red into the bark of a tree, or yellow into the river torrent. She was working at a great design of tropical river running through a tropical forest, where spotted deer would eventually browse upon masses of fruit, bananas, oranges, and giant pomegranates, while a troop of naked natives whirled darts into the air. Between the stitches she looked to one side and read a sentence about the Reality of Matter, or the Nature of Good. Round her men in blue jerseys knelt and scrubbed the boards or leant over the rails and whistled, and not far off Mr Pepper sat cutting up roots with a penknife.[9]

We can see quite well that Woolf is seeking to give that multi-layered apprehension of experience, which she does so effortlessly in the passages I looked at earlier in *To The Lighthouse*. But between the design of the embroidery with its 'tropical river running through a tropical forest', 'the little black volume' speaking of 'the Reality of Matter and the Nature of Good', 'the men in blue jerseys kneeling and scrubbing', and 'Mr Pepper cutting up roots with a penknife', are yawning vacancies not transitions. Woolf has not yet found her way to present subject and object so that the constituents 'may take on the one or the other aspect'. As a consequence there is no employment for the reader as 'a fellow worker'; he remains, for most of the time, a faintly bored spectator.

If *The Voyage Out* marks one extreme in the relationship of the reader with Woolf's fiction, *The Waves* (1931) marks the other. In saying this I have in mind the reaction to the novel described by

Elizabeth Hardwick:

> I was immensely moved by *The Waves* when I read it recently and
> yet I cannot think of anything to say except that it was wonderful.
> The people are not characters, there is no plot in the usual sense.
> What can you bring to bear: verisimilitude to what? You can
> merely say over and over again, very beautiful, and that when
> you were reading it you were happy.[10]

For Elizabeth Hardwick the novel has disappeared, in Bradley's
terms 'the object' has been absorbed in 'the feeling'. *The Waves* has
choreographed the reader's meditations and left no margin for
critical discourse – at least for Miss Hardwick this has been the case.
For the reader who dislikes *The Waves*, the pattern of response will
tend to reverse the emphasis. There is only 'the object', it is quite
self-sufficient; if there is any 'reading' of it to be done, Woolf has
already done it, not simply through a surrogate voice, Bernard, but
in the total structure of the book. Again there seems no margin for
critical discourse. I am not wishing to endorse, at this point, either
one or the other of these views, but simply to indicate that the nature
of Woolf's most ambitious novel has been to create in its readers a
response of such marked intensity, whether of identification or
rejection, that the act of critical judgement is made to seem an act of
supererogation. It would be to misconceive the situation to think it
better if the novel were to prompt a more 'balanced', a more
discriminatory, response. The rhetoric of the novel is peremptory
and exclusive; it makes the reader think of himself as 'the writer', so
that 'the feeling' *in* the novel becomes indistiguishable from feeling
about the novel.

Virginia Woolf's last novel, *Between the Acts* (1941) has exerted a
special appeal for the contemporary reader. In contrast to *The
Waves* where critical judgement seemed hard to find, *Between the Acts*
actively solicits such judgement; among the various pleasures it
offers the reader is the sense of his own critical awareness of the effect
the novel is making upon him. It puts on parade an interest in the
problematics of fiction – what is illusion? What is reality? What is
meaning? Integral to the novel's appeal is a meditation on the
extent, and on the limitations of art. *Between the Acts* has certainly
something of the social vivacity of the novels of Woolf's middle
period – *Mrs Dalloway* and *To The Lighthouse* – but it is immeasurably more watchful and self-aware. There is the steel of determi-

nation behind the novel's high spirits. For a certain kind of reader, its expert self-awareness, its assurance of touch, will be a sign of Woolf's mature art; but for another, the novel will make an impression not of knowledge, but of knowingness, not of mystery but mystification. A passage like the following suggests something of the equivocation of the novel's appeal. It is the conclusion of the description which contrasts two pictures which hang in the dining room, one picture being of an ancestor, the other of an anonymous lady.

> He was a talk producer, that ancestor. But the lady was a picture. In her yellow robe, leaning, with a pillar to support her, a silver arrow in her hand, and a feather in her hair, she led the eye up, down, from the curve to the straight, through glades of greenery and shades of silver, dun and rose into silence. The room was empty.
> Empty, empty, empty; silent, silent, silent. The room was a shell singing of what was before time was; a vase stood in the heart of the house, alabaster, smooth, cold, holding the still, distilled silence of emptiness, silence.[11]

Such a passage is warmly hospitable to interpretation, without being insistent, and we are left free to muse upon two kinds of art, the relation of art to time, the eloquence of the unspoken. While such reflections give the passage a sheen which is part of the pleasure it seeks to give, we might also feel that it is all too casual, too carefully parenthetical. In the passage I looked at earlier from *The Voyage Out*, the reader was made to feel that Woolf was in difficulty about negotiating transitions; in *Between The Acts* (as the very title indicates) the negotiation of transitions has come dangerously close to being an end in itself.

I have left to a final paragraph that phase of Woolf's work where I believe her relation with her reader to have been at its happiest, a phase where the reader is invited to participate, but allowed freedom for manoeuvre. It is the period characterised by *Mrs Dalloway*, where the reader is free to explore the resonances between Septimus and Clarissa, and *To The Lighthouse*, where the reader can see Mrs Ramsay for himself, and then meditate upon her different significance in relation to Mr Ramsay and Lily Briscoe. Both novels define and create gaps which the reader can inhabit with pleasure, because they emerge from dramatic conflicts within the novel and are not (however cunningly) inscribed into it.

Asked to give a title descriptive of the reader's role in *Mrs Dalloway* and *To The Lighthouse*, I think 'The Reader as Guest' would come close to the mark; an invited presence, a participant, avoiding the roles of onlooker and surrogate host. It is fitting that the image which lingers most memorably in *To The Lighthouse* should be that dinner party.

> Now all the candles were lit, and the faces on both sides of the table were brought nearer by the candle light, and composed, as they had not been in the twilight, into a party round a table, for the night was now shut off by panes of glass, which, far from giving any accurate view of the outside world, rippled it so strangely that here, inside the room, seemed to be order and dry land; there, outside, a reflection in which things wavered and vanished, waterily.[12]

'Here, inside . . . there, outside'; the equilibrium is finely managed, but it is an equilibrium which the reader experiences first as a feeling within the novel and then, as the novel shapes itself in the recreating memory, a feeling about it, so that it becomes, in the paradoxical sense intended by Bradley, 'an object of affection'.

Notes

1. Virginia Woolf, 'The Novels of Thomas Hardy', *Collected Essays*, ed. L. Woolf (London: Chatto & Windus, 1966) Vol. I, p. 258.
2. Virginia Woolf, *To The Lighthouse* (1927; rpt. London: Hogarth Press, 1932) Sect. I, Ch. 19, pp. 184-5.
3. Ibid., pp. 186-7.
4. Ibid., Sect. I, Ch. 9, pp. 86-7.
5. Ibid., Sect. I, Ch. 13, pp. 114-15.
6. T. S. Eliot, *Knowledge and Experience in the Philosophy of F. H. Bradley* (London: Faber and Faber, 1964) pp. 22, 25.
7. Leonard Woolf, *Downhill All the Way: An Autobiography of the Years 1919-1939* (London: Hogarth Press, 1967) p. 109.
8. Virginia Woolf, letter dated 7 Feb. 1909, *The Flight of the Mind: The Letters of Virginia Woolf, Vol. I 1888-1912*, eds. Nigel Nicolson and Joanne Trautmann (London: Hogarth Press, 1976) pp. 382-3.
9. Virginia Woolf, *The Voyage Out* (1915; rpt. London: Hogarth Press, 1929) p. 30.

10. Elizabeth Hardwick, 'Virginia Woolf and Bloomsbury', *Seduction and Betrayal* (London: Weidenfeld & Nicolson, 1974) p. 136.
11. Virginia Woolf, *Between the Acts* (London: Hogarth Press, 1941) pp. 46-7.
12. Woolf, *To The Lighthouse*, Sect. I, Ch. 17, p. 151.

4 A Writer's Life

Lyndall Gordon

I

'Come to lunch', Virginia Woolf invited her brother-in-law, Clive
Bell. 'Eliot will be there in a four-piece suit.' It was easy to
caricature Eliot's respectable façade; later, when she knew him
better, she was more searching. 'How he suffers!' she noted when he
came to tea on 4 February 1935:

> Yes: I felt my accursed gift of sympathy rising . . . Suddenly T.
> spoke with a genuine cry of feeling. About immortality: . . . he
> revealed his passion, as he seldom does. A religious soul: an
> unhappy man: a lonely very sensitive man, all wrapt up in fibres
> of self torture, doubt, conceit, desire for warmth & intimacy. And
> I'm very fond of him - like him in some of my reserves &
> subterfuges.[1]

In this quick sketch, Virginia Woolf circles the essence of Eliot. Both
these writers had similar views of lives; both wanted to express the
obscure corners of character and experience and, secondly, to give
shape to the lifespan. In turn, we might use these views as guidelines
for biographic studies of themselves. This kind of study would be,
ideally, complementary to standard biography in that it would
concentrate on the invisible moments of a writer's life that terminate
in the work. Emerson said: 'The life of a great artist is always thus
inward, a life of no events'.[2] I shall look at ideas for this kind of
biography in the works of Virginia Woolf, glancing at similar ideas
in Eliot, and then suggest how they might be applied to a writer's
life.

Virginia Woolf was given to dashing comments on people that
could be fanciful or malicious. We must distinguish, from these, her
genuine attempts at imaginative truth. Some of her most brilliant

attempts came early with her incisive portraits of her parents in the 'Reminiscences' (1907-8) where, interestingly, she is less critical of Leslie Stephen, and perhaps more just, than in later portraits of her father. Moreover, between 1908 and 1910 she wrote some perceptive biographic reviews, approaching a life through its least public phase. Both Virginia Stephen (in June 1910) and Strachey (later) were amused by Lady Hester Stanhope's advance on the East in 1812-13 in male clothes, riding astride. Strachey's traveller is no more than a ridiculous eccentric, flourishing all the manners of power without power itself. He filled gaps of understanding with gorgeous oriental clothes. But Virginia Stephen pointed *to* the gaps: what drove Lady Hester abroad? Where Strachey dwelt on the grandeur of her three years in the home of her uncle, William Pitt, Virginia Stephen saw, from Lady Hester's account of her triumphs, that she must have made herself disliked:

> With scanty education but great natural force, she despised people without troubling to give them a reason for it. Intuition took the place of argument, and her penetration was great.

Real powers fermented in her. But since there was no scope for these in England, she indulged her fantasy of power in the East and, said Virginia Stephen, 'drove herself as near madness as one can go by feeding a measureless ambition upon phantoms'.[3]

One model in these early years was Jane Carlyle whose letters, Leslie Stephen had told her, were the best in the language. In one of Virginia Stephen's admiring reviews, in 1905, she remarked on Jane Carlyle's quick sense of the essential in character 'which is creative as well as critical and, in her, amounted to genius'.[4]

She described her mother's similar insight in the 'Reminiscences' and again in *To the Lighthouse*. At dinner Mrs Ramsay's eyes go round the table, exploring the minds of her guests

> like a light stealing under water so that . . . the reeds in it and the minnows balancing themselves, and the sudden silent trout are all lit up, hanging, trembling.[5]

Her eyebeam lights up an invisible self. It is an exercise of that gift to see through all lies which the beam of the lighthouse had briefly exposed. The biographer behind her novel, the artist behind her easel reproduce the action of the lighthouse. Lily Briscoe's painting of Mrs Ramsay searches out the source of her authority in her inner life. Seeking what is screened by the Victorian mother's arresting beauty, she pares it away and paints her as a wedge shape of darkness. Later, Virginia Woolf said that the painter, Walter Sickert, was the best of biographers for

> when he sits a man or woman down in front of him he sees the whole of the life that has been lived to make that face . . . None of our biographers make such complete and flawless statements.[6]

In 1909 Virginia Stephen wrote a fictional review of a biography of an imaginary Victorian writer, Miss Willatt. The unpublished 'Memoirs of a Novelist' provided a theoretical base for later experiments in fiction. It fulfilled her wish 'to write a very subtle work on the proper writing of lives . . . It comes over me that I know nothing of the art; but blunder in a rash way after motive, and human character . . .'.[7] Miss Willatt, Virginia Stephen imagines, was a writer who died in 1884. Her books now lie on the topmost shelves of seaside libraries. One must take a ladder to reach them and a cloth to wipe them off. Virginia Stephen deliberately picks an unpromising subject, a not very appealing woman whose talents were less than minor. (Miss Willatt thought it indecent to describe what she knew, her family, so 'invented Arabian lovers and set them on the banks of the Orinoco'.) Miss Willatt so fits the stereotype of the silly spinster that she makes the greatest possible demands on her biographer's powers of discernment.

Her fictitious biographer, Miss Linsett, has no powers of discernment. She dwells sentimentally on the balls of the 1840s, not realising that a large, awkward creature like Miss Willatt would have wished to hide her body. Miss Linsett obscures her subject with other contemporary platitudes: tender regrets at the death of her father. Virginia Stephen (as fictitious reviewer) dismisses this twitter:

> Happily there are signs that Miss Willatt was not what she seemed. They creep out in the notes, in her letters, and most clearly in her portraits. The sight of that large selfish face, with the capable forehead and the surly but intelligent eyes, discredits all the platitudes on the opposite page; she looks quite capable of having deceived Miss Linsett.
> When her father died (she had always disliked him) her spirits rose . . .

Miss Linsett makes the father's death in 1855 the end to one chapter and Miss Willatt's removal to London the beginning of the next. In other words, the biographer's plan depends, whenever possible, 'upon changes of address', which confirms the reviewer's suspicion that she 'had no other guide to Miss Willatt's character'. What Miss Linsett misses is the decisive moment in the life: Miss Willatt's sudden decision, at thirty-six, to give up the sham of philanthropy for writing.

Miss Willatt's work among the poor provokes long accounts of charitable societies. Digression is, again, the result of a biographer's inability to discover what is interesting about a writer's life which is without public importance or historic action. Other typical fillers are the pedigree (Miss Linsett takes thirty-six pages over the history of the family, 'a way of marking time during those chill early pages') and the slow approach to the grave. Here, once more, the narrative slackens to a funeral pace. Miss Linsett lingers with relish over the excruciating details of her subject's last illness and leaves her, in the end, buried in extraneous facts.

With this early satire on literary biography, Virginia Stephen bounced herself away from a stale tradition in much the same way as Jane Austen's early satire, 'Love and Friendship', cuts free from stale sentiment. 'Memoirs of a Novelist' warns in particular against excessive detail which could blur crucial moments and, above all, against the mental slot. In the same year (1909), reviewing the Carlyles' love–letters, Virginia Stephen repeats this warning: 'the more we see the less we can label' and again, 'the further we read the less we trust to definition'.[8] In 'Memoirs', the attentive reviewer can glimpse a live woman – flawed, ambitious, restless and intransigent – but cannot rescue the rest of Miss Willatt's story, for such women, in the past, 'have been rolled into the earth irrecoverably'. Here, the young Virginia Stephen is circling the potential subject on which she was to cast the lighthouse beam of her great novels: the obscure, middle-aged woman.

To seek out the invisible life is a well-tried idea in the novel and biography, but where Virginia Woolf is original is in a certain tactic of restraint: she injects silence. Terence Hewet, the unfledged novelist in *The Voyage Out* wants 'to write a novel about Silence . . . the things people don't say. But the difficulty is immense'.[9] At about the same time, Eliot, too, came upon silence as a way of presenting elusive corners of experience. In 'Silence', an unpublished poem dated June 1910, he describes how, while walking one day in noisy

city streets, he sees them shrink and divide.[10] His everyday
preoccupations, his past, all the claims of the future are wiped out by
a commanding silence. 'Silence' is Eliot's first and perhaps most
lucid description of the timeless moment. He concludes that there is
nothing else beside it.

Silence, in both cases, suggests experience where language fails.
In Eliot, there is the untranslatable silence of religious vision. He
uses silence, also, to jerk the reader awake, a silence so painfully
abrupt that it brings us to judgement. We are forced to recognise
flesh as ridiculous or loathsome, if possible to be discarded. In
contrast, what we see in Virginia Woolf's silence is far less pre-
determined. Her silence simply circles certain characters – Rachel,
Jacob, Mrs Dalloway – and then she recedes softly, leaving 'a zone
of silence' to reverberate with unstated suggestion. In 1930, in an
introductory letter to the writings of the working-class members of
the Co-operative Women's Guild, Virginia Woolf said: 'These
voices are beginning only now to emerge from silence into half-
articulate speech. These lives are still half-hidden in profound
obscurity'.[11]

Like these real women, the fictional Mrs Ramsay harbours an
indecipherable silence. Virginia Woolf's model of womanhood
originated with her mother, but her mother purified, not only of the
dramatic plot of her outward life and the passing platitudes of
Victorian womanhood, but purified of the artifice of language itself.
Lily, alone with Mrs Ramsay in the dark bedroom,

> imagined how in the chambers of the mind and heart of the
> woman . . . were . . . tablets bearing sacred inscriptions, which if
> one could spell them out, would teach one everything, but they
> would never be made public.

Biographer and artist in Lily unite to ask: 'What art was there,
known to love or cunning, by which one pressed through into those
secret chambers?'[12]

A biographic problem latent in the portraits of Rachel Vinrace
and Mrs Ramsay is given explicit formulation in *Jacob's Room*. This
book has something in common with 'Memoirs of a Novelist' which
was intended as the first in a series of fictional biographies. Both
works are less concerned with Miss Willatt or Jacob than with their
biographers' problem: that, if the invisible life is ultimately
unknowable, is not biography pointless, its failure inevitable?

All through *Jacob's Room*, his biographer talks directly to the reader. We two push ourselves forward – busy, agog, distractable – while our subject slips out of sight. The would-be biographer is

> vibrating . . . at the mouth of the cavern of mystery, endowing Jacob Flanders with all sorts of qualities he had not at all . . .; what remains is mostly a matter of guesswork. Yet over him we hang vibrating.[13]

The biographic obsession is comic in its futility. The deliberately fragmented narrative with its curt sentences, its tantalising glimpses – Jacob lying on his back in Greece – force the reader to share in the biographer's effort and failure. What is so impressive is this honesty about failure. As 'Memoirs of a Novelist' warned against the usual mental slots, so Jacob's biographer refuses to content herself with the usual stories; the Tom Jones story, say, of the young man who couples with the plausible flirt, Florinda. Jacob does perform the Tom Jones routine and others, but we sense that whatever is silently furled within him would have bypassed banality with the passing of youth. *Jacob's Room* thus suggests that if a subject is unknowable is it not logical to risk the act of imagination that would give to the subject a coherent form? At the same time, a biographer must be truthful enough to exhibit the broken areas, the silent spaces. At the Parthenon, Jacob gazes at marble figures whose backs were left unfinished. On this model, Virginia Woolf devised a kind of biography that would give it the formal restraints of a suggestive art.

Virginia Woolf thought biography should leave something to the imagination. When she composes her portrait of her mother in *To the Lighthouse* she treats external biographic facts as mere punctuation (Mrs Ramsay does die, most disconcertingly, in brackets) and strikes boldly for invisible states of mind that uphold action. She asked, first, what was her mother to herself? It was an inspired stroke to let the beam of the lighthouse catch her, in a rare moment, alone. The scene is deliberately understated, unanalysed, a model of biographic tact. Secondly, Virginia Woolf asked what was the private scene of her parent's marriage? Again, imagination had to take her beyond the child's memory. As the portrait progressed she feared it was too made up and was relieved when her sister confirmed its accuracy when the book came out in May 1927. She wrote to Vanessa Bell:

I'm in a terrible state of pleasure that you should think Mrs
Ramsay so like mother. At the same time, it is a psychological
mystery why she should be: how a child could know about her;
except that she has always haunted me . . . .[14]

II

As silence circled the untried spaces of character, so Virginia Woolf
plotted the hidden shape of the lifespan. Both she and Eliot marked
off the lifespan by what Eliot called 'essential moments' and
Virginia Woolf, 'moments of being'. Whenever Eliot wrote about
lives, he was not so concerned with public circumstance as with
what he called 'unattended moments':

The awful daring of a moment's surrender . . .
By this, and this only, we have existed[15]

To find these moments, the biographer must pare away the trivia of
the external life for Virginia Woolf believed that 'there are only a
few essential hours of life'. She, too, thought the biographer might
shed 'the regimented unreal life' to fasten on the definitive
moments. For Eliot, these moments are when, rarely, he loses
himself in a religious vision. They are transforming moments,
invitations to a new life. For Virginia Woolf, in contrast, the
definitive moments look back into the past. 'If life has a base that it
stands upon' it is a memory. Her life as a writer was based on two
persistent memories: the north Cornwall shore and her unconventional Victorian parents.

Early one morning, lying in the nursery of her family's summer
home at St Ives, she heard 'the waves breaking, one, two, one, two
. . . behind a yellow blind' and knew, she said, 'the purest ecstasy I
can conceive'.[16] Years later, she wanted the waves' rhythm to sound
all through *To the Lighthouse* and *The Waves*. Is there a link between
the moment in the nursery and the commanding intuition of her
maturity, that the rhythm of human processes, if attended to
without the interference of timetables, will have something in
common with the wavelike rhythms of the physical universe, waves
of sound, light, the sea? That one, two, rise and crash came to
represent, certainly, the recurring creative possibilities of the
lifespan and its finality.

The other crucial memory, of her parents, provoked endless analysis. There is a photograph of Julia Stephen reading with her younger children in about 1894. The photograph breathes the perfect stillness of the children's absorption. More than thirty years later there is a similar scene in *To the Lighthouse*. As the Victorian mother reads aloud, she observes a son's eyes darken, sees a daughter drawn by an imaginative word, and concludes 'they were happier now than they would ever be again'. The family dead haunted Virginia Woolf's imagination. 'The ghosts', she wrote in her diary at the age of fifty, 'change so oddly in my mind; like people who live, & are changed by what one hears of them'. With these changes in understanding came the need to compose their portraits in her fictions. She said more than once that her books were not exactly novels; they were fictional elegies.

For Virginia Woolf the essential hours were concentrated in early childhood, but there were later turning points: in 1905, when, quite by chance, she may have come upon a form for the modern novel while tramping in Cornwall; in 1907-8, when she discovered the creative uses of autobiography; in 1926, when she spied 'the fin' of a submerged life that she must pursue and proclaim in its entirety in *The Waves*; and, finally, the 'soul's change' of 1932 when she resolved to speak out for her sex. Such crucial points, she noted in her diary, no biographer could guess from external events. Luckily, her bent was so continually autobiographic that the array of recently-published works and the unpublished papers, taken together with the established works, do give an account of the hidden moments on which her life turned. These allow us to see Virginia Woolf not so much as she appeared to others, to her family and Bloomsbury, but as she appeared to herself.

Virginia Woolf demonstrates how to do such lives in *The Waves*. There she follows six lives simultaneously from childhood to maturity. The six lives rise on the crest of the moments with an imaginative residue. The art of living lay in the recognition of these moments which are not the preserve of the gifted but are common to all lives. What made these six lives distinctive, though, was that they did not force their internal rhythms to coincide with set biographic schemes of marriage and career. Bernard, reviewing these lives, decides that all the Victorian stories of birth, school, marriage and death simply are not true, that lives turn on 'moments of humiliation and triumph' that occur now and then but rarely at times of official crisis or celebration.

Bernard trusts that the lines of six lives will be coherent if he cuts out what Virginia Woolf called, in her private shorthand, 'waste' (by which she meant the appointment book, official honours and doings). Four years later, Eliot was to write the same theory into *Burnt Norton*. He, too, used the word 'waste' for the empty stretches of the lifespan that are not worth recording in the light of a sublime moment:

Ridiculous the waste sad time
Stretching before and after.[17]

Eliot was so single-minded that the inner coherence of his life is easy to see. From 'Silence' on, the religious life is the ideal that propels his existence so that each poem redefines the position won in the previous poem. To him, 'the life of a man of genius, viewed in relation to his writing, comes to take a pattern of inevitability, and even his disabilities will seem to have stood him in good stead'.[18]

The shape of Virginia Woolf's life is less easy to see because its pattern is inclusive. She did not drop life for art so quickly as the cerebral young man of 'La Figlia che Piange'. Her diary spurts all the time, bathing her with experience. Her proximity to life and her responsiveness is so unflagging that she had no need, like Yeats, to generate feeling through the actor's mask or, like Eliot, to break, agonisingly, through a crust of comfortable deadness. In Eliot's case, so much had to be discarded to make his life conform to the pattern of the religious life. Virginia Woolf sought, on the other hand, a pattern that could admit 'everything', every stage of the lifespan with its plethora of moments. The clue to the governing pattern of her career may lie in *The Waves*. There, she divided the lifespan into stages which, her notes for the book suggest, would prove 'that there are waves . . . by wh. life is marked; a rounding off, wh. has nothing to do with events. A natural finishing'.[19] This may be the pattern of her creative life: a wave ridden to its crest, then sometimes a trough, but always another wave rising far out.

Bernard wishes, he tells the reader, 'to give you my life'. It is a composed life like those of his five friends. However unconventional the theory in *The Waves* – the concentration of moments, the refusal of 'waste', the repetition of a coherent pattern – the compositional principle remains intact. Bernard restores meaning to the often humdrum process of living. His method ensures that the weight of his multiple-biography should fall on the constructive moments on which effective lives turn. It also ensures attention to the destructive moments when effort, and may be life itself, seem pointless. For Virginia Woolf to rise from her own trough (when, engulfed in depression, she spied 'the fin'), she had to ask, through her six samples, what resources do we have against the biological or psychological minimums of existence?

In middle age, Bernard sank to his lowest point. The great wave of renewed energy that followed came through ordinary acts of imaginative sympathy that flowered in the biographic masterpiece of Bernard's old age. His creative tide rises to flood the caves of memory as he shapes figure after figure. Working from the givens of nature – the limpet clinging to a rock, the beast stamping, the nymph of the fountain – he retells memories until they take their final set. Here is another compositional principle, analagous to the statue image in *Jacob's Room*: under Bernard's expert touch, the six friends harden as statues who can outlive their time. He fixes their lives, at their very moment of pulsation, like Yeats' marbles of the dancing floor.

A third compositional principle follows from the early tactic of silence. Bernard is an accomplished phrase-maker but, as he grows older, he begins to distrust sentences that come down with all their feet on the ground because, he believes, conclusiveness falsifies truth. The reader must learn to live with 'the fin', as Virginia Woolf did, with what is unknown or barely seen. In this way, the six friends attend to one another's unvoiced intent: they – and since they comprise our species – *we* are natural biographers and, as we exist in community, we exist by composing others.

III

The autobiographical writer is an ideal subject for this kind of biography. In *Orlando*, Virginia Woolf said in her most extravagant manner: 'Every secret of a writer's soul, every experience of his life, every quality of his mind is written large in his works'. More is known about Virginia Woolf's own life than about that of almost any writer. Quentin Bell's superb biography gives a complete and candid record of her life and an immediate sense of what it was like to know Virginia Woolf day by day. Yet she told Ethel Smyth in 1938 that she was 'trained to silence'. In an unpublished piece she said: 'There is a silence in life, a perpetual deposit of experience for which action provides no proper outlet and our words no fit expression'.[20] Is there, then, something we still do not know, perhaps cannot know?

She reserved, I think, a side of herself for her novels alone. The writer's life is an invisible life, parallel but distinct from her public career. The death of Rachel in *The Voyage Out* and the mental solitude of Septimus Warren Smith in *Mrs Dalloway* and of Rhoda in *The Waves* are Virginia Woolf's backward, transforming looks at her own muted side, potentially creative, potentially distorted and always threatened with extinction. To follow the history of Virginia Woolf's muted self is to follow the more muted characters in her novels.

But can we legitimately read back from the work to the life? 'Somewhere, everywhere', said Virginia Woolf, 'now hidden, now apparent in whatever is written down is the form of a human being'.[21] To detect this is a very delicate undertaking. Eliot forbade it in 'Tradition and the Individual Talent' (1919) where he argued the writer's separation from the work. But this celebrated position he contradicted in other essays. In 'Ben Jonson' (also 1919) he declared that 'the creation of a work of art . . . consists in the process of transfusion of the personality, or, in a deeper sense, the life of the author into the character'. In 'John Ford' (1932) he admitted that the work alone would 'give the pattern . . . of the personal emotion, the personal drama and struggle, which no biography, however full and intimate, could give us'.[22]

No biography? Yet there is a composed kind of biography, implied throughout Eliot and Woolf, that would bring us closer than any other to the sources of creativity. This writer's life would have to rock back and forth between the life and the work, coming to rest always on the work. The sequence would depend not primarily on chronology but on the sources of creativity as they emerge one after another so as to focus at all times on the development of an artist. I have looked, first, at Virginia Woolf's parents as they were and then at the way she remembered them in *To the Lighthouse,* seen close up in their own time, then, after a passage of years, from the mature perspective of a modern artist. The play of actual and composed character, of actual and composed event, continues in the second stage, the long twenty-year apprenticeship. The young writer's mental solitude, her odd education and recurring illness offset a young woman's journey towards knowledge and death in *The Voyage Out.* Then, in the third stage,

Virginia Woolf's mature efforts to compose her life – her waves of renewed experiment – are balanced by the formal diagram of the lifespan in *The Waves*. Virginia Woolf composed her life as deliberately as she composed her work. She presents a case of a writer whose life is not merely a background but is a major source for her work. She turned her early losses, her memories and moments of bliss into art which, at the same time, casts its perspective on her life.

What kind of book, Virginia Woolf asked in 1916, 'will stand up and speak with other ages about our age when we lie prone and silent'? And she hinted that autobiographic writers of her own time were creating almost a fresh branch of literature, some classic form, as yet unrealised. 'I perceive', she said in the second draft of *The Waves*, 'that the art of biography is still in its infancy or more properly speaking has yet to be born'.[23]

It should be possible to do as Virginia Woolf urges, to distinguish between the barren fact and 'the fact that suggests and engenders',[24] but only with the utmost caution, keeping in mind Montaigne's excellent advice and warning:

A sound intellect will refuse to judge men simply by their outward action; we must probe the inside and discover what springs set men in motion. but since this is an arduous and hazardous undertaking, I wish fewer people would meddle with it.[25]

Notes

1. Virginia Woolf, diary entry dated 5 Feb. 1935, *The Diary of Virginia Woolf*, eds Anne Olivier Bell and Andrew McNeillie (London: Hogarth Press, 1982) Vol. IV, p. 277.
2. Ralph Waldo Emerson, *The Journals and Miscellaneous Notebooks of Ralph Waldo Emerson*, eds William H. Gilman, *et al.* (Cambridge: Harvard University Press, 1964) Vol. VII, pp. 248-9.
3. Virginia Woolf, 'Lady Hester Stanhope', *Books and Portraits*, ed. Mary Lyon (London: Hogarth Press, 1977) p. 196.
4. Virginia Woolf, 'The Letters of Jane Welsh Carlyle', The *Guardian*, 2 Aug. 1905, p. 1295. Unsigned.
5. Virginia Woolf, *To the Lighthouse* (1927; rpt. London: Hogarth Press, 1932) Sect. I, Ch. 17, p. 165.
6. Virginia Woolf, 'Walter Sickert', *Collected Essays*, ed. Leonard Woolf (London: Chatto & Windus, 1966) Vol. II, p. 236.
7. Virginia Woolf, Holograph ms, 17 pp., Monks House Papers (University of Sussex) B. 9(a). This was the first piece of fiction that Virginia Woolf submitted

for publication. She offered it to the *Cornhill Magazine*, the journal her father had edited. Reginald Smith turned it down.

8. Virginia Woolf, 'More Carlyle Letters', *Times Literary Supplement*, 1 April 1909, p. 126. Unsigned.

9. Virginia Woolf, *The Voyage Out* (1915; rpt. London: Hogarth Press, 1929) p. 262.

10. T. S. Eliot, Holograph Notebook, Berg Collection, New York Public Library. Eliot was twenty-one and his final undergraduate year at Harvard. The city streets were presumably those of Boston.

11. Virginià Woolf, 'Memories of a Working Women's Guild', *Collected Essays*, ed. L. Woolf (London: Chatto & Windus, 1967) Vol. IV, p. 148.

12. Woolf, *To the Lighthouse*, Sect. I, Ch. 9, p. 82.

13. Virginia Woolf, *Jacob's Room* (1922; rpt. London: Hogarth Press, 1929) Ch. 5, pp. 117-18.

14. Virginia Woolf, letter dated 25 May 1927, *A Change of Perspective: The Letters of Virginia Woolf, Vol. III, 1923-1928, eds.* Nigel Nicolson and Joanne Trautmann (London: Hogarth Press, 1977) pp. 382-3.

15. T. S. Eliot, The Waste Land, *Collected Poems 1909–1962* (London: Faber & Faber, 1963) p. 78.

16. Virginia Woolf, 'A Sketch of the Past', *Moments of Being*, ed. J. Schulkind (University of Sussex Press, 1976) pp. 64-5.

17. T. S. Eliot, 'Burnt Norton', *Collected Poems 1909–1962* (London: Faber & Faber, 1963) p. 195.

18. T. S. Eliot, 'The Classics and the Man of Letters', *To Criticize the Critic* (London, Faber & Faber, 1965) p. 147.

19. Virginia Woolf, Notes (3 Nov. 1930), *The Waves: The Two Holograph Drafts*, ed. J. Graham (London: Hogarth Press, 1976) p. 758.

20. Virginia Woolf, Monks House Papers, B. 11.

21. Virginia Woolf, 'Reading', *Collected Essays*, Vol. II, p. 29.

22. T. S. Eliot, *Selected Essays* (London: Faber & Faber, 3rd enlarged edition, 1951) pp. 157; 203.

23. Woolf, Holograph of *The Waves*, op. cit., p. 684.

24. Virginia Woolf, 'The Art of Biography', *Collected Essays*, Vol. IV, p. 228.

25. Michael de Montaigne, 'Of the Inconsistency of Our Actions', *The Complete Essays of Montaigne*, trans. Donald M. Frame (Stanford University Press, 1965) p. 244.

5 Diminishment of Consciousness: a Paradox in the Art of Virginia Woolf

John Bayley

Two small pictures – landscapes – hang in a public room in Somerville College, Oxford. Approaching for a closer look the visitor almost immediately concludes they are better seen from a distance and withdraws accordingly. There is something sad about those pictures, which are by Roger Fry.[1] All the dynamism of an epoch, all its life-giving enthusiasms, seem to have drained out, and left them bleak and lonely in this arid academic setting. To see them is to think of a time past, not of an art all-suffusing and continuously present. No story still animates them, no secrecy glows out of them. As he looks and leaves the spectator may be struck by the thought that they are both very like, and very unlike, the novels of Virginia Woolf.

The novels survive, the pictures do not: that would be the crudest way of putting it. But the 'something sad', the lack of a secret and a story: this they have in common. And the pictures may remind us too of a memorable picture in Virginia Woolf's first novel, *The Voyage Out*. The hero and heroine of the novel, who have, as it were, forgotten that they are Clive Bell and the author (when I first read the novel I didn't know it either), are standing together in front of a looking glass. They are in love; they are engaged; 'but it chilled them to see themselves in the glass, for instead of being vast and indivisible they were really very small and separate, the size of the glass leaving a large space for reflection of other things'.[2]

I once felt strongly, and still feel whenever I re-read it, the charm of that novel, its pathos and curious power. It is a seminal novel – another good first novel, Elizabeth Bowen's *The Hotel*, was obviously inspired by it – and for Virginia Woolf herself it was a voyage many times undertaken. She often returned to the same characters and patterns of relations, though never portraying them so directly as she portrayed Morrells and Bells and Stephenses and Stracheys in *The Voyage Out*. And the awareness of the hero and heroine as they look in the mirror will become again, in the later novels, an awareness like a landscape by Roger Fry, one about which a story cannot be told, which can hold no secret, bring no new world into being. The last thing this awareness can do, or wishes to do, is organise itself into those demarcated chess-squares of make-believe which in the interest of order and artifice suspend the simple candour of the self.

That candour is proclaimed by Virginia Woolf as the ground of her art. We meet it on the first page of *To the Lighthouse*, when we learn that James Ramsay 'belonged, even at the age of six, to that great clan who cannot keep this feeling separate from that'.[3] It is a sign of the elect. Virginia Woolf had mixed feelings about D. H. Lawrence, but in his novels she identified 'the same pressure to be ourselves', the pressure, that is, which rejects the novelist's conjuring trick, his attempt to project the reader into another consciousness, to charm him into other conventions of being, hypothetical areas of feeling. Such an area would be that invented by Henry James for his heroine Milly Theale in *The Wings of the Dove*, and Virginia Woolf referred to it as if James were a particularly skilful prestidigitator, whose art is both to display and to conceal. In *The Wings of the Dove* there is 'a great flourishing of silk handkerchiefs, and Milly disappears behind them'.[4]

Love is the great area of fictional invention: a story always has to be made up about it. But, as with life itself, her artist's consciousness must not pretend, must not try to keep this feeling separate from that. Life, as Bernard says in *The Waves*, is 'not susceptible to stories': to describe it demands a note of perpetual intimacy, the use of a 'little language such as lovers use'.[5] Terence Hewet and Rachel Vinrace, the lovers of *The Voyage Out*, talk together in this language; but they do not take themselves for granted as a 'romance' and a story, as do Arthur and Susan, the humbler engaged couple in the novel. Hewet is thinking of writing a novel about 'Silence, or the things people don't say'. Or should it be the things enlightened people can't write? Arthur and Susan have a coherent story about their future, to which the falsity of fiction lends its proper decorum, but Rachel and her lover are together because they belong to that clan who cannot keep their feelings separate. Suddenly she cries 'Let's break it off, then', and the words have done 'more to unite them than any amount of argument'.

The novelist aids and abets our living in different worlds and in artificial modes of experience. He invents tales more real than those we tell ourselves, tales vain, erotic, morbid, improbable, and – if he is good at his business – true. But for Hewet and Rachel, characters in a novel for whom life is the thing, they are absurd. This novel's specification is that other people make up stories. Rachel and Hewet – you and I – do not.

But Hewet is divided and uncertain. Should he also try to write 'real' fiction? His dilemma expresses that of *The Voyage Out* itself. He laughs at the novel but how much does he need it? He and Rachel are already 'shaping the world' in which they will be married. She too laughs at the 'sheer nonsense' of the books on the table; 'novels, plays, histories', they are all 'trash', all made up. 'Read poetry Rachel, poetry, poetry, poetry! . . .' urges Hewet; and picking up a piece of trash on the table he begins to read aloud, 'his intention being to satirise the short sharp bark of the writer's English'. She pays no attention, for it has occurred to her that 'the world is composed of vast blocks of matter', and that he and she are 'nothing but patches of light, soft spots of sun wavering over the carpet and up the wall'. She is answering him in her own way, for the novel he is reading out is composed of 'blocks of matter', invented and fabricated, carefully fitted together. Because they are alive he and she lack any comparable reality. She is a pianist who thinks in sounds, not words; he in forms and silences. To her he is contemptuous of the ploys of fiction: 'No one dreams of reading this kind of thing now – antiquated problem plays, harrowing descriptions of life in the East End – oh no, we've exploded all that'.

Hewet voices the natural superiority of each generation's new literary programme. But his words also disclose the dangerous paradox at the heart of his creator's belief. Consciousness, true to itself, must create, while forgoing the temptation to make things up. Because it preferred to live its relationships and situations, Bloomsbury depreciated fiction, patronised the conventional and traditional human need to live at once in many worlds, mostly those of fancy and dream. Honesty demanded action, not imagination. The enlightened and agnostic consciousness resents dualisms. Take a minor contemporary instance. A young woman writes to the advice column of a magazine to say how upset she is that her sex fantasies are masochistic and submissive, whereas in actual life she does not in the least want to be dominated by brutal men. Of course not, replies the agony aunt, but relax. Your fantasies and your life are two different things – why not live comfortably in both worlds? Sound advice maybe – most novel readers do. And a tension between fantasy and reality is at the heart of most novelists' business.

To Virginia Woolf it meant nothing: and yet it means much to the structure and success of her first novel. Rachel rejects 'love' as she rejected religion, and yet life urges her toward its pretences, as it urges the novel itself. What she feels for Hewet, and for Helen, is something different. She is compelled to answer the formal congratulations sent on her engagement, producing 'phrases which bore a marked likeness to those she had condemned'. The humour and the pathos of the long scene between her and Hewet arise out of the author's vigorous struggle – more open and more vulnerable here than later in her career – with the dilemma of consciousness and story. She must be true to her own sense of things; speak only what she finds and feels. And yet it is a function of the novel both to parody and to dramatise consciousness, to reveal both its secrecies and its pretences, to hallow its falsity. That is what Joyce was doing in *Ulysses*, the novel which Virginia Woolf so much feared and resented.

She also resented E. M. Forster, while liking and perhaps even needing him, and the resentment was mutual, for Forster, who in *The Art of the Novel* spoke so much of faking, understood that what is true in a novel is also what is faked, because this is the way its art works in two worlds. While faking, the novelist must take his invention seriously, very seriously indeed, and the ways in which he does this seemed to her absurd. 'If they didn't feel a thing why did they go and pretend to?' cries Rachel, appalled by the hypocrisies of religion and of what other people call falling in love. The shrewdness, humour and commonsense of Virginia Woolf is of course 'in charge' of Rachel's reactions, even in that point of her development as an artist, and yet Rachel's attitude to life is in a large degree expressive of her creator's attitude to art. It is often because the artist 'doesn't feel a thing' that he is able to make us feel them so acutely, and the consciousness of her own art could never fathom the mystery of that contract. When she 'fakes', as in *Orlando*, she does so openly, delightedly; the fantasy does not take itself seriously for a moment and breaks off when it becomes bored.

Orlando is not another world but simply the Bloomsbury world projecting itself into humourous extravagance, as Virginia Woolf did in her own conversation. One of the reasons for Bloomsbury's continued vitality among us is that its communal attitude closely resembles that of the modern artist, critic and reader – no pretences, no distances, no mysteries – just three persons concerned working together on the production and appreciation of a work of art. A representative modern novel such as Italo Calvino's *If On a Winter's Night a Traveller* has a great deal in common not only with *Orlando* but with all Virginia Woolf's later work.

I must touch again on her relations with the contemporary scene, but let us note now the sustained attack in *The Voyage Out* on what she calls there fiction's 'sprightly and slightly ridiculous world'. Of course she loved that world, loved it more and more as its conventions threatened less and less her own developing art. She loved, for instance, Sir Walter Scott, most determinedly 'unfictive' of novelists, whose worlds absorb us because they are so wholly, so ridiculously invented, and yet can take their own truth to life so completely for granted. She could never do that, but *The Voyage Out* is to my mind the most interesting of her novels because of the ways in which old-style, fiction possesses or haunts her involuntarily at times in spite of her continual attacks on and feints away from it. The death of Rachel is profoundly moving. It is one of the most absolute deaths in English fiction. It is moving because it yields with such abandon to the novel's old power to move us. And yet it also renounces the novel.

This duality is at the heart of her work. Rachel dies, in effect, so as not to become a 'character'. Had she been one, fiction could have taken charge of and naturalised her death, making it like that of Hector or Little Nell or Jo the crossing sweeper. Forster refers to it in his essay on Virginia Woolf with a mixture of distaste and respect:[6] it was not death in the novel as he understood it; the neat functional deaths that dot his pages and culminate in that of Mrs Moore in *A Passage to India*. It reveals all the solitary pathos its author concealed: the death of her brother, her own breakdowns. But this pathos is strangely allied to comedy, in an unstable relation which makes *The Voyage Out* by far the funniest of her novels. Rachel dies as a kind of feminine gesture, to avoid having to take part in an art form shaped and dominated by the masculine principle.

In their great scene together Hewet reads Rachel, to their mutual derision, an extract from a novel which sounds as if it were by Hugh Walpole (the hero is called Hugh), which treats in a pompous manner of modern marriage, combining luscious fantasies with a pseudo-shrewd analysis of the difficulties of a male-female relationship. At first the couple have 'jolly companionship and stimulating revelations . . . shouting *Love in a Valley* to each other across the snowy slopes of the Riffelhorn' (and so on and so on, says Hewet – I'll skip the descriptions). But soon she begins to give tea-parties and he goes back to 'his talks with old Bob Murphy in his smoky book-lined room, where the two men unloose their souls to each other'. When he tries to speak frankly to her he finds her 'lying on the great polar-bear skin in their bedroom, half-undressed, for they were dining with the Greens in Wilton Crescent, the ruddy firelight making the diamonds wink and twinkle on her bare arms and in the delicious curve of her breast – a vision of adorable feminity'. Notwithstanding, their problems get worse. Hugh takes a week-end ticket to Swanage and has it out with himself on the downs above Corfe. 'Fifteen pages or so which we'll skip. The conclusion is . . .' yes, as Hewet's reading promises, there was a story, and an appropriate outcome.

And one not so wholly different, as Virginia Woolf knew, from the way she tried to manage things in her second novel, *Night and Day*. To save Rachel from marriage, and from looking seductive in the ruddy firelight, there was only one way out. Otherwise she would be projected into life, forced into a story, and the wonderfully touching tableau of her falling in love with Hewet would dissolve and disappear. As it is, it is preserved by the indifferent solitude of comedy, by the many other things that are reflected separately in the glass. Rachel's disappearance is made the more absolute by the ensuing comic exchange between Mr Perrott and Evelyn, the girl he loves, who exclaims at him: 'I'm positive Rachel's not dead'. 'Mr Perrott would have said almost anything that Evelyn wanted him to say, but to assert that he believed in the immortality of the soul was not in his power'.[7]

The loss of Rachel is not only moving in itself but is the novel's comic gain. And it brings us back to the duality so essential to Virginia Woolf's best work. It seems to me that one can connect her snobbish and worldly interests, her social triumphs and anxieties, with her attitude to the traditional novel, its comedies and convictions. Some of her more refined admirers, such as the French critic Maurice Blanchot, cannot bear to think of this side of her at all. 'That a writer of such extreme refinement should be susceptible to trivialities of this kind is most puzzling'.[8] M Blanchot is easily puzzled. For him she was the most refined of poetic sensibilities, and indeed poetry was what she strove for, the 'poetry, poetry, poetry' which Hewet recommends to Rachel. But she adored *Vanity Fair*; she adored the absurdities and dishonesties of the world, and not only adored them but was compromised by them. When they erupt into her work it springs to life. It is very significant that Rachel is so much taken by the Dalloways; absurd as they are they offer life to her. 'I liked the Dalloways, and I shall never see them again'. Rachel does not, but we shall. Like the novel itself the Dalloways, that 'sprightly and slightly ridiculous' pair, beckon seductively, larger than life, more dynamic, making up the story of themselves outside the bare honesty of the receptive consciousness.

In *Mrs Dalloway* Virginia Woolf sought to bring the lady inside that consciousness, balancing her world against the other world, that of Septimus. Mrs Dalloway's disparate and separate existence becomes one with her creator. Brilliant as the effect is, it is less various than in *The Voyage Out*. Being brought in from the novel, being taken over, diminishes the Mrs Dalloway who is so instantly alive, as Jane Austen would have made her live, in *The Voyage Out*. There she is the embodiment of the novel character; the two sides of her creator's outlook confront each other in her exchanges on board ship with Helen Ambrose. '"Don't you feel," she wound up, addressing Helen, "that life's a perpetual conflict?" Helen considered for a moment. "No", she said. "I don't think I do."' This is not only Mayfair confronting Bloomsbury, but the consciousness of the novel – Mrs Dalloway is always 'seeing herself' in some context, perhaps in her drawing-room in Browne Street with a Plato open on her knees – coming up against that of the non-novel. No wonder the pause that followed was decidedly uncomfortable. In her pioneering book on Virginia Woolf, Joan Bennet takes the exchange straight, assuming that it represents two points of view, as it were between Forster's, Wilcoxes' and Schlegel's.[9] But I think it is much funnier than that implies, as well as more significant—a Mrs Dalloway wholly absorbed into and treated as the stuff of fiction, where indeed those perpetual conflicts are always in progress, talking to Vanessa or Virginia Stephen. Fiction, its pretensions, its falsities and its charms, is being displayed in the context of what for the writer is reality.

And yet the whole scene is done in the manner of Jane Austen,

Mrs Dalloway's favourite novelist. Fiction, through her, gets its revenge, as it does continually throughout *The Voyage Out*. The battle between the two keeps the novel itself effortlessly alive. It is a struggle more subtle and comprehensive thàn that between men and women, between the fashionable and the poetic life, though it is closely related to these. The comedy of the sex battle is one of the joys of *The Voyage Out*, and a great part of the fun is the way it is constantly referred to fiction. Hewet reads from one absurd novel off Rachel's table; the sensible Miss Allan refers to another which she is reading, and which is complacently identified by another character as *Maternity*, by Michael Jessop. Even maternity men take over, just as they have taken over the novel, culture, education, politics, as the Dalloways have taken over Jane Austen. 'Rachel', says Mrs Dalloway, 'cannot bear our beloved Jane'. Her husband pronounces that she is 'incomparably the greatest female writer that we possess . . . and for this reason: she does not attempt to write like a man'. The joke of course is that Jane Austen could do nothing else, which is really why they admire her. The Aunt Tom of her sex, she assiduously sparkled, invented and contrived, as Addison and Fielding had taught her, and for much of *The Voyage Out* Virginia Woolf knows she is doing the same. Rachel and Helen 'after the fashion of their sex', are 'highly trained in promoting men's talk without listening to it'. The triumph of *The Voyage Out* is the use to which the novelist puts a similar sort of high training.

As her 'Common Reader' essay shows, Virginia Woolf never changed this attitude to Jane Austen. 'Moons and mountains', she wrote, remained inaccessible to her;[10] and it was to realise the idea of those moons and mountains in art that Virginia Woolf herself strove, by an act of will. Brought up in a masculine environment, which had formed her cultural consciousness and style, she yet strove in her art for an idea of femininity. Essentially she is a combative writer, not a dreamy passive, poetic one; and in her later books it is possible to feel that she makes too conscious an effort to embody herself as feminine poetic, Shakespeare's mute sister who has found a voice. The urge was in her: it was in her culture and society. But the masculine games of invention, the tough dualistic struggle between self and fiction, suit her better. Perhaps for this reason her style has to harden into poetry, into what for her was poetry; it does not retain the lively instability and flexibility of tone that we find in *The Voyage Out*.

Or one could say that style becomes a manner; a manner that shuts out other possibilities. The main reason for the failure of *Night and Day* is its lack of that play with and parody of the novel which gives such different perspectives on experience to *The Voyage Out*. Although parody there usually takes a comedy form, it is just as much in evidence in the moving scenes between the lovers, and in the tragic sequence of Rachel's death, an almost unbearably protracted version of those death-bed scenes with which the Victorian novelist wrung his reader's heart-strings. Parody is at the heart of invention, the agent that lends to a fiction the resources of multiple consciousness, resources variously exploited in *Hamlet*, in Pushkin's *Eugene Onegin*, in *The Turn of the Screw*. The good novelist's world of consciousness develops naturally in collaboration with these resources. Virginia Woolf attempted consciously to free herself from them.

Parody was not escaped thereby, for her later manner becomes a kind of self-parody. In seeking to represent the reality of consciousness it finds such a consciousness cannot escape from itself. The impersonalising functions of parody are usurped by mechanism, by art-work. Rachel died in order that she should not take part in a novel, and the function and substance of the novel are taken over in *The Waves* by the device of a single consciousness divided into different voices, by the pageant in *Between the Acts*. The household of *Between the Acts* goes straight back to *The Voyage Out*, except that the humour and observation of the early novel seemed to tremble always on the edge of another dimension, the dimension of fiction, which filled it with curiosity and hope. So perceived, so drenched in sensation, so glittering with reality is the household of Poyntz Hall, that the pages about them read like an aborted Balzac. But silence falls as Mrs Manresa stops talking with her voice and eyes, stops preening and approving the eternity of her adolescence, as Isa stops turning her consciousness into poetry and fiction ('My husband, the father of my children'). In *The Voyage Out* the characters' fictions about themselves blended and interacted with the main fiction. In *Between the Acts* the two are quite separate. Love and hate, jealousy and rivalry, sit silent with nowhere to go. The novel is now 'Silence, or the things that didn't happen'. The pageant has become what is made up and invented, an inversion of the foolish novel that Hewet was reading to Rachel before the end of *The Voyage Out*.

The characters of Virginia Woolf's last novel are as vibrantly alive as those of her first – even more so, for they are seen with a greater experience of life – but they are now quite lacking in the comic or tragic potential with which the fusion of fictional modes

endowed those in *The Voyage Out*. In *Between the Acts* observation
separates itself wholly from the manipulations and manners of art.
Written down as if in a notebook – the stable married couple with
their different interests and their different sexual day-dreams, the
woman who charms attended by her homosexual, the lesbian who
gets up pageants for village occasions – all seem waiting to step out of
the observed world into the other world of fiction. In the odd, wry
harmony of *The Voyage Out* they came and went between the two.
But in *Between the Acts* art-work is imposed on observation, as if to
complete the picture: it does not meet and mingle with it. The
'poetry' in the characters is attached to them like balloons coming
out of their heads, and so are their emotions – hatred for one's
husband, love for one's husband. These flat facts going nowhere but
decorated with the devices of beginning and ending ('Then the
curtain rose. They spoke.') produce an oddly and it seems an
unintentionally melancholy impression. Consciousness seems to
have lost its agility, its power to move between worlds and enhance
the life of each by contrast.

The helpless manner becomes a real helplessness. That has much
to do with Virginia Woolf's honesty and integrity, as much as with
her bouts of despair and her qualms about the way her art was going.
It seems deliberate, a matter of sexual choice. She must continue to
move away from the free make-believe of the masculine world into
the present limitations of the female one, with its unco-ordinated
mixture of the flat, the farcical, and the poetic. As each recedes the
picture must remain blank. The strange emptiness and sadness that
hangs like a grey mist over the animated scenes of *Between the Acts*
seems the result of this arrestment.

Consciousness in fact rejoices in sequence, endlessly repeating to
itself 'and now, and now . . .' and fiction turns this into its own
Arabian Nights, the mainspring of artifice. *To the Lighthouse* structures
itself on time passing, and the later novels portray time as poetry
while rejecting all implications of sequence that animate a fictional
art. There is thus a kind of misunderstanding in the foreground of
her method between the way she presents time and the natural way
in which time gets into fiction. G. E. Moore said he couldn't
understand the notion of time held by his Cambridge colleague
Mactaggart, because time for him meant that he had eaten his
breakfast and would soon be having his lunch. *The Years* depends
upon the idea of time passing, but the simple expectations aroused
by sequence are replaced by an idea of time that is blank and empty.

The Years disappointed critics because after *The Waves* it seemed a return to the conventions of the novel, a conducting of families through time in the manner of Bennet's *The Old Wives' Tale*. Virginia Woolf herself agonised over this. It is still an absorbing and wonderful book – the first half especially draws us in – but what may strike the reader now is how completely it demonstrates her emancipation, her escape into the 'novel-essay', into her own way of doing things. Yes, the reader might think, this is indeed what living is like, so why do novels make all their fuss? Yet such a feeling is not liberating but curiously cheerless, and it destroys curiosity. In gaining this kind of consciousness we seem to have lost all that consciousness feeds on. This brilliant unremitting helplessness, which sees everything and on which nothing is lost, has none the less taken the potential out of things.

That potential is the art of implication, in which, as James knew well, good fiction is soaked. The reader feeds avidly on what the writer withholds from him, on what he can make of a nudge or a hint. Virginia Woolf has no dimension of the implied. And yet the method of *The Years* seems to cry out for it. Kitty Lasswade, for instance, shares with Eleanor Pargiter the same craving for passivity; for sinking into the solitude of a taxi or train, where someone else is responsible. But Kitty, nicknamed the 'Grenadier', is a forceful woman who has made a splendid marriage, has children, one her favourite. How did it come about? What are her relations with her husband? What is he like? Since we receive no encouragement our interest droops. Two promising characters, the brother and sister-in-law of Colonel Pargiter, suddenly appearing after the first third of the book, are as suddenly disposed of by death. Perhaps, like that of Rachel herself, their potential was too unmanageable?

Of course the history of the book's development, out of what Virginia Woolf called 'novel-essays' about the Pargiters, and the role of their class and kind, both in the subjection and the emancipation of women, goes far to explain the intractable nature of her problem. Polemical essays are illustrating an imaginary novel, not, as in *The Voyage Out*, living in a sort of involuntary comedy relation with the novel. In her essay 'The New Biography' she wrote that though the truths of fact and fiction are both genuine they are antagonistic. 'Let them meet and they destroy each other . . . the imagination will not serve under two masters simultaneously'.[11] An ominous claim, which it would occur to very few novelists to make, for the fusion of the two is taken for granted in their craft, as it almost accidentally was in *The Voyage Out*. It seems that Virginia Woolf is referring to the polemical side of her art, and to its passive side. On the one hand she is fighting for female emancipation. The young Pargiters – 'parget' is a dialect word meaning to smooth and plaster over a surface – are committed to getting at the truth, and to stay 'boxed up together telling lies' in big stuffy London houses. But on the other hand her truth of fiction requires passivity, simply to be conscious of what is going on, to surrender oneself accurately to feeling and impression.

We think of Virginia Woolf as a creator of new aesthetic forms in fiction, the forms of modernism. But her later novels now look more and more like the rather forlorn stepchildren of the old doctrine of Naturalism. This venerable heresy, now publicly discredited but still influential among working novelists who have hardly heard of it by name, forswore all pretence and make-believe and took as its central tenet the need to show things as they really were – a call to social struggle as well as aesthetic honesty. But there is also a passive side to such realism. Individuals are in the grip of vast historical and biological forces; there is little they can do but be honest, a duty laid especially on the writer.

In our time the reaction against realism has led to the concept of the novel as a wholly manipulated artefact; the novel that does not pretend to be anything else, advertising throughout its lack of connection with things as they are. It was once taken for granted that Virginia Woolf's novels were like that, but *The Years* especially now looks like realism, particularly if we compare it with Proust or with Anthony Powell's sequence, *A Dance to the Music of Time*. The way characters are constructed reveals the difference. We should never want to meet Mr Pickwick or Père Goriot or Mrs Gamp. They are creations made for fiction only; to be enjoyed only inside it. The characters in *The Years* can be met with any day, and they have the same interest, or lack of it, in the novel as they have in real life. Only a realist could be so disturbed about fiction meeting fact – 'let them meet and they destroy each other'. Virginia Woolf has rigorously kept her characters non-fictional, and has supplied the fictional element by art-work, and by the standardised consciousness – there is only one way to go round – that is passed from hand to hand throughout the novel, as need arises. That consciousness dissolves implication and potential. The individual consciousness of fictional creatures like Charlus or Widmerpool remains unknown to us, as is withheld, and the idea of its potential keeps us absorbed in their sayings and doings. The realist method of strict honesty will not perform this fictional trick.

The only truly fictional characters in the mature novels of Virginia Woolf are those who remain unsupplied by standard consciousness, like Crosby, the parlourmaid in *The Years*, and the old woman in the house opposite seen going to bed by Mrs Dalloway. In seeking to strip aside the rendering of pretence and tell the truth realism is necessarily reductive. The characters in *The Years* are taken from life, whereas Rachel in *The Voyage Out* comes as much or more from literature, and the result is that Rachel is the more interesting character. The people in *The Years* are, so to speak, returned to life, whereas Rachel's death both ends and confirms the novel. There is no fiction to be disowned in *The Years*, but one of the many sorts of novel both exploited and disowned in *The Voyage Out* is the *bildungsroman* used by Jane Austen, though she would not have known the term. Rachel's consciousness expands and learns to think and act through meeting other more or less contemporary literary heroines – H. G. Wells' Anna Veronica, Nora slamming the door at the end of *The Doll's House*. From them she acquires a fictional potential, unrealised, but always present to the reader.

The old doctrines of realism found an unexpected home in the feminist novel. Uninfluenced by men, women did not live in two worlds, they did not posture and pretend and make things up: they experienced reality simply and as it was. In one sense, as Virginia Woolf admits, both through a character in *The Voyage Out* and in her essays, they lacked the self-confidence to make things up, but this gave all the more authenticity to their rendering of experience. Dorothy Richardson and Jean Rhys exhibit the same kind of passiveness; women's role was still divided; they might be protesting in life but in fiction they recorded. The feminist novel in other forms is still very much alive, and that lends interest to its theoretical origins. As Harold Rosenberg rather grimly observed, 'dead art movements are the normal life of art'. We can understand the divisions and difficulties in Virginia Woolf's art better if we see it developing not forwards into the modernist aesthetic but backwards into realism.

'Dead art movements are the normal life of art'. Unlike much of the work of her contemporaries Virginia Woolf's novels lie outside the scope of that comment. The old pretences of the novel may originally have been banished from her pages, but they are back with us again today. We walk through her pages, and particularly through those of her masterpiece, *The Voyage Out*, as if through a gallery, still full of live portraits and compositions, of gods and men like Mr Dalloway waving swords and making speeches, of goddesses and great ladies like Mrs Dalloway resisting or indulging some mortal partner. It is a far cry from there to the sad little room in Somerville College, with its two landscapes by Roger Fry.

Notes

1. The two paintings, both titled 'Landscape', are dated 1906.
2. Virginia Woolf, *The Voyage Out* (1915; rpt. London: Hogarth Press, 1929) Ch. 22, pp. 355-71. Much of the discussion in this paper will centre around this chapter, which is entirely devoted to the long scene between Rachel and Terence following the announcement of their engagement.
3. Virginia Woolf, *To the Lighthouse* (1927; rpt. London: Hogarth Press, 1932) Sect. I, Ch. 1, p. 11.
4. Virginia Woolf, *A Writer's Diary*, ed. Leonard Woolf (London: Hogarth Press, 1953) entry dated 12 Sept. 1921; the entry on Lawrence is dated 2 Oct. 1932.
5. Virginia Woolf, *The Waves* (1931; rpt. London: Hogarth Press, 1946) p. 169.
6. E. M. Forster, 'The Early Novels of Virginia Woolf', *Abinger Harvest* (London: Edward Arnold, 1936) pp. 125-34.
7. Woolf, *The Voyage Out*, p. 442.
8. Maurice Blanchot, – 'Outwitting the Demon – A Vocation', *The Sirens' Song*, ed. Gabriel Josipovici, trans. Sacha Rabinovitch (Brighton: Harvester Press, 1982) p. 87.
9. Joan Bennet, *Virginia Woolf: Her Art as a Novelist* (Cambridge University Press, 1945) p. 10.
10. Virginia Woolf, 'Jane Austen', *The Common Reader* (London: Hogarth Press, 1929) pp. 168-83.
11. Virginia Woolf, 'The New Biography', *Collected Essays*, ed. Leonard Woolf (London: Hogarth Press, 1967) Vol. IV, p. 234.

6 Self-Defence and Self-Knowledge: the Function of Vanity and Friendship in Virginia Woolf

T. E. Apter

I

Night and Day opens with a description of Katherine Hilbery pouring tea 'in common with many other young ladies of her class'. If someone were to open the door and see her, she would appear as a perfect participant of the party, yet only one-fifth of her mind is so occupied. Anyone looking at her, that is, would identify her with one-fifth of her mind. Katherine's awareness of others' mis-reading of her character cuts in two ways: it makes her lonely, alienating her from others; but it also protects her from the annihilation she would suffer should someone truly look at her, but see nothing. Time and again Woolf's characters seek the protection invisibility offers: Mrs Dalloway's knowledge of her multiplicity thrives upon her being 'invisible; unseen; unknown'. Bernard, in *The Waves*, would accept the death of the self that is to be married, if only 'this margin of unknown territory' is untouched; and Mrs Ramsay's strength is dependent upon her ability to retreat to a wedge-shaped core of darkness, something invisible to others. But these well-defended retreats cannot be permanent residences. The attitudes and views of others will have their powers felt. However much a character believes he should be confident that such views are false, they insidiously attack confidence and identity. Thus Katherine is left with the contradictory beliefs that 'the only truth which she could discover was the truth of what she felt' and that her own view is 'a frail beam when compared with the broad illumination shed by the eyes of all the people who are in agreement to see together'.

With various degrees of sophistication, and with various degrees of success, Virginia Woolf dwells upon the paradoxes and conflicts surrounding the secrecy of our self-knowledge and the necessity of a shared identity. In *The Voyage Out*, where sensitivity is seen as an aberration, Rachel discovers that 'to feel anything strongly was to create an abyss between oneself and others who feel strongly but perhaps differently'. When Rachel declares that Cowper's praise of the scent of broom sickens her – for it reminds her of the flowers at her mother's funeral – her Aunt Lucy says, 'Nonsense . . . don't say such foolish things, dear. I always think [broom] a particularly cheerful plant'. It is nonsense, then, to respond in a manner that deviates from convention. To protect her individual feelings, Rachel believes it would be best to play the piano, and forget all the rest; but her alliance with Hewet arouses in her other deep feelings, whose intrusion she cannot survive. In *Night and Day*, however, the alliance that lies outside conventional definitions does offer Katherine Hilbery the 'wonderful chance of friendship', which, she hopes might offer the ability to step from the active, daylit part of her self to that part which is contemplative and dark as night – to step from one to the other, erect, and without essential change.

In *Jacob's Room* this hope of friendship is put in abeyance by the prevailing difficulties of anyone knowing another person. Here Woolf develops her conception of the personality as unbounded: it can be seen in any number of ways; different aspects can be highlighted, endless meanings can be found. The list of true statements about a person can never be complete; and, as an additional complication, we view people according to our own desires and needs, thereby diminishing the chances of assembling an adequate picture. We deal with people as with shadows, and love is based upon ignorance and misapprehension. Nonetheless we persist in love, in need, and in the effort of realisation. Thus Betty Flanders confronts the question of what remains of her dead husband:

> Had he, then, been nothing? An unanswerable question, since even if it weren't the habit of the undertaker to close the eyes, the light so soon goes out of them. At first, part of herself; now one of a company, he had merged with the grass, the sloping hillside . . . the lilacs that drooped in April . . . over the churchyard wall. Seabrook was now all that . . .[1]

He seems to disappear as she considers how his own perceptions, and the memories, impressions and symbols created from them have ended with his death. Yet she then confirms his continuing reality as she feels him to be part of what she sees. His merging with the grass, and the identification of the church bell with the sound of his voice, do not indicate a mystical union with God or nature, but rather show how Mrs Flanders has been marked by her husband, how she completes him.

In common with many other people, Virginia Woolf frequently asks what a person really is in terms of what remains of him after his death. But for her this is not a religious question about the status of the soul. It is a question which arises as death thrusts us on our own devices to define the meaning another person has for us. In the retrospective and intensified appreciation involved in grief conventional identity is useless. We want to break through the prejudices and needs which distort knowledge of another, and we need to achieve a multiple vision. One would want fifty pairs of eyes to see with, Lily Briscoe realises, as she tries to capture Mrs Ramsay's personality. Lily's painting becomes a means of investigating how the world appeared to Mrs Ramsay, and therefore of how she made the world appear to others. It is not new facts about a person we need, it is a reassessment of old information. Thus Lily 'was only trying to smooth out something she had been given years ago folded up; something she had seen'. But no one can consolidate his or her knowledge of Jacob, and the bleakness of his death rests on what remains – a handful of incomplete impressions.

In *The Years* again the characters suffer alienation, defeat and paralysis because knowledge of others is impossible. Disparate images of a person, which might, under happier conditions, lead to multiplicity, here lead to a mental numbness. After a period of separation one character is recognisable only by a gesture here and there, and recognition goes no further than a vague sense of familiarity. North realises that to Sara he is simply 'my cousin from Africa' and Sara, in turn, strikes his consciousness 'in sections; first the voice; then the attitude'. Peggy, reflecting upon various facts about her Aunt Delia, concludes that she is unable to describe people not because there is something essentially private about another person, but because she is incapable of integrating her impressions of another person. The inability to know another person does not stem from the inability to receive sufficient information, but from the inability to make use of information; and the fear, common to so many of Woolf's characters, of confronting another person, is the fear of receiving data one cannot process and of being oppressed by the futility of mental effort.

In *Jacob's Room*, however, knowledge fails because our views of others depend upon what we are, what we need and want. Characters are prone to gross perceptual mistakes, as well as to more subtle misunderstandings. Seeing a couple making love on the beach, the young Jacob runs towards a rock he supposes is his nanny, since he wants his nanny. Rarely does he see the complex, independent reality of another person, and when this realisation is forced upon him it comes not only as a shock but as an attack. He sees Florinda walking arm in arm with another man, thus destroying his self-interested assumption that she is incapable of deception. As he sees her more clearly, he himself is drenched in light:

> You could see the pattern on his trousers; the old thorns on his stick; his shoe-laces; bare hands; and face.
>   It was as if a stone were ground to dust; as if white sparks flew from a livid whetstone, which was his spine; as if the switchback railway, having swooped to the depths, fell, fell, fell.[2]

Woolf uses 'spine' here, as she does in *The Waves*, as a focus of affect and perception. The new vision paralyses him and makes him a helpless observer of his own disintegration. His ignorance, then, was a defence against self-knowledge, in particular the knowledge of his bias, self-deceit, and isolation. For it is always as a solitary, unacknowledged spectator that Jacob comes to see some truth about another; and when he does so he experiences the same frozen illumination that strikes him when others observe him; it isolates and constricts him in the same way, and similarly thrusts him against false conceptions.

The determining force of Jacob's thoughts is to realise, in spite of these difficulties, his individuality. 'I am what I am, and intend to be it', he declares; but Jacob knows this self does not have an absolute existence. It must be created in face of the falsehoods which it suffers and of which it is guilty. Solitude is essential to this task. Fleeing the 'shock, horror and discomfort' of a professor's luncheon, Jacob finds immediate relief in a solitary walk by the river:

> for he draws into him at every step . . . such steady certainty, such reassurance from all sides, the trees bowing, the grey spires soft in

the blue, voices blowing and seeming suspended in the air, the springy air of May, the elastic air with . . . whatever it is that gives the May air its potency, blurring the trees, gumming the buds, daubing the green. And the river too runs past, not at flood, nor swiftly, but cloying the oar that dips in it and drops white drops from the blade, swimming green and deep over the bowed rushes, as if lavishly caressing them.[3]

We can see here precisely what solitude offers, and why it is important. The trees are bowing; the spires are soft, all colours are blurred or muted so that there is a lessening of focus and clarity; yet this softening is seen to be part of the air's potency: as ordinary boundaries are diminished, thought grows more powerful. The movement of the river – 'not at a flood or swiftly' – mirrors the individual consciousness finding its own pace, whereby images and impressions no longer paralyse the perceiver, but generate further movement of the imagination and therefore provide the opportunity of self-realisation.

This luxurious privacy is seen to be a necessity to sanity; it is the safety valve of the creative self, which is so often set upon by shifts, contradictions, falsehoods and injustice. It is the assurance that consciousness remains inviolable, so it occurs not simply when one is alone, but when one is released from others' views. This is what Mrs Dalloway enjoys as she sews: 'Quiet descends upon her, calm, content, as her needle, drawing the silk smoothly to its gentle pause, collected the green folds together and attached them, very lightly to the belt'. This lulled state results in a deceptive passivity in which thoughts become significantly selective, and in which individual integration is possible.

When a person confronts others he is under attack because the self is not, as Jacob would have, self-contained or self-controlled. The creative capacity of individual perception involves a keen, involuntary sympathy with the views of others. Also, as it looks outward, it changes the world. Thus Clarissa Dalloway suggests that she may live on in all those things she has looked upon lovingly, and thus Mrs Ramsay haunts the house at Skye. This lending of the self to what it perceives expands and enriches the self, but it also fragments and threatens it. If such self-extension offers immortality, it also offers mortality. For the people who complete one can do so in any number of ways. The unbounded definitions of the self, the way others can mould, distort, or ignore aspects and qualities, put personal identity at risk. Assurance of some invisible part of the self, and solitude, offer essential protection, but these defences are never perfect, and never sufficient.

The party in Woolf's fiction serves as a focus for the desire and dread of breaking beyond the safety of privacy. Peter Walsh realises, as he wonders whether to attend Clarissa's party:

> For this is the truth about our soul, . . . our self, who fish-like inhabits deep seas and plies among obscurities . . . suddenly she shoots to the surface and sports on the wind-wrinkled waves; that is, has a positive need to brush, scrape, kindle herself, gossiping.[4]

Yet this need can be met only at a cost. Entering the house 'the cold stream of visual impressions failed him now as if the eye were a cup that overflowed and let the rest run down its china walls unrecorded. The brain must wake now. The body must contract now, entering the house, the lighted house . . . the soul must brave itself to endure'.[5] Now the impressions he had noted with relish must be ignored. Now he must abandon individual creativeness to become someone who is observed, and therefore someone who is re-defined, and therefore in need of new defences. The body which must contract is the 'body' which, while Clarissa sews, 'listens to the passing bee; the wave breaking; the dog barking' and it is the 'body' which to Septimus, seems drowned. 'Body' here does not indicate the physical aspect of the person, but substance, or assembly of the self.

And how does the soul 'brave itself to endure'? What kind of protection does it need? What changes must it undergo? As Peter Walsh enters the house he takes out his pocket knife – not a worn-out masculine symbol here, but a tool with which to pare down his perceptions, to preen his identity, and to defend himself against others' views. Here at the party he must treat his failure to become a writer as an amusement (for it is little more to other people), just as Sally Seton must feign contentment with her life, by bragging about her sons. It is vanity – that is, the compulsion to protect oneself by appearing enviable – that makes them behave in this way; but vanity is not a frivolity; it is self-preservation. Survival depends on one's ability to make oneself as strong, definite and clear as we appear to others. One is therefore compelled to use the same language others use in censuring and limiting us, though we ourselves usually employ more flattering terms. Vanity brings with it paranoia, making the characters keenly sensitive to what others might be thinking. Hence the paradox and danger of the party: it is a meeting of those people who complete one, but it is also a place where the vacillations of identity may become confusing and exhausting, thus stimulating vanity as a defence. Yet normally preservation of one's identity depends upon awareness of multiplicity and complexity. The challenge of the party is often defeated by the defence it renders necessary, for vanity telescopes the self, usually using a single quality or triumph as a convenient handle. And the very falseness of this defence puts one at further risk. We see the excruciating detail of self-defeat in the stories now collected in *Mrs Dalloway's Party*.[6] Lily Everit in 'The Introduction' tries to construct her identity in opposition to all the doubts thrust upon her at the party, by focussing solely on her recent success in an essay on Swift. The stars marked on the essay become hard and fixed, like jewels inside her. Yet this assurance is itself a sign that her identity is in grave danger. She clings to it 'as a drowning man might hug a spar in the sea' and the diamond-like sharpness of her being soon dissolves into a 'mist of alarm and apprehension'. Seeing herself through the eyes of a confident young man she realises that it is absurd to suppose a mere child like herself could understand Dean Swift. Nor is it only this self-definition that is destroyed, but also that being 'by which she knew and crept into the hearts of her mother and father and brothers and sisters'. The single self, which is false, is easily destroyed, taking with it all meaningful identity. In its place Lily finds that the fine dress, the twisted and coiled hair, appear as her true self, and thus she becomes a victim in the world of public action and thought which she had sought to challenge with her intellectual triumph. Prickett Ellis, in 'The Man who Loved His Kind', similarly defends himself against the superior fashion and confidence of those at the party by defining himself in terms of his work on behalf of the common man. His love for the common man becomes a mark of self-esteem, and a hammer to smash against his present companions. Mabel Waring, in 'The New Dress', believes she has protected herself from such painful inferiority to others' wealth and fashion by choosing a quaint, inexpensive but becoming dress – a belief which deserts her as she stands in the cloak-room at Mrs Dalloway's. Seeking reassurance, she makes herself ridiculous. She tells people she feels dowdy, and when they offer the obligatory compliments, she sees they are lying. If they spontaneously admire her, she believes they are disguising their amusement or revulsion; and if they say nothing, she feels they are too ashamed, on her behalf, to mention it.

Vanity is not a sin which is punishable; it is punishment itself, leading one through a hell of false constructions and inevitable downfalls. It is an attempt to defend the ego against attacks from others, yet it destroys the self by insisting that it can be clearly defined. The sister of vanity is of course envy, which also works against the self, infecting and distorting the vision which is crucial to identity. Thus Mabel Waring sees everyone around her as 'meagre, insignificant, toiling flies' and then realises that she sees herself as a fly in contrast to other beautiful creatures. It is envy, too, that cripples Elizabeth Dalloway's friend, Doris Kilman, who destroys the world she observes. We become what we behold; and as Doris Kilman stands in the street, the scene is 'beaten up, broken up by the assault of carriages, the brutality of vans, the eager advance of angular men, of flaunting women. . .' Anger brutalises her vision, justifying her hostility and envy, sealing her off from spontaneous appreciation and development.

Envy builds prisons with the bricks of vanity, and the characters whose vanity works, succeed in locking themselves within. It is therefore a triumph for Peter Walsh, and a triumph for Mrs Dalloway's party, when, after joining forces with Sally Seton in an attempt to label Clarissa a snob, he suddenly sees her gift: 'To be; to exist; to sum it all up in the moment as she passed'. The description is neither profound nor original, but it is significant because it releases Peter Walsh from the limiting definitions he had been thrusting upon her, thereby limiting his vision in order to protect his pride.

But what would happen if vanity failed us completely? What if we should lose any ability to define ourselves narrowly and clearly, and to thrust similar, but less flattering definitions upon others, should they hurt or threaten us? What if we were unable to pare down perceptions and to use, from time to time, conventional language? The undefended self is seen in Septimus Warren Smith who becomes everyone's victim because he cannot use, even temporarily, the self-righteous clarity found in normal life. His insanity was triggered by the death, during the War, of his friend, Evans. He believes he looked upon Evans's death with indifference, yet what he actually does is to realise the public's indifference. Lucrezia protests that everyone has friends who were lost in the War, but her argument which is convention's argument, is both mad and demonic: it is normal, she assumes, for men to be killed, and since it happens frequently, grief is inappropriate. Thus, when Septimus feels nothing, he is looking upon his friend's death with the eyes of the world, and the eyes of the world drive him insane. Nor can the world tolerate this offence. Not only do Sir William Bradshaw, the self-righteous perpetrator of established views, and Dr Holmes, convention's modest servant, exacerbate his pain and isolation, but Lucrezia, too, wishes him dead. 'I am alone!' she cries by the fountain at Regent's Park; but her desperation arises because she is not alone, because others' views affect our own; his nightmare becomes hers, and poisons everything for her, even the trees and the sky.

Evans's death proved to Septimus that conventional language is unacceptable. He can no longer use this language, and therefore no longer has any protection against it. His only defence is death, as Clarissa realises:

> A thing there was that mattered; a thing, wreathed about with chatter, defaced, obscured in her own life, let drop every day in corruption, lies, chatter. This he had preserved. Death was defiance. Death was an attempt to communicate, people feeling the impossibility of reaching the centre which, mystically, evaded them; closeness drew apart; rapture faded; one was alone. There was an embrace in death.[7]

Yet the corruption, lies and chatter do not destroy Mrs Dalloway, for she, unlike Septimus, can preserve her self; she has access to a solitude in which she can seek her own meaning, in which the disjointed and violent impressions she receives can be integrated and assembled. Lacking this safety valve, Septimus receives impressions as a cushion receives pins, nor has he any opportunity to heal these attacks upon his consciousness. Whatever he sees appears as a symbol in language he cannot understand, and the self, which must be self-created through memory, image and imagination, cannot survive without a language.

II

Clarissa 'felt herself everywhere: not "here, here, here"; and she tapped the back of the seat; but everywhere . . . so that to know her, or anyone, one must seek out the people who completed them . . .' Thus, though people suffer greatly from others' views, they also need them. What is the solution to this conflict between the need to find confirmation and expansion through others, and the need to diminish the self in the face of others' views? One solution proposed by Woolf is the sympathy and persistent truthfulness found in Mrs Ramsay whose personality cuts through others' vanities and wooes them from their defensive simple-mindedness. She obliterates the alienation presented in *Jacob's Room* as a general human condition because she has the ability to see people as more than shadows, and Woolf is very good at showing precisely how she comes to know others. The assertion that Mrs Ramsay 'knew without having learnt' does not mean that she has some inexplicable access to knowledge, or that she is strong on women's intuition – which would simply be to absolve her from giving reasons for her knowledge. Mrs Ramsay's knowledge of others is based upon her observation of them – a task Jacob found cruel and threatening, as his ideas of others were bound up with his own needs. For Mrs Ramsay such observation is natural and direct. Reading Grimm's tale about soldiers with kettle drums to her son James, she watches his eyes darken and thinks, 'Why should he grow up, and lose all that'? When she finishes the story she sees another change in his eyes – 'something wondering, pale, like the reflection of a light, which at once made him gaze and marvel'. She sees the lighthouse has been lit and thinks, 'He will remember this disappointment all his life'. Her understanding is based upon what she sees in his eyes, what she sees objectively around her, and what has gone before. At dinner she knows from the twitching of their lips that her children have been sharing a joke, and she notes Prue's new development by 'the faintest light . . . on her face . . . some excitement, some anticipation of happiness'. People are safe with her. She will see the reality of those hidden, semi-articulate areas which are essential to true selfhood or identity.

But there are not many Mrs Ramsays, and most of Woolf's characters must learn to live in a world without her. Their salvation must be found in friendship, though friendship is never easily won or easily maintained. In *Night and Day* the hope was that friendship would offer the ability to step from the active, social part of the self to the dark, contemplative part, proud and erect, without essential change; but Woolf was subsequently to analyse friendship more subtly, and to give up her assumption that the shifting aspects of the self could ever be experienced without confusion and ambivalence. In *Jacob's Room* her praise of friendship reads like an eulogy of solitude: it is 'still, deep, like a pool. Without need of movement or speech it rose softly and washed over everything, mollifying, kindling, and coating the mind with the lustre of pearl', thus reminding one of the relief Jacob found in his solitary walk by the river. But in *The Waves* Woolf abandons these static, perfect images of friendship, and integrates its benefits to the loss we often feel in others' presence. She shows how it works, what puts it under stress, and how its rewards are achieved. The conception of friendship here deployed is closely linked to her assessment of the role creative perception plays in constructing personal reality, and to her view of how images become symbols. The friends in *The Waves* are bound by their shared imagery. They can make sense of their lives and realise its symbols only with one another's help. There is little emphasis on mutual affection. Indeed, the people for whom they might be expected to have the strongest emotional bonds are virtually omitted from the novel – parents, siblings, spouses, children. The psychology of these characters is not a Freudian drama of traumas, but an accumulation of images and their attempts to assemble images and to understand their meaning. These characters form a group because the vision of each helps form the bedrock of the others', either because symbols are shared, and thereby modified or expanded by the others, or because each sees himself more clearly in contrast to the others. '"I love", said Susan, "and I hate. I desire one thing only. My eyes are hard. Jinny's eyes break into a thousand lights. Rhoda's are like those pale flowers to which moths come in the evening. [Bernard's] grow full and brim and never break".'[8]

Susan of course is not remarking so much on the appearance of her friend's eyes, but on what they see; and in understanding what they see, she comes to know something more about the way she sees and, therefore, about what she needs and what she is. This method of association and contrast is maintained through separation, for each has become a mental inmate of the others. Thus, as Bernard looks out of the window and watches the merging crowds, and notes the contrast between an elderly woman and the warmth of the lighted window she stands beneath, he reflects that Neville would not appreciate this contrast, and that Neville, undeterred by disjointed impressions, has a chance to succeed as a poet. Through Neville, Bernard sees his own reasons for failure. Bernard then thinks of Louis, and a different set of images arise:

What malevolent yet searching light would Louis throw upon this dwindling autumn evening . . . His thin lips are somewhat pursed; his cheeks are pale; he pores in an office over some obscure commercial document . . . But I seeking contrasts often feel his eye on us, his laughing eye, his wild eye, adding us up like insignificant items in some grand total . . .[9]

After noting what Neville would not see, Bernard considers what Louis would see, choosing Louis's vision here because its diminishing mockery matches his self-deprecating contrast between his failure and Neville's success. Also, in response to his own defensiveness, Louis allows Bernard to reflect on the defensiveness of another and to focus, also, on Louis's failure to realise his potential.

The one character in *The Waves* who does not speak is Percival, and he does not require a voice because his life is created by action, which is immediate and definable. There is not one piece of paper, Bernard reflects, between Percival and the sun. That is, he has no burden of semi-articulacy, with the contemplative darkness necessary to its resolution. For the other characters, however, language is essential to self-development and the establishment of identity – a language created from images and impressions, which allows the self to be reflected. This need is emphasised by the repeated glosses over external context. The language required for an investigation of the self is a metaphorical language, and metaphor becomes the primary language, and the primary reality. The reader is continually directed towards what the characters see or hear, but one cannot distinguish between that which the character perceives, and that which he takes it to be. There is no point, in this novel, to such a distinction. It is not that the characters fail to see the world, or persist in seeing only symbols, but what they see in the world is symptomatic of what they are. Louis hears a great beast's foot stamping – a dog? what? – what he hears is the measure of his own anger and frustration. Bernard, the story-teller, admires an intricate web, glistening like a complex tale vividly mapped. Susan sees leaves gathered round the window like pointed ears – of corn, presumably – feeling the completeness of her desire for fertility. Neville who, unlike Bernard, does not suffer distraction, admires the bird's eyes through tunnels in the grass, admiring a sort of tunnelled vision. Rhoda sees light falling, as she continually feels herself to be falling. They seek images which speak of themselves. And the primacy of this imagery is enforced by the manner in which it is shared among the characters. Louis feels himself to be rooted to the earth, and when Jinny kisses him she smells 'earth mould'. Rhoda feels that only in darkness will her tree grow, and that this shows her to be succouring a death-wish is seen as Neville makes use of the tree symbol: hearing the cook speak about a murder, he sees a tree with greaved silver bark, and decides to call this vision 'death among the apple trees'.

As the friends meet to bid farewell to Percival, Bernard reflects on what it is that binds them and brings them together. 'Love', he concludes, is too small a word to mark their feelings:

> We have come together . . . to make one thing, not enduring – for what endures? – but seen by many eyes simultaneously. There is a red carnation in that vase. A single flower as we sat here waiting, but now a seven-sided flower, many-petalled, red, puce, purple-shaded, stiff with silver-tinted leaves – a whole flower to which every eye brings its own contribution.[10]

This is the basis of their mutual sympathy, and of Bernard's sense that his is the brow that was struck when Percival died, that on his neck is the kiss Jinny gave to Louis, and that he falls with Rhoda to her death. The characters do not have the same consciousness, or share similar consciousness – 'the virginal wax that coats the spine melted in different patches for each of us' – yet the consciousness of each forms part of the others' reality, each helping to complete the flower which is both imaginative – 'puce, purple-shaded' – and linked to the implacable reality of their mortality – with its silver-tinted leaves, like the leaves of the death tree.

Because their perceptions are interdependent, and because perception is crucial to self-knowledge, Percival's death changes each of them. Their grief is depicted not primarily in terms of what they feel, but in terms of how they now see. Neville believes the lights of the world have gone out. His own past is cut off from him, since this was a shared past, which can no longer be fully shared. Bernard tries to conjure up the world Percival no longer sees: he tries to become guardian of the lost world upon which he depends. But it is Rhoda who suffers the greatest set-back. Her fear of external objects now becomes hatred of them. The faces that pass her appear ugly and deformed. She tries to clutch at the beauty she once saw, but instead is plunged into a depression in which 'envy, jealousy, hatred and spite scuttle like crabs over the sand'. Without the balance of Percival's bright vision, her imagination destroys itself:

'Like' and 'like' and 'like' – but what is this thing that lies
beneath the semblance of the thing? Now that lightning has
gashed the tree and the flowering branch has fallen and Percival,
by his death, has made this gift, let me see this thing. There is a
square; there is an oblong. The players take the square and place
it upon the oblong . . . The structure is now visible; what is
inchoate is here stated; we are not so various or so mean; we have
made oblongs and stood them on squares. This is our triumph,
this is our consolation.[11]

The metaphorical investigation of the self which reveals its individuality and multiplicity is now abandoned in favour of that
system of abstract figures which terrified her at school, presenting as
it did a system with rules impersonally and rigorously applied. Now
that Percival has died she is at the mercy of an external system, and
the logic of this is death.

   The profound intimacy these characters experience does not
protect them from the ordinary vicissitudes of communication in
which the self is misunderstood and constructs in defence another
false self. Neville knows that to his friends he is only Neville, while to
himself he is immeasurable selves, 'a net whose fibres pass im-
perceptibly beneath the world . . . I detect, I perceive'. As perceiver
one is infinite; as perceived one is constricted. Louis, as a child, feels
protected by his identification with the earth, but 'now something
passes the eyehole. Now an eye-beam is slid through the chink. Its
beam strikes me. I am a boy in a grey flannel suit . . .' and as Neville
shows Bernard his poem, Bernard suffers the humiliation of 'being
contracted by another person into a single being'. These friends, too,
are torn between the dread and the excitement of meeting. Louis
sees that they torture Rhoda: 'She dreads us, she despises us, yet
comes cringing to our sides because for all our cruelty there is always
some name, some face, which sheds a radiance and lights up her
pavements and makes it possible to replenish her dreams'. And as
Neville notes the 'acid green' of Susan's eyes, he remembers there is
always someone who, when the friends meet, refuses to be submerged. This resistance is like an assertion of superiority, and
Neville responds by reminding himself of his own merit and success:
egoism stimulates egoism. Yet here the vanity, as, inevitably, it
crumbles, does not lead to a see-sawing of identity, but to a release
from the ego. Here the initial vanity is a kind of purgatory in which
healing is possible. And the reward for the collapse of the ego

freedom from time and space, and a supreme, imaginative objectivity which allows them 'to see things without attachment, from the outside, and to realise their beauty in itself . . .'

But in Bernard's final soliloquy this joyful detachment is modified, and the constricted, observed, vanity-prone self is given a new weight. Initially Bernard re-experiences the release and glory he and his friends felt, once the self had been extinguished: 'lightness has come with a kind of transparency, making oneself invisible and things seen through as one walks . . .' He remembers Percival, and finds himself persuading Rhoda, already dead, not to take her life. Realising how his life is shared, he believes that personal desire and curiosity are finally eclipsed, making him 'immeasurably receptive, holding everything, trembling with fulness, yet clear, contained'. Pure contemplation, and pure truth, seem to be achieved until he bangs into a pillar box and is laughed at by any passer-by. The self identified as 'Bernard' returns to mock him: 'the wave has tumbled me over, head over heels, scattering my possessions, leaving me to collect, to assemble, to heap together, summon my forces, rise and confront the enemy'. Under the compulsion of another's gaze he again observes details of his surroundings: 'Listen: a whistle sounds, wheels rush, and the door creaks on its hinges, I regain the sense of complexity and the reality and the struggle, for which I thank you'. The constriction forced upon him by another's gaze, therefore, stimulates his perceptions. Self-defence forces him back to the immediacy and vividness on which the mind feeds. We see here clearly that problems with others' views is not resistance to a fortuitous intruder whom we would be better off without, but part of what allows us, or even pushes us towards, awareness and self-awareness. Release from the ego offers a glorious impression of truth, but we thrive, too, on the struggles between our sense of what the self really is, and the defences we construct against others' views of us. These struggles can sharpen perceptions which then are re-selected, re-moulded in solitude.

Of course Woolf's novels are not philosophical tracts, but they do contain concepts of the self and its defences which are pertinent to understanding her fiction and which also add to the interest her fiction has today. She presents tantalising connections between what we see ourselves to be and how we see the world, between the mechanisms by which we defend ourselves against others' views of us and our craving for self-confirmation through friendship. She shows how we are profoundly concerned with others' viewpoints, and how this concern extends beyond rational assessment or respect for these views. She shows how our dependence on others for personal identity is not a sign of weakness or shallow narcissism, but a means of facing the reality of our connection to other people – a connection, which, like all attachments, confronts gains and losses, compelling difficult manoeuvres and compromises. In an age labelled by many as 'narcissistic', therefore, she throws new light on the psychological functions of vanity, and shows how if it succeeds in failing only a little, it is not at odds with deep friendships and self-knowledge.

Notes

1. Virginia Woolf, *Jacob's Room* (1922; rpt. London: Hogarth Press, 1929) p. 22.
2. Ibid., p. 153.
3. Ibid., p. 56.
4. Virginia Woolf, *Mrs Dalloway* (1925; rpt. London: Hogarth Press, 1947) p. 177.
5. Ibid., p. 181.
6. Virginia Woolf, *Mrs Dalloway's Party: A Short Story Sequence*, ed. Stella McNichol (London: Hogarth Press, 1973).
7. Woolf, *Mrs Dalloway*, p. 202.
8. Virginia Woolf, *The Waves* (1931; rpt. London: Hogarth Press, 1946) p. 11.
9. Ibid., p. 66.
10. Ibid., p. 91.
11. Ibid., p. 116.

7 Virginia Woolf and Pre-History

Gillian Beer

I

The primeval and the prehistoric have powerfully fascinated many twentieth century writers, notably Conrad and Eliot. The idea of origins and the idea of development are problematically connected in that of pre-history. And in the twentieth century the unconscious has often been presented in the guise of the primeval. These associations have been engendered by the most powerful new metaphor of the past 150 years. The development of the individual organism has always been a rich resource for metaphor; but evolutionary theory, and in particular, Darwin's writing, suggested that species also developed and changed. The analogy between ontogeny (individual development) and phylogeny (species development) has proved to be the most productive, dangerous, and compelling of creative thoughts for our culture, manifesting itself not only in biology, but also in psychology, race-theory, humanism, and in the homage of our assumptions about the developmental pattern of history.

What were the particular difficulties raised for Virginia Woolf by the idea of pre-history and what particular new meanings did she make from it?

The problem of what is truly 'natural and eternal' and what is susceptible to change is one difficulty that expresses itself in Virginia Woolf's work. Social and historical factors claim for themselves 'natural' and 'eternal' authority; social determinism claims to be biological determinism. A wry footnote to *Three Guineas* shows Virginia Woolf tussling with the problem of the imputed permanent characteristics of man and woman and the possibility of change:

The nature of manhood and the nature of womanhood are frequently defined by both Italian and German dictators. Both repeatedly insist that it is the nature of man and indeed the essence of manhood to fight. . . . Both repeatedly insist that it is the nature of womanhood to heal the wounds of the fighter. Nevertheless a very strong movement is on foot towards emancipating man from the old 'natural and eternal law' that man is essentially a fighter . . . Professor Huxley, however, warns us that 'any considerable alteration of the hereditary constitution is an affair of millennia, not of decades.' On the other hand, as science also assures us that our life on earth is 'an affair of millennia, not of decades', some alteration in the hereditary constitution may be worth attempting.[1]

So the nature/nurture question is one associated question, here alleviated by the immense span of time that science promises to humankind in which to attempt 'alteration in the hereditary constitution'.

But there are other ways, more diffused, expressed more as form, less as argument, in which the primeval and problems of development move through her writing. Virginia Woolf grew up a Victorian. She was already a young adult before the twentieth century. She did not simply reject the Victorians and their concerns, or renounce them. Instead she persistingly re-wrote them. Surviving our parents is a hard lesson to learn (parent-texts as well as parent-people), but essential if we are to survive at all. One way is to ignore them, another way is elegy, a third is to liberate them so that they become elements in a discourse and an experience which, bound in their historical moment, they could not have foreseen. Re-writing sustains and disperses, dispels, restores, and interrupts. How does she re-write that major figure in her own upbringing, her own 'development', Charles Darwin ?

Before going further we need to consider her attitudes to 'history' and to discriminate some meanings of pre-history. Is pre-history and the primeval in her work simply part of her strong interest in history? In the last entry recorded in *A Writer's Diary* Virginia Woolf writes:

No: I intend no introspection. I mark Henry James' sentence: observe perpetually. Observe the oncome of age. Observe greed. Observe my own despondency. . . . Suppose I bought a ticket at the Museum; biked in daily and read history. Suppose I selected one dominant figure in every age and wrote round and about. Occupation is essential.[2]

She didn't do it, of course. Instead she drowned. History here for Virginia Woolf is a life-line to pluck her out of the deep waters of introspection.

'History', almost in a text-book sense, is a recurrent theme in her work. *Orlando* jubilantly fantasises the possibility of the self surviving history, looking different, gendered differently, but not much changed from century to century. *A Room of One's Own* creates a counter-history in the image of Shakespeare's sister, and *Night and Day* and *The Years* follow those long contours of family saga which allow the writer to record changes in how it felt to be alive. History in her writing is a matter of textures (horse-hair or velvet), changing light (flambeaux or gas-light), not of events or 'dominant figures of the age'. In 'A Sketch of the Past' she writes of the problems of memoir or biography:

> Consider what immense forces society brings to play upon each of us, how that society changes from decade to decade; and also from class to class; well, if we cannot analyse these invisible presences, we know very little of the subject of the memoir; and again how futile life–writing becomes. I see myself as a fish in a stream; deflected; held in place; but cannot describe the stream.[3]

Such analysis, such discriminations, are the business of the historian. But *her* representations of history have something of the picture-book in them, figures held in superb but picturesque moments – a series of tableaux, a pageant. And that, of course, is the image she turns to in her last novel, *Between the Acts*.

> From behind the bushes issued Queen Elizabeth – Eliza Clark, licensed to sell tobacco. Could she be Mrs Clark of the village shop? She was splendidly made up. Her head, pearl-hung, rose from a vast ruff. Shiny satins draped her. Sixpenny brooches glared like cats' eyes and tigers' eyes; pearls looked down; her cape was made in cloth of silver – in fact swabs used to scour saucepans. She looked the age in person. . . . *For a moment she stood there, eminent, dominant, on the soap box with the blue and sailing clouds behind her.*[4]

History is stationary, inhabited by replaceable figures whose individuality is less than their community with other lives lived already 'with the blue and sailing clouds behind'. This paradox is at the heart of her representation of history: with all her acute sense of the shifts in material and intellectual circumstances, she figures human beings as unchanging, standing in for each other across the centuries. This sense of the inertness of the human condition means that history for her is playful, a spume of language. In *Between the Acts* it seems to Isa that the three great words are Love, Hate, Peace. And nothing else matters. The strangeness of the past is all on the surface. At base, it is familiar.

Playfully and with great intensity, such problems create the fabric of thought and association in *Between the Acts*. Mrs Lynn Jones wonders what happened to the home of her youth.

> Change had to come, she said to herself, or there'd have been yards and yards of Papa's beard, of Mama's knitting. . . . What she meant was, change had to come, unless things were perfect; in which case she supposed they resisted Time. Heaven was changeless.
> "Were they like that?" Isa asked abruptly. She looked at Mrs Swithin as if she had been a dinosaur or a very diminutive mammoth. Extinct she must be, since she had lived in the reign of Queen Victoria. . . .
> "The Victorians," Mrs Swithin mused. "I don't believe" . . . "that there ever were such people. Only you and me and William dressed differently."
> "You don't believe in history," said William.
> The stage remained empty. The cows moved in the field. The shadows were deeper under the trees.[5]

Virginia Woolf's first and last novels, *The Voyage Out* (1915) and *Between the Acts* (1941), are the two works which engage most directly with ideas of the primeval. In *The Voyage Out* it is necessary to travel to remote countries to discover it. The primitive is still figured as outside self. But in *The Waves*, and even more in *Between the Acts*, the prehistoric is seen not simply as part of a remote past, but as contiguous, continuous, a part of ordinary present-day life.

In recent years 'pre-history' has become a useful technical term for describing those conditions of production and of reception which determine the relationship between text and reader. (What do we know about the conditions of production and how does this knowledge define our reading?) The term 'pre-history' is also sometimes used to describe the means by which a work of fiction creates its own past, suggesting a continuity between an unrecorded previous existence for the characters and the language of the text that makes them be. That is, it can be used as a way of claiming a non-linguistic, prior presence for people whom we simultaneously know to be purely the verbal products of a particular act of writing. But there is a further sense of the term which seems particularly apt to Virginia Woolf's work: pre-history implies a pre-narrative domain which will not buckle to plot. Just as Freud said that the unconscious knows no narrative, so pre-history tells no story. It is time without narrative, its only story a conclusion. That story is extinction. Once there were primeval forests, massive land creatures, sea-beasts crawling in the swamp. Now they are gone.

In their place is mankind and its recorded history of war, politics, empire, its unrecorded history of generations obscured by profound oblivion. Virginia Woolf was always distrustful of narrative, finding herself unable to make up plot or accept its resolutions.[6] She was fascinated by recurrence, perpetuity, and both by the difficulty of forgetting and by the fragmentary vestiges which are remembered. In an early draft of *The Waves* she writes:

> I am not concerned with the single life but with lives together. I am trying to find in the folds of the past such fragments as time preserves . . . there was a napkin, a flowerpot and a book. I am telling the story of the world from the beginning, and in a small room, whose windows are open.[7]

The single self in the small room with windows open to the outer world attempts to make again from fragments the continuity of time. She seeks to 'explicate', that is, to 'unfold', the folds of time, to renew the lapsed materiality of the past.

'The story of the world from the beginning' has been, in the past hundred years or so, seen predominantly as a story of development and succession. In *Civilization and Its Discontents* Freud accepts an evolutionist basis for psycho-analysis but distinguishes between organic and mental evolution:

> As a rule the intermediate links [in organic evolution] have died out and are known to us only through reconstruction. In the

realm of the mind, on the other hand, what is primitive is so commonly preserved alongside of the transformed version which has arisen from it that it is unnecessary to give instances as evidence.[8]

That is very much the position of Conrad in *Heart of Darkness*. Virginia Woolf, however, emphasises the extent to which the 'primitive is preserved alongside the transformed version' in the material as well as the mental world. She tempers the triumphalist narrative of development and meditates instead upon ways in which the prehistoric permeates the present day. Sometimes this becomes an opposing comedy to the Tennysonian insistence that we let 'the ape and tiger die' and move beyond the animal:

> There is the old brute, too, the savage, the hairy man who dabbles his fingers in ropes of entrails; and gobbles and belches; whose speech is guttural, visceral – well, he is here. He squats in me. Tonight he has been feasted on quails, salad, and sweetbread. He now holds a glass of fine old brandy in his paw. He brindles, purrs and shoots warm thrills all down my spine as I sip. It is true, he washes his hands before dinner, but they are still hairy. He buttons on trousers and waistcoats, but they contain the same organs. . . That man, the hairy, the ape-like, has contributed his part to my life.

That passage from Bernard's final soliloquy in *The Waves* is succeeded by the morphological ecstasy of

> I could worship my hand even, with its fan of bones laced by blue mysterious veins and its astonishing look of aptness, suppleness and ability to curl softly or suddenly crush – its infinite sensibility.[9]

The example of the hand was one that Darwin used in *The Origin of Species* to track the identity of structures across species and to establish continuity with our uncouth progenitors, hard to acknowledge as kin.

The ready, inter-metaphorical movement to and fro between the development of the individual and the development of the species makes for new relations and anxieties. It informs the thinking of the past hundred years. Though we take it for granted, Virginia Woolf like Freud, belonged to a generation in which its novelty of meaning was still perceptible. It is the idea which allows Freud, in 'The Wolf-Man', for example, to speak of 'the pre-historic period of childhood', and which earlier had led T. H. Huxley to explain the lack of experimental evidence for the evolutionary process thus: 'the human race can no more be expected to testify to its own origins than a child can be tendered as witness to its own birth'.[10] Both quotations emphasise oblivion, the impossibility of recording. Darwinian theory required that we accept forgetfulness and the vanishing of matter, and yet insisted at the same time on descent from a remote and changed precursor. Origins can never be fully regained nor rediscovered. Origins are always antecedent to language and consciousness. That same emphasis upon lost and unreclaimable origins, upon antecedent oblivion, is found in Freud's working of Darwinian theory. But there is also, in Freud and in Woolf, a counter-insistence on perpetuity and on the survival of what precedes consciousness, precedes history.

In *Moses and Monotheism* (which Virginia Woolf was reading as she worked on *Pointz Hall*, the first title for *Between the Acts*) Freud writes:

assume that in the history of the human species something happened similar to the events in the life of the individual. That is to say mankind as a whole also passed through conflicts of a sexual-aggressive nature, which left permanent traces but which were for the most part warded off and forgotten; later, after a long period of latency, they came to life again . . . Since it can no longer be doubted after the discovery of evolution that mankind had a pre-history and since this history is unknown (that is to say, forgotten), such a conclusion has almost the significance of an axiom . . . the effective and forgotten traumata relate, here as well as there, to life in the human family.[11]

The gossips in *Between the Acts* muse crudely on these connections:

No, I thought it much too scrappy. Take the idiot. Did she mean, so to speak, something hidden, the unconscious as they call it? But why always drag in sex . . . It's true, there's a sense in which we all, I admit, are savages still. Those women with red nails.[12]

The coinage of evolutionary ideas and of Freudianism is here brought to the surface and daringly trivialised. I say 'daringly' because she thus draws attention to and simultaneously deflects us from the depth of these issues in her own creativity.

Oddly little attention has been given to the possible reading relationships between Woolf and Freud, as opposed to Freudian plumbings of Woolf's neuroses. The Hogarth Press published translations of Freud from 1921 on. Virginia Woolf was reading him in the 1930s. Once, in Freud's old age, they met, and he handed her a narcissus. Frank Sulloway, in *Freud: Biologist of the Mind*, makes the point that what distinguished Freud from earlier psychologists was his adoption of an evolutionist as opposed to a psychologistic description of the mind. Pre-history is anterior to knowledge. It lies beneath the polarisations and emplotments of knowledge. It lies, as it were, *beneath* history in that same spatial-geological metaphor that Freud used to describe the relationship of consciousness and the unconscious which lies beneath. The unconscious is both prior in time and beneath in space. It is not known, but equally not gone, nor voided. It escapes registration.

One of the features of Virginia Woolf's style is her fascination with taking language out towards obliterativeness, towards things she feels cannot be described, like the clouds near the beginning of *Between the Acts* and the sky whose blue cannot be symbolised:

> Was it their own law, or no law, they obeyed? Some were wisps of white hair merely. One, high up, very distant, had hardened to golden alabaster; was made of immortal marble. Beyond that was blue, pure blue, black blue; blue that had never filtered down; that had escaped registration. It never fell as sun, shadow, or rain upon the world, but disregarded the little coloured ball of earth entirely. No flower felt it; no field; no garden.[13]

The blue 'had escaped registration'. The escape from registration was an ideal, a necessarily unachievable ideal, of her writing. Virginia Woolf is fascinated by the persistence of pre-history as well as its impenetrable distance. The sky, the clouds, changing, unchangeful, are outside history, there from the beginning of time.

These objects of meditation (absence of origins, survival of the primeval, the impacting of race in individuals), haunt Woolf and help to explain certain of the shapes her narratives take, and certain of the exemplary renunciations she makes. Her scepticism about developmental narratives and about irreversible transformations are part of her debate with her Victorian progenitors, her Victorian *self.* Leslie Stephen attributed his loss of faith quite directly to reading *The Origin of Species.* Virginia Woolf, in her career as a writer, assays the forms for experience offered by evolutionary theory. One insistence of evolutionary theory was on changed forms which could not be reversed. Perhaps in the light of the dominant forms for understanding experience developed by her father's generation, her resistance to the idea of transformation has particular meaning.

It is certainly striking how little transformation means in her work. Certainly there are *oscillations* to and fro between metaphor and the material world. There are momentary illuminations, mistaken identities. But transformations, in her writing, can always be reversed. Indeed I wonder whether her much discussed frigidity is a necessary renunciation of climax and of the obliterativeness of climax. It is a way of keeping everything persistingly elated, never completed. In our reading experience of Virginia Woolf, one of the most striking attributes of her style is the sensuous arousal it creates in the reader even while it constantly evades moments of completion. She eschews the authoritarian inevitability of sequence implied in plot. Instead, her writing offers constant shifts between discourses from moment to moment. She has abraded some of the conventional notions of 'development' apparently authenticated by evolutionary story, and in doing so she is responding with great subtlety to the other implications of Darwin's myths.[14]

Let me turn now to *The Voyage Out*, the first of her novels, since this bears traces not only of a struggle with Victorian narrative, but of Woolf's own reading of Darwin's writing. *The Voyage Out* still uses the form of the *bildungsroman*. The particular shape that she uses here is that of the voyage which is to be also a voyage of self-discovery. In *bildungsroman*, typically, the hero learns by means of his growing-up experiences both to know his self and to accept its limitations, to conform to the demands made on the ego by society. A typical form for romantic narrative is that of the circular voyage – away from home until at the furthest point of distance the meaning of home is understood and the return can be accomplished. That narrative was brought into question by other early twentieth century writers as well as Virginia Woolf; by Conrad, in *Heart of Darkness*, where the voyage up river and into the jungle takes you back into the primeval, into the primal self whose core of darkness is indescribable and can never be taken into narrative. Certainly, as Conrad expresses it, it can be explicated only through negations:

unfathomable, immeasurable. These are the forms through which he measures the density of the forest and the activity of the primitive self. Like Freud, Conrad condenses unconscious and prehistoric.[15] We see another reading of the voyage, later, in *A Passage to India* where Forster shows the voyage out into Empire and beyond it, the discovery that the *extent* of India reaches beyond the power of human language to record or British imperial power to suppress. For Virginia Woolf, the *Voyage Out* had a particular meaning.

The book has a closely realistic surface. Rachel Vinrace goes out on her voyage of pleasure and discovery to South America. The narrative implies self-development and promises an according with society's expectations. But in this, we are disappointed. Development is thwarted. Rachel dies. There is no voyage back. The book offers an enquiry typical of women's plot: can the heroine survive her own growth? Initiation into society for women involves initiation into descent. They will become vessels of descent, not borne aloft by the boat that carries them, but themselves bearing and carrying: child-bearing. At the moment of entry into sexual life, Virginia Woolf's heroine falls ill and dies. Rachel's voyage to South America is extended into a special voyage of exploration upriver into the primeval forests. It is on this voyage that Rachel and Terence declare their love, and on this voyage also that she contracts the fever from which she dies.

In these passages describing the forest Virginia Woolf draws directly on another book about a voyage: *The Voyage of the Beagle*, Darwin's account of his early travels round the globe which provided him with the experience and evidences from which emerged his theory of evolution by means of natural selection. Some of the passages of description of the South American forests in Darwin seem to provide 'local colour' for Virginia Woolf - though I shall argue that they provide more than that. His incandescent, sometimes eerie descriptions chime in closely with hers.

> In vain we tried to gain the hill. The forest was so impenetrable that no-one who had not beheld it could imagine so entangled a mass of dying and dead trunks. I am sure that often for more than ten minutes together our feet never touched the ground and we were frequently ten or fifteen feet above it, so that the seamen as a joke called out the soundings. At other times we crept one after another on our hands and knees under the rotten trunks. In the lower part of the mountain noble trees with winter's bark and the

laurel-like sassafras with fragrant leaves, and others the names of which I do not know were matted together by a trailing bamboo or cane. Here we were more like fishes struggling in a net than any other creature.[16]

That is Darwin. This is *The Voyage Out*:

As they moved on the country grew wilder and wilder. The trees and the undergrowth seemed to be strangling each other near the ground in a multitudinous wrestle; while here and there a splendid tree towered high above the swarm, shaking its thin green umbrellas lightly in the upper air. . . .
    As they passed into the depths of the forest the light grew dimmer, and the noises of the ordinary world were replaced by those creaking and sighing sounds which suggest to the traveller in a forest that he is walking at the bottom of the sea. The path narrowed and turned; it was hedged in by dense creepers which knotted tree to tree, and burst here and there into star-shaped crimson blossoms. . . . The atmosphere was close and the air came at them in languid puffs of scent.[17]

Darwin similarly emphasised the mingling of life and death in the atmosphere of the forests:

The day was beautiful and the number of trees which were in full flower perfumed the air and yet even this could hardly dissipate the gloomy dampness of the forest. Moreover the many dead trunks that stand like skeletons never fail to give these primeval woods a character of solemnity absent in countries long civilised. Death instead of life seemed the predominant spirit.[18]

The return to primary forms may reveal a squandering of life rather than its renewal. Virginia Woolf's writing seems to be quite alert to its own inter-textuality here, to be conjuring another pre-history. Darwin's book records the period in his life when, setting sail as an orthodox Christian, he had, by the time he returned to England, begun to conceive the theories which were to change our ways of perceiving experience. *The Voyage of the Beagle* is the pre-text to *The Origin of Species*, its pre-history.
    In *The Voyage Out* the scene immediately after that in the forest is full of Darwinian echoes and Darwinian references. An immense amount of sexual force has been generated which spills about among

the other characters. People crudely use some of the more specious
extensions of evolutionism. Mrs Flushing laughs at the idea of
disinterestedness and love. 'Savin' yourself' is all that matters.

> 'One reads a lot about love – that's why poetry's so dull. But what
> happens in real life, eh? It ain't love!' she cried.
> . . . 'Tell them about the bath, Alice.'
> 'In the stable-yard,' said Mrs Flushing. 'Covered with ice in
> winter. We had to get in; if we didn't, we were whipped. The
> strong ones lived – the others died. What you call the survival of
> the fittest – a most excellent plan, I daresay, if you've thirteen
> children!'[19]

The intellectual Hirst is beset by the silence: 'These trees get on one's
nerves – it's all so crazy. God's undoubtedly mad. What sane person
could have conceived a wilderness like this, and peopled it with apes
and alligators?' In the following chapter Rachel and Terence come
upon the remote tribe of 'soft instinctive people' where mother 'drew
apart her shawl and uncovered her breast to the lips of her baby',
watching them the while; Helen, also watching them, 'standing by
herself in the sunny space among the native women, was exposed to
presentiments of disaster'.

> The cries of the senseless beasts rang in her ears high and low in
> the air, as they ran from tree-trunk to tree-top. How small the
> little figures looked wandering through the trees! She became
> acutely conscious of the little limbs, the thin veins, the delicate
> flesh of men and women, which breaks so easily and lets the life
> escape compared with these great trees and deep waters.[20]

The sense of unchanging life and of the sheer chanciness of survival
are more important here than descent. And the abrupt cutting off of
her heroine's life is her challenge to developmental narrative.

II

Darwin's early writing elated Virginia Woolf, I think. The young
Darwin, like the young Rachel, is discovering the world and in some
of the same regions. But he, active, independent, completes the

circular journey. She, surrounded by protectors, hemmed in by reserve, has the journey curtailed by death. Virginia Woolf's resistance to transformation does not deny death, but in this book death is received as silence and diminution, not transformation. The individual life is muffled. The flesh easily lets life escape 'compared with those great trees and deep waters'.

Evolutionary theory had made a new myth of the past. Instead of the garden, the swamp. Instead of fixed and perfect species, forms in flux. It also renewed the peculiar power of the sea as the first place of life. Most myth systems had given the sea a primary place in the formation of life; now scientific theory historicised this concept. The sea resists transformation. Yet the sea is never old; it is constantly renewing itself. That, I think, was important for Virginia Woolf, and became increasingly so. Her fascination with the sea and with the primeval and prehistoric may be related to her search for a way out of sexual difference, or, equally, for a continuity with lost origins. Her mother died when she was twelve. Because of this loss, and her own gender, the mother in her work is conceived as origin, the father as intervention. In an early version of *The Waves* she wrote of the waves as 'sinking and falling, many mothers, and again, many mothers, and behind them many more, endlessly sinking and falling'.[21] Mothers – matrices: re-formation, not transformation; the acceptance of oblivion: these are connections crucial to Virginia Woolf's writing. The search for lost origins had been powerful throughout the nineteenth century. Darwin himself may have had an unrecognised personal incentive in his impulse to work back towards ultimate origins, and to re-populate the past of the world by means of natural history. His own mother died when he was eight and he was troubled by the scantiness of his memories of her.

What I want to argue is that the need to discover origins, the vehement backward plumbing of history, the insistence on causality and judgement, was *allayed* for Virginia Woolf by her awareness of the survival of pre-history. The continued presence of sea, clouds, leaves, stones, the animal form of man, the unchanged perceptual intensity of the senses, all sustain her awareness of the simultaneity of the prehistoric in our present moment. This absolves her from the causal forms she associates with nineteenth century narratives.

She is drawn most to what is perpetually changing: and I give equal force here to both elements, perpetual and changing. A passage strikingly related to her imagination of the waves of the sea is to be found in Ruskin's *Modern Painters* where he writes:

Most people think of waves as rising and falling. But if they look at
the sea carefully, they will perceive that the waves do not rise and
fall. They change. Change both place and form, but they do not
fall; one wave goes on, and on, and still on; now lower, now
higher, now tossing its mane like a horse, now building itself
together like a wall, now shaking, now steady, but still the same
wave till at last it seems struck by something, and changes, one
knows not how, becomes another wave.[22]

For Ruskin, waves change, but are not transformed. They become
other waves. This absence of transformation, the acceptance of
sustained obliteration and continuity, becomes of great moment in
Woolf's later writing.

Writing for her can less and less claim infinity of recall. By the
time she reaches her last work she is content with gaps and
contradictions. In *Between the Acts* the characters themselves are
vestiges of creation, the language is fraught with citation, pastiche,
and allusion. 'Orts, scraps, and fragments are we': the image shifts
from its context in *Troilus and Cressida*, away from the idea of the
greasy remnants of a meal, becoming instead an archaeological
image suggesting lost cultures, the detritus of an unremembered
past. Yet the phrase itself, through its recurrence in the text, is a
binding chant, linking unlike together in kinship and difference.
Merely to look at the work on the page signals difference when we
come to *Between the Acts*. Whereas in the sub-marine world of *The
Waves*, 'that mystical eyeless book', as she calls it, we are 'deflected,
held in place' by the way in which the language of the book covers
every space, the writing occupies the page, in *Between the Acts* white
spaces abound, unprinted, unrestored.

Between the Acts is set in June 1939, just before the coming of the
war. In it, she deliberately substitutes 'we' for 'I'. She was writing it
from 1938 onwards. She was writing it through the coming of the
war. In a contemporaneous work, 'Little Gidding', Eliot wrote that
'History is now and England'. In *Between the Acts* history is the past.
The present is pre-history in a double sense. Whenever the action of
the historical pageant falters it is saved by the unwilled resurgence of
the primeval: the shower of rain, the idiot, the cows bellowing for
their lost calves. At the same time, the book describes a moment
which may be the last of this culture. The planes swoop overhead.
June 1939 is the pre-history to a coming war which, the book makes
clear without hysteria, may mark the end of this society:

'It all looks very black.'
'No one wants it – save those damned Germans.'
There was a pause.
'I'd cut down those trees . . .'
'How they get their roses to grow!'
'They say there's been a garden here for five hundred years . . .'[23]

In the intense comedy of *Between the Acts*, with its shifty lexical play, its apocalyptic imminence, its easy vacillation between the domestic and the monstrous, we reach her most unsettling meditation on the meanings of pre-history. Since Darwin, humankind could no longer take for granted its own centrality or its own permanence.

It is from the period of composition of this work that Virginia Woolf's one direct reference to Darwin in her diaries occurs. We know from references in *To the Lighthouse* that she used him naturally as an example of the apex of human achievement. ('We can't all be Titians and we can't all be Darwins.') In October 1940 the Woolfs' house in Tavistock Square was bombed. She and Leonard Woolf went up to London to salvage some of their possessions.

A wind blowing through. I began to hunt out diaries. What could we salvage in this little car? Darwin and the silver, and some glass and china.[24]

The diaries, Darwin, some silver, glass and china. It is an intriguing list and a revealing one. Later she records: 'I forgot the Voyage of the Beagle'. I have already shown, I hope, that the problems bequeathed by Darwin's narratives troubled Virginia Woolf creatively in ways that led her to subtle appraisals and meditations on his work. There is no need to assert the prevalence of evolutionary ideas during Virginia Woolf's lifetime and we know that Darwin's writings had had direct effects upon her early family circumstances. We all live within post-Darwinian assumptions now, and hence, paradoxically, we are not alert to the extent to which imaginatively we take for granted shapes for experience suggested by his theories and their extensions. We need therefore to measure the level of awareness at which Virginia Woolf was engaging with Darwin and the implications of his work. We need to do this in order to clarify the particular difficulties he posed for her as a writer and to perceive the new forms that her re-writing of these difficulties created. In the Diary passage we have external evidence that she valued his books. And in *Between the Acts* we have her fullest exploration of the new relations of experience to pre-history which had been fuelled by Darwin's theories. Those theories were indefatigably extended by the two succeeding generations in terms of development, race-theory, the unconscious.

> 'Once there was no sea,' said Mrs Swithin. 'No sea at all between us and the continent. I was reading that in a book this morning. There were rhododendrons in the Strand; and mammoths in Piccadilly.'
> 'When we were savages,' said Isa.
> Then she remembered; her dentist had told her that savages could perform very skilful operations on the brain. Savages had false teeth, he said.[25]

Much of the wit of the book depends upon its turning aside any notion of development as implying improvement. And because so much of it takes the form of thought, past and present lie level, culled as needed by the individual's associations. The novel is a spatial landscape, not a linear sequence. The pastiches of the pageant set periods of the past alongside each other and beside the present. Most of the people in the book say 'Adsum' for their ancestors. Bart's dog is still a wild dog. Bart himself appears a monster, with his rolled newspaper for snout, to his small grandson. The child is convinced, the grandfather is comically offended. The single disturbingly graphic scene of traditional 'action' brings to the surface of the text the matter of pre-history: children, savages, the coming war, the devouring chain of life are all expressed in the awkward scene where Giles acts, running counter to the indications of book and title, 'Between the Acts':

> He kicked – a flinty yellow stone, a sharp stone, edged as if cut by a savage for an arrow. A barbaric stone; a pre-historic. Stone-kicking was a child's game. He remembered the rules.[26]

He stamps on toad and snake: 'It was birth the wrong way round – a monstrous inversion. . . . The mass crushed and slithered. The white canvas on his tennis shoes was bloodstained and sticky. But it was action. Action relieved him'. The four-square allegorisation of violence, of the oncoming of war and greed, is forcefully set apart from the method of most of the book in a way which apes its own subject-matter. It is vividly heraldic. In contrast, there is the sly habit of the narrative of pointing, and thus making enigmatic, simple statements by the intervention of 'he said' or 'she said'. The word 'origin' is a favourite for such play:

> Lucy rapping her fingers on the table said: 'What's the origin – the origin – of that?'
> 'Superstition,' he said.

> 'What's the origin,' said a voice, 'of the expression "with a flea in his ear"?'[27]

In this work interruption is as important as association. Spaces on the page give room to the unrecorded areas between the acts of language. And characters and narrative discourse alike persistently break in upon thought as well as speech. In the same mode, the prehistoric breaks in upon the present as well as surviving within it. At the end of the book 'the great carp himself, which came to the surface so very seldom' is momentarily visible as a flash of silver. At the end of the vicar's speech 'Every sound in nature was painfully audible; the swish of the trees; the gulp of a cow; even the skim of the swallows over the grass could be heard'. Characters break in on each other's vivid reveries. The book is permeated with Lucy Swithin's reading of H. G. Wells[28]. Virginia Woolf here amalgamates his *The Outline of History* with his *Short History of the World* and writes her own version rather than quoting Wells directly. Old Mrs Swithin, so pious, repetitive, and faithful, has an imaginative life swarming with sensual images of power and birth. During the book's twenty-four hours, she inhabits the repeated present of the day of pageant, and the primeval worlds of her book's description. The two sometimes flow together, are sometimes disjunct, are each other's unacted part. Wakened early by the birds

> she had stretched for her favourite reading – an Outline of History – and had spent the hours between three and five thinking of rhododendron forests in Piccadilly; when the entire continent, not then, she understood, divided by a channel, was all one; populated, she understood, by elephant-bodied, seal-necked, heaving, surging, slowly writhing, and, she supposed, barking monsters; the iguanodon, the mammoth, and the mastodon; from whom presumably, she thought, jerking the window open, we descend.

That last thought is taken into narrative discourse to describe 'the great lady in the bath chair' later: 'so indigenous was she that even her body, crippled by arthritis, resembled an uncouth, nocturnal creature, now nearly extinct'. This passage continues:

> It took her five seconds in actual time, in mind time ever so much longer, to separate Grace herself, with blue china on a tray, from the leather-covered grunting monster who was about, as the door opened, to demolish a whole tree in the green steaming undergrowth of the primeval forest.[29]

Two pages later the small boy grubbing in the ground, his perceptions unchanged from primitive man, is terrified by 'a terrible peaked eyeless monster moving on legs, brandishing arms'. It is known by us as his grandfather joking, with a newspaper. Lightly, through comic juxtaposition and pastiche, she concurs with Wells' more sonorous description of 'our ancestors' who are also us.

> His ancestors, like the ancestors of all the kindred mammals, must have been creatures so rare, so obscure, and so remote that they have left scarcely a trace amidst the abundant vestiges of the monsters that wallowed rejoicing in the steamy air and lush vegetation of the Mesozoic lagoons, or crawled or hopped or fluttered over the great river plains of that time.[30]

No wonder Cleopatra is Mrs Swithin's marvellously unexpected 'unacted part' – Queen of the Nile – in which all first life seethed and grew. 'You've made me feel I could have played . . . Cleopatra!' As Wells wrote:

> wallowing amphibia and primitive reptiles were the very highest creatures that life had so far produced. Whatever land lay away from the water or high above the water was still altogether barren and lifeless. But steadfastly, generation by generation, life was creeping away from the shallow sea-water of its beginning.[31]

Wells's romantic language infuses that of Mrs Swithin and invigorates the book with its sensual movement: 'Amidst this luxuriant primitive vegetation crawled and glided and flew the first insects'. Diverse scopes of the past are interlaced: hot images of empire thread the work, particularly in Bart's memories of his youth in India. The word 'savages' keeps recurring, tempered, made sceptical, reinvoked. The untamed dog who either cringes or bites, the fish stirring the pond, the membranes of plants, all suggest the primeval pouring through the present.

The swallows lace Africa and Europe, connecting England's present with its pre-history:

> 'They come every year,' said Mrs Swithin . . . 'From Africa.' As they had come, she supposed, when the Barn was a swamp. . . .
>
> Before there was a channel, when the earth, upon which the Windsor chair was planted, was a riot of rhododendrons, and humming birds quivered at the mouths of scarlet trumpets, as she had read that morning in her Outline of History, they had come.[32]

That is one aspect of the continuance of pre-history; the elegant survival of swallows reassures and sustains a consonance between different time modes in the work. There are other, less beautiful continuities, presented as cliché, as covert allusion, as gossip. Immediately after the description of the swallows we have Mrs Manresa in 'the little game of the woman following the man', connected through Cobbet's observation: 'He had known human nature in the East. It was the same in the West. Plants remained – the carnation, the zinnia, and the geranium'. William Dodge, in the next paragraphs, masturbates as Giles approaches:

> 'The idiot?' William answered Mrs Parker for her. 'He's in the tradition.'
>
> 'But surely,' said Mrs Parker, and told Giles how creepy the idiot – 'We have one in our village' – had made her feel. "Surely, Mr Oliver, we're more civilized?"
>
> '*We?*' said Giles. '*We?*' He looked, once, at William. He knew not his name; but what his left hand was doing.[33]

Giles has blood on his boots. Isa obsessively recalls the scene of rape she read about in the newspaper. The 'sister swallow' is linked, through myth, with the raped woman, and the rape is trivially re-enacted in Giles's insistence in this same passage on the double standard: 'It made no difference; his infidelity – but hers did'. The sexual drive of individuals, though masked by diverse cultural signs, remains fiercely unchanged: 'Venus toute entière à sa proie attachée'. Racine's metaphor, almost cannibalistic in its intensity, is part of the immovable repertoire of Isa's thought – Isa, whose *acts* in this book consist merely of receiving a cup of tea from the hand of the gentleman farmer.

It is as though, compacted yet spacious, the matter of the past is more fully *there* the more remote it is. The captious pastiche of the pageant's language presents snatches of English history as a series of linguistic gestures, and tropes. But the remote past of pre-history crowds the everyday present in its untransformed actuality. It is as though she concurs with Freud's observation that individual and masses 'retain an impression of the past in unconscious memory traces' and 'there probably exists in the mental life of the individual not only what he has experienced himself, but also what he brought with him at birth, fragments of phylogenetic origin, an archaic heritage'.[34]

The parallel between ontogeny and phylogeny in Freud's argument here, which Virginia Woolf read as she worked on the novel, strengthens her own imagery of individual and mass. 'Drawn from our island history. England I am', begins the pageant. Why are pre-history, 'unconscious memory traces' and 'our island history' of such importance in the work?

The allusions to all levels of the past function as 'beot', in *Beowulf's* term. Repetition, encrustation, recurrence, continuity – all are under threat.[35] Plot in this book is the coming of war, the impending obliteration, which makes the ordinary at last *visible* in all its richness. When Miss La Trobe, at the end of the pageant, holds up the mirrors to the audience, they cannot see anything but shallow images of themselves. But we, as outer audience, replenish the emptiness they experience, even while we share it. 'Orts, scraps, and fragments are we.' The entire life (historically bound, and synchronically present) which has been figured in the work is under threat, and momentarily sacred.

Miss La Trobe imagines the scene for her next play:

It was growing dark. Since there were no clouds to trouble the sky the blue was bluer, the green greener. There was no longer a view – no Folly, no spire of Bolney Minster. It was land merely, no land in particular. She put down her case and stood looking at the land. Then something rose to the surface.

'I should group them', she murmured, 'here.' It would be midnight; there would be two figures, half concealed by a rock. The curtain would rise.[36]

The landscape of sky and land, from which all particular relics of England have been obliterated, could as well be at the beginning of the world as now. The two figures are anonymous, progenitors perhaps, only perhaps. She is 'singing of what was before Time was'. At the end, the book itself repeats Miss La Trobe's project. It takes us back before the beginning of history but it takes us there through reading endoubled:

'England,' she was reading, 'was then a swamp. Thick forests covered the land. On the top of their matted branches birds sang . . . .' [Bartholomew] looked leafless, spectral, and his chair monumental. As a dog shudders its skin, his skin shuddered . . . . 'Prehistoric man,' she read, 'half-human, half-ape, roused himself from his semi-crouching position and raised great stones.'

The old people retire to bed. Giles and Isa are left alone. 'The Record of the Rocks . . . begins in the midst of the game', writes H. G. Wells. 'The curtain rises on a drama in the sea that has already begun, and has been going on for some time.'[37]

Giles and Isa, in the final paragraphs, are linked with other species, and with other texts preoccupied with the force of the primeval.

From that embrace another life might be born. But first they must fight, as the dog fox fights with the vixen, in *the heart of darkness*, in the fields of night. . . . It was night before roads were made, or houses. It was the night that dwellers in caves had watched from some high place among rocks.

Then the curtain rose. They spoke.[38]

With the image of the rising curtain and of the bared landscape of night Virginia Woolf simultaneously enregisters the artfulness of history, the perpetuity of the material world. Language, like fishes, rises to the surface. 'Then something rose to the surface', we are told of Miss La Trobe. 'Ourselves', thinks Mrs Swithin as she looks at the fish. But the Dover sole is eaten for lunch. The deftness of the book is in its refusal ever quite to become elegy or threnody. It hopes for survival and gives space to the disruptions of comedy. Simultaneity and conglomeration are, it seems, comic as well as comforting:

> So one thing led to another; and the conglomeration of things pressed you flat; held you fast, like a fish in water. So he came for the week-end, and changed.
>   'How d'you do?' he said all round; nodded to the unknown guest; took against him; and ate his fillet of sole.[39]

Nothing in this work is renounced. But equally nothing is claimed for ever. Levels of discourse persistingly shift, accept their own inadequacy. Not for nothing is Mrs Swithin, who holds history and pre-history together, nicknamed 'Old Flimsy'.

In an almost exactly contemporaneous work, composed equally under the impact of the coming of war, Eliot was writing:

> The river is within us, the sea is all about us;
> The sea is the land's edge also, the granite
> Into which it reaches, the beaches where it tosses
> Its hints of earlier and other creation:
> The starfish, the horseshoe crab, the whale's backbone;
> The pools when it offers to our curiosity
> The more delicate algae and the sea anemone.

In 'Dry Salvages', of which a draft was finished on 4 January 1941, Eliot repudiates 'superficial notions of evolution/Which becomes, in the popular mind, a means of disowning the past'. He continues in a passage, which chimes in with those I have cited from Freud as well as Woolf, responding as they all are to Darwin's writing:

> . . . the past experience revived in the meaning
> Is not the experience of one life only
> But of many generations, not forgetting
> Something that is probably quite ineffable:
> The backward look behind the assurance
> Of recorded history, the backward half-look
> Over the shoulder, towards the primitive terror.[40]

At first, that passage sounds very close to *Between the Acts*, but what is important is that for her that 'backward half-look over the shoulder' does not result in terror. She looks 'behind the assurance of recorded history' *for* assurance.

Pre-history can be described only in the mirror of history, since language and history are inextricable. Yet, outside language and analysis, origins are all about us. She is no longer thrusting back to the past; she has renounced the search for origins. At one level, that is a political act which disengages her from the racial madness of the time. The medium of her work is largely choric, gossip, emerging from 'mass observation'.

> 'No, I don't go by politicians. I've a friend who's been to Russia. He says . . . And my daughter, just back from Rome, she says the common people, in the cafés, hate Dictators . . . Well, different people say different things' . . .
>
> 'And what about the Jews? The refugees . . . the Jews . . . People like ourselves, beginning life again . . . But it's always been the same. . . .'[41]

In her earlier work, when attention is called to it, the present moment has been empty, as at the conclusion of *Orlando*. Here the present moment lightly engages all the past. She refuses that metaphor which assumes that pre-history is deeper, grander, more sonorous, than the present moment, and instead disperses it throughout the now of *Between the Acts*. The book holds the knowledge that cultures and histories are obliterated, that things may not endure. The immediate history of England is interrupted and threatened by the insistent murmur of aeroplanes moving overhead in preparation for war. Is man 'essentially a fighter'? Does the primeval validate war?[42] Clouds, sky, swallows, pike, sea, earth, appetites and perceptions, figure the simultaneity of pre-history and the present, and yet also sustain the idea of a future. The engorged appetite of empire, the fallacy of 'development' based on notions of dominion or of race, are given the lie by the text's insistence on the untransformed nature of human experience – lightly dressed in diverse languages – absurdly knit together by rhymes. Here she registers for once the fullness of the present, not as moment only. The urgency of the connection between militarism and masculine education which Virginia Woolf asserted in *Three Guineas* is here articulated as part of a text which goes beyond it to emphasise the alternative insights offered by Darwin into kinship between past and present forms, the long pathways of descent, the lateral ties between humankind and other animals, the constancy of the primeval. For us living in an age where we can foresee the possibility of a post-nuclear world inhabited at most by sea, grass, scorpions, and sky, the salutary comedy of *Between the Acts* realises its fullest intensity.

Notes

1. Virginia Woolf, *Three Guineas* (1938; rpt London: Hogarth Press, 1943) pp. 326–7. For Julian Huxley's views·see, for example, his presidential address to the Zoology section of the British Association in 1936 on 'Natural Selection and Evolutionary Progress'.
2. Virginia Woolf, *A Writer's Diary*, ed. Leonard Woolf (London: Hogarth Press, 1953) p. 365.
3. Virginia Woolf, 'A Sketch of the Past', *Moments of Being*, ed. J. Schulkind (University of Sussex Press, 1976) p. 80.
4. Virginia Woolf, *Between the Acts* (London: Hogarth Press, 1941) p. 101–2.
5. Ibid., p. 203.
6. For a related discussion of Virginia Woolf's evasion of plot, see my article 'Beyond Determinism: George Eliot and Virginia Woolf' in *Women Writing and Writing About Women*, ed. Mary Jacobus (London: Croom Helm, 1979) pp. 80–99.
7. Virginia Woolf, *The Waves: The Two Holograph Drafts*, ed. J. Graham (London: Hogarth Press, 1976) I, p. 42.
8. Sigmund Freud, *Civilization and Its Discontents* (London: Hogarth Press, 1930; rev. ed. 1963) p. 5.
9. Woolf, *The Waves* (1931; rpt. London: Hogarth Press, 1946) pp. 205, 206.
10. T. H. Huxley, 'Lectures on Evolution', *Science and Hebrew Tradition* (London: Macmillan, 1893) p. 73.
11. Sigmund Freud, *Moses and Monotheism* (London: Hogarth Press, 1939) pp. 129–30.
12. Woolf, *Between the Acts*, pp. 232–3.
13. Ibid., p. 30.
14. For an analysis of Darwin's narrative language and of his myths, see my study, *Darwin's Plots* (London: Routledge & Kegan Paul, 1983).
15. For discussion of Conrad's reading of evolutionary theory see Ian Watt, *Conrad in the Nineteenth Century* (London: Chatto & Windus, 1979).
16. Charles Darwin, *The Voyage of the Beagle* (London: J. M. Dent, n.d.) p. 308.
17. Virginia Woolf, *The Voyage Out* (1915; rpt. London: Hogarth Press, 1929) p. 327; 331.
18. Darwin, *Voyage*, p. 321.
19. Woolf, *Voyage Out*, pp. 335–6.
20. Ibid., p. 349–350.
21. Woolf, *Waves: Holograph Drafts*, I, p. 64.
22. John Ruskin, *Modern Painters, Vol. III* (1856; rpt. New York: John Wiley, 1881) Part iv, Ch. 12, 6, 11, p. 161. Ruskin is another Victorian 'father' to be set beside Walter Pater; see Perry Meisel, *The Absent Father: Virginia Woolf and*

Walter Pater (New Haven: Yale University Press, 1980), and my 'Hume, Stephen, and Elegy in *To the Lighthouse*', *Essays in Criticism*, Jan., 1984.
23. Woolf, *Between the Acts*, p. 177.
24. Virginia Woolf, diary entry dated 20 Oct. 1940, *The Diary of Virginia Woolf*, eds Anne Olivier Bell and Andrew McNeillie (London: Hogarth Press, 1982) Vol. V. In *Between the Acts* itself, Darwin is named at the end of Isa's reading-list, p. 26.
25. Woolf, *Between the Acts*, p. 38.
26. Ibid., p. 118.
27. Ibid., pp. 33, 145.
28. H. G. Wells, *The Outline of History: Being a Plain History of Life and Mankind* (Rev. ed. London: Cassell, 1920). The quotations are all from Ch. 3, on 'Natural Selection'.
29. Woolf, *Between the Acts*, pp. 13–14.
30. Wells, *Outline of History*, p. 24.
31. Ibid., p. 14.
32. Woolf, *Between the Acts*, pp. 123, 130.
33. Ibid., pp. 132–3.
34. Freud, *Moses and Monotheism*, pp. 151, 157.
35. Roger Poole, in *The Unknown Virginia Woolf* (Cambridge University Press, 1978) convincingly establishes connections between *Three Guineas* and *Between the Acts*.
36. Woolf, *Between the Acts*, pp. 245–6.
37. Ibid., p. 255; Wells, *Outline*, p. 11.
38. Woolf, *Between the Acts*, p. 256; my italics.
39. Ibid., p. 59. Compare the quotation from 'A Sketch of the Past' on p. 3.
40. T. S. Eliot, 'Dry Salvages' *Four Quartets, Collected Poems 1909–1962* (London: Faber & Faber, 1974) pp. 205, 208–9.
41. Woolf, *Between the Acts*, p. 144–5.
42. Compare Woolf's comments on militarism and evolution quoted at the beginning of this essay.

Panel Discussion 1

Gillian Beer (Chair), Bernard Bergonzi, John Harvey, Iris Murdoch

GB: I thought we might start by asking each of the three panellists how they find the presence of Virginia Woolf in their own practice as novelists. Is she somebody who can now simply be bypassed? Or is she still a recalcitrant being, a recalcitrant *writing*, which needs to be circumvented, written through, obliterated, transcribed? I'll start by asking Bernard Bergonzi.

BB: What's the question, Gillian?

GB: Do you still *need* Virginia Woolf, or can you do without her? [laughter]

BB: Well I *did* do without her for a long while, I think. That is to say, I read her, a number of her books, when I was quite young – about nineteen or twenty. And then there was a great occlusion of her reputation in the fifties, and she seemed to have pretty well sunk without trace. What is interesting is the way the reputation has come up again so much in the last twenty years, hence this well-attended Centenary Conference.

I suppose I went back to her texts for professional reasons: I found myself lecturing on her, every year on *To the Lighthouse* – a book which I really came to admire through the process of teaching it. I think we're all familiar with that activity – how books which you take up as a chore, because you have to, you can actually come to respect and admire. Of course it can go the other way too, alas. But I think probably my dealings with Mrs Woolf have been of that critical and professional kind. Insofar as I have written a bit of fiction myself, I don't think there was any presence of Virginia Woolf in it or near it; the sources of that were quite other.

JH: I should likewise say that I hadn't, before writing myself, enormously read or drawn on Virginia Woolf, though over the years I have been reading and enjoying her. I should say also, that what I find myself enjoying more and more *is* the writing, and the variety of the writing – including the criticism, and some of the Memoirs, especially the 'Sketch of the Past'. Of the fiction, the novel which I do go back to again and again is the one that I suppose everyone does, *To the Lighthouse*.

How one might nowadays be influenced by it I don't know. One returns to it I think chiefly to appreciate the art with which it arranges and focusses the family experience that it is based in. It does seem to me almost *the* exemplary novel about a father. I know that Mr Ramsay isn't to be assimilated entirely to Leslie Stephen; that Virginia Woolf leaves out his main achievements and a number of his good qualities, and exaggerates other features of him and some of those exaggerated features seem to be ones where his character especially overlaps with hers. One gathers that the anxiety about whether or not he's a failure, with its constant, exorbitant demands for reassurance and support, and for constant encouragement, was something which was marked in her as well as in him. And I'd have thought that for various reasons one would feel that the novel is not exactly a portrait of – or doesn't even try to be portrait of – the real person that her father was. But it *is* a portrait of, as it were, the daimon of her father that she's nurtured inside herself over the years, which needs to be, in a way, exorcised, *negotiated* especially. And it seems to me that what she does in the novel is to negotiate that partly invented image of her father, about which she has intense, varied feelings, about which she's divided, seeking really a right order for the memories of him, or the images of him, which her imagination gives her.

I prefer the word 'order' to 'structure' because I think the right order is both the right structure and the right sequence. The novel is a sequence, and one can see that it has worked as a sequence in bringing her to the right attitude in the way that, along with the predominantly malign images that you have in the early parts of the novel, she increasingly finds a place for *benign* images of him. As, for instance, when the boat has been becalmed and all the bad passions of the family seem to be about to burst out; and then the wind fills the sails and takes the boat forward, without any of the explosions from Ramsay that have been expected, but instead, simply with his mysteriously raising his hand very high and then lowering it, as if he were conducting some secret symphony. Towards the end you do get a progression of extraordinarily eloquent images of him, each of which comes with, as it were, a just surprise.

It seems to me a model of the sort of fiction in which you try to meet again and find a better rapport with someone who has been enormously important in your life. Ramsay clearly has that kind of hold or power in Virginia Woolf's imagination and I think her dealing with him is exemplary if you compare it with other novelists who have done anything like it – for instance, it compares very well with D. H. Lawrence's dealing with his father in *Sons and Lovers*.

I put my emphasis on the father because I'm not one of the admirers of Mrs Ramsay. It seems to me she's sufficiently there for the role she has in the novel; but that seems primarily to be kind of luminous *value* by which Ramsay is to be measured and mainly found wanting. I know she is criticised as well as idealised, but it still seems to me that this is mainly what she is. And one gets an odd indication of this in the curious way in which her absence in the third part of the novel seems somehow bigger than her presence in the first part.

                                                                                . . .

GB: Thank you. . . . I think that one important point that's already been raised is the question of *consensus* of reading. Perhaps that very high place in the canon that *To the Lighthouse* is given is because it is a novel where on the whole people think that there is a consensus of reading. I would like to raise the problem of whether we should, precisely for that reason, look suspiciously at it. But perhaps before we develop that argument, I could turn to Iris Murdoch to hear something of her reaction to Virginia Woolf.

IM: I'm not quite sure how to begin. I don't feel that she comes at all near my own work, though I admire her very much. She is usually associated with the term 'stream of consciousness', which we've been thinking about in relation to both the previous talks [Hermione Lee's and Allen McLaurin's], and when I first read her when I was at school I was interested in this conception. But I was chiefly, I think, concerned with her as a *novelist*. I mean, she may have *hoped* that she was going to have – or thought she *might* if she were really free – no humour or characters or plot, but she *did* have these things! And I think one's reflection upon the characters – and we've just heard Mr Harvey talking about this – is one of the main sources of interest in her. The 'stream of consciousness' method is in many respects, of course, more familiar to us now as a way of portraying character. The change in people's attitude to her is interesting to a critic, to a historian, also perhaps to a philosopher; we now see a very different, at least I now see a very different Virginia Woolf, from the one we saw earlier.

The matter of her feminism is a rather delicate one, I think, which one has to pick up with a good deal of care. Perhaps we both recognise her feminism now and are critical of it. That is, we see, on the one hand, that she's a fighter for the position of women (and the reference to Jane Harrison I find interesting). On the other hand, there's an awful lot in her stories which is to do with portraying a feminine sensibility in contrast to a masculine intellect, or a feminine generosity in comparison with a male egotism; and I don't think that I see the world in quite those terms. Nor do I think that the liberation of women should be associated with such distinctions.

So I think that she is of continuing interest, to critics of course, and to thinkers generally. And she's a great extraordinary phenomenon really. I mean, the notion of stream of consciousness is now everywhere among us, and is practised in a great many ways, but there's nobody quite like her. And this phenomenon remains with us in the great open free society of the novel, where people do, in spite of critics, do all sorts of different things.

GB: I think the point you made at the end there is certainly one we all ought to bear in mind. . . . An inhibition at the moment with Virginia Woolf is the tendency to see her always in the intellectual group of Bloomsbury. I would rather like to see her alongside some other modernist writers like Henry Green, or even Ivy Compton-Burnet. I wonder what you, Bernard, would think about that kind of grouping?

BB: Yes, well it's very curious the way her reputation was occluded, as I said, for a long time, and then came up again; and one can trace the sort of stages of the ascent. And I think the Bloomsbury cult which perhaps reached its peak a few years ago, that this *was* rather factitious. And yes, I think you're right, this didn't do her any good; to be all the time placing her into that particular historical/social/cultural context. I suppose, yes, as Iris says, the feminism is something which has made her now so much the focus of attention. I recently read, I think it was for the first time, her *A Room of One's*

Own, which I suppose is one of the main planks in her use by feminists, which is a very eloquent, polemical book. I really don't know how usable I would find it if I were a late twentieth century woman. I mean, clearly some of the arguments are very inspiring; I think the whole notion of patriarchy seems to have been taken out of that book, the way she uses it. But I would have thought many of her other arguments and assumptions are very much of an earlier milieu and period. But certainly that's another thing which has helped her reputation now.

   And then there's the minute latter-day interest, not just in stream of consciousness, but in all modes of narrative. A fairly recent critical discovery has been that you can write *endlessly* about, not a single book, but two or three pages, by the sort of minute analysis of narrative modes; and as sophisticated and subtle a writer as Virginia Woolf offers a great deal of scope here. But that takes it a long way from the kind of interest John Harvey spoke of; a purely *human* interest in how you get your father sorted out or focussed in a work of fiction. That is a solid, traditional interest in characters, psychology and so on – which I think still appeals – but there's a lot of latter-day interest in Virginia Woolf of a rather technical kind that is fascinated by the sheer complexity of her narrative. In short, Virginia Woolf has become a great object of academic *study*. Bearing in mind her dismissive comments about the academic study of English, there's a deep irony about this: what would she have made of all of us, sitting here, in these deliberations? That's a deeper question. I don't know whether anyone would like to sketch in an answer to that . . . .

GB: I'm not really sure I much care what she'd have made of us. It seems to me that a writer writes, the writing becomes usable in a variety of ways, and that those uses are determined by historical moments. She certainly potentiated in her novels elements that she would not necessarily herself have recognised; just as, I think, she potentiated in her novels re-readings of the Victorian writers; she dispersed them into a kind of discourse that they certainly couldn't have recognised or composed for themselves. I think that in the same way there is a dispersal of the parents in *To the Lighthouse*. So when we get to *Between the Acts* and she says 'Dispersed are we' (or rather 'it is said' and it is said deliberately at several removes in that narrative) the saying is not at all negative. Dispersal may be something that we can draw from Virginia Woolf that she had very little awareness of in her career, but which she needed and which she performed.

In the same way, the question about her adoption by – well you called it, and I think Iris called it, feminism – clearly one would have, if one were going to try to plot her reputation, to distinguish quite acutely between different forms of feminism. For instance, Elaine Showalter takes her strongly to task for the androgynous drive of her theory and her writing and says that we should instead be setting up a complete opposition between male and female, and should be engaging in something more like gyno-criticism, something in which we study only women writers. Whereas I think I don't agree with Showalter there, because it seems to me that one of the things that Woolf does, and allows us to do, is to get outside some of these binarisms, such as male-female, so that we don't need to take necessarily a kind of post-Leech view of myth, as always implying *Night and Day*. All right, I know she uses all these oscillating contraries in her own work. But it does seem to me that she prepares us also simultaneously to question this particular kind of oscillation of contraries.

Getting away from oppositions which create despondency, that's one of the things that I (reading her as a woman who writes, though who doesn't write novels) find that she allows me to think about, and develop. But I don't claim it as something that only feminist criticism permits, but as available to any of us reading her – in the eighties. We're here, after all, reading her in the eighties, not in the twenties or thirties.

M: I'm not quite sure what I should be picking up here, but perhaps I could just say a few things that I think. This matter of myth is very much in people's minds now, and I think should be, partly because of our attitude toward religious myth, and the demythologisation of religion, and wondering what myth does for us, and so on. One has to remind oneself with a novelist, that this is a work of art and that the novelist is making up his own myth; and that one has to look at all these things in the context of the whole work. This is important in relation to the imagery that she uses, and the method of her stream of consciousness. I think this is a terribly deep and difficult problem. Hermione Lee very eloquently and movingly presented this image of a perceived thing which becomes the thought and feeling, and how these things are, as it were, glued together – which is in itself, in a way, an image of art. Somebody could say, though perhaps it would be misleading, about Virginia

Woolf, that she was always writing about art. That she was thinking about this peculiar transformation.

Now, I think this is a difficult thing to judge. If somebody says to me offhand, well now, what makes you enjoy reading Virginia Woolf? I might say, 'She's full of marvellous metaphors; there are the most wonderful images which one wants to remember'. And in this respect she is like a poet. But again, it's very important that she's not a poet. . . . One has to try both to enjoy the magic – and she's a great magician – and also to try and assess the truth of what is being said. Is it something deep that's being said? Is it something interesting? Is it something true? And this is where the fact that it is a story is important; it is about characters, and the contrast which John Harvey made between the figure of Mrs Ramsay and the figure of Mr Ramsay brings this out I think. That Mrs Ramsay is a sort of luminous value – one might compare her, *mutatis* a great many *mutandis*, with Cordelia in *King Lear*, who is both a person and a kind of luminous symbol. Well now, some people, and I think I rather half feel this myself, react against Mrs Ramsay. They think there's a bit too much luminosity based on not enough *stuff*, and that Mr Ramsay is a more interesting and *realistic* (let the word come in here) character.

And one has to think of this tremendous presentation in terms of images, as something which has also to be seen as part of a work of art, written in discursive prose. And that the *transformation* – and this is where the difficult bit comes that I can't really explain – the transformation of the image into a kind of *thing* (this is a way people sometimes talk about some kinds of poetry, perhaps T. S. Eliot does) . . . this is something which can be seen to be valuable for itself. But the *truth* of it, the truth-conveying aspect of it, the reality-conveying aspect of it, or the sense in which it is something which transcends its mere charm, will depend upon its relation to the whole narrative. So the stories are important, and indeed the plot is important. I do think that it is an important objection to some of the novels, or to parts of some of the novels, when various plots are suggested, that the sort of truth-structure within which the stream of consciousness is going to gain its finest quality, is inhibited, is not present, because of the absence of some kind of dominating intellect, which of course Virginia Woolf is deliberately inhibiting.

JH: I think the point which I'd like to make especially is that in *To the Lighthouse* particularly the concern for truth involves the presence of irony. I think, by the way, that Virginia Woolf is always, to an extent, a realist, that she is a realist in the sense that there always seems to be some check and test on her characters as to whether each next step they take is plausible. I think that applies, for instance, even in *The Waves*, the novel which, in its style of language, can seem furthest away from any realistic mode. Still, the characters of Jinny, Bernard and so on, seem to be checked against an idea Virginia Woolf has as to how each of them would feel in reality, however stylised and poetic their speeches are.

I think this kind of appraisal of the characters in the fiction, against some fairly direct sense of the world as it is, is operating all the time. But I agree with Iris Murdoch that it does often seem to operate weakly, and in *The Waves* I think it operates weakly. I think what enables it to operate more strongly in *To the Lighthouse* is the presence of irony. You get in that novel, I think especially with Mr Ramsay, a variety of response, a variety of ironic inflections. Its noticeable, for instance, that in almost any one of those long sentences which Mr Ramsay inspires, Virginia Woolf will start off with a fairly hostile irony – that at times he'll sound like Mr Gradgrind in Dickens – and yet the sentence will wind its way round and inside Ramsay's ego, and see things somewhat in his perspective also, so that the irony takes a different tinge, more sympathetic, and is at times benign.

Involved with the irony there is also the extraordinary mobility of viewpoint that you get in *To the Lighthouse* as Virginia Woolf moves constantly from character to character, and circles and returns, enters one person's passion and another person's fancy, then recedes to a distance and sees things in a long perspective: she's so mobile that the reader is constantly engaged, as she is, in comparing and appraising.

The ironic inflections that keep entering the prose do, I think, work as indirect but constant checks as to truth, and this is why I think that because there is less irony there is less truth in her subsequent fiction (except of course for *Between the Acts* which is ironic everywhere). In this connection I'd like to take up another point that Gillian made, and question the value of dispersal. Dispersal is certainly something that Virginia Woolf is interested in, and one would want to take more of a stand in relation to it than simply to say that it is a good object of study. Because I'd have thought that the strength of *To the Lighthouse* is that she doesn't attempt to disperse the discrepant features of, for instance, Ramsay, but keeps them together; while in, for instance, *Mrs Dalloway*, she took the decision at a fairly early stage to disperse the conception she had originally had – of a person for whom the social world had very strong holds and in whom the genius of a hostess was strong, but for whom all that social busyness could collapse into solitary and suicidal dejection. That conception which, it seems to me, could have led to a character who would have been both as much in her heart and under her skin as Mr Ramsay, and which could have generated as fine a fiction, was dispersed into Mrs Dalloway on the one hand and Septimus Smith on the other. It seems to me that more is lost than is gained with that dispersal. Again, *The Waves* seems dominated by the idea that the several characters in it are the dispersed parts of a kind of ideal, whole person, whom in a way is figured by the dead Percival, but whom one is also meant to imagine being composed by the remaining lives. And it seems to me here again that the conception doesn't work.

. . .

GB: Could I . . . come back to you, Bernard? Because it seems to me that a real, a quite crucial disagreement is coming out, which is that if I were asked for the novels which I most value in Virginia Woolf's work, they would be two of those that have so far come in for the greatest demurral, that is *Mrs Dalloway* and *The Waves*, and then I think I'd go on to *Between the Acts*. And that probably is to do with the deep attachment that I have – which I think is something more than an object of study – to the idea of *dispersal*. Or, if you like, to *permeation*, getting away from the ordering of plot, which relies on certain authoritarian knittings up, and instead allows things to move out and not necessarily be completed. I wouldn't myself see this as in any way a reneging on plot, but rather as a new form of narrative which queries our implicitly patriarchal concepts of plot. Thus I would be interested to hear what Bernard, for instance, would say if he were composing a canon of Virginia Woolf – which books would go into it as the ones which he would most wish to read again?

BB: Well, I suppose if one is compiling a canon – which I might say I don't find a terribly interesting activity – but if one were to then yes, it would be *To the Lighthouse* I think. But as people have been talking, as John Harvey was talking about realism and so on certain thoughts were coming together in my mind – which is that we have come increasingly to fit Virginia Woolf into a sort of mod

ernist pantheon, and to say that she embodies the modernist aesthetic, which is all sort of tied up in a convenient shorthand – myth,
timelessness, narration dissolved into epiphanies and moments and
gestures toward transcendence, the undermining of conventional
narrative – all of that. At this point, you know, I start thinking like a
Marxist, which I am not, but they are the necessary opponents in
my own inner dialogues, . . . I can see ways where she clearly does
fit very significantly into twentieth century history: *Mrs Dalloway*,
among other things, is a novel about what happens to English life
after the First World War; that War is a visible, rather terrible
presence in the book in Septimus Smith, who dies. But when she
comes to *To the Lighthouse* she seems to move away from that kind of
realism, she seems to move much more to myth, to transcendence,
epiphanies and all the rest of it . . . . And I'm often fascinated by
that momentary appearance the First World War makes in *To the
Lighthouse*, in square brackets I think, in that sort of middle section
which is a kind of brief summary of what's gone on. One of the
young men has died, other young men have too – all of this is just so
summarily treated that I'm sometimes rather shocked by this. How
could she, as it were, dispose of such a historical disaster and
catastrophe in such a brief compass. It seems rather a sort of
aesthetic indifference.

But thinking about it again, one can see that it's a sufficient clue to
something. . . . In other words, one way of looking at *To the
Lighthouse* is to relate it to certain other major English novelists of the
twenties which have the First World War as a kind of invisible
presence. *Women in Love* is one obvious example. As Paul Delaney
said in his recent book, it's one of the greatest war novels in which
the War is never actually mentioned. Forster's *A Passage to India* is
another one, which is set far away in space, and is not very clear
about its time, but probably before the War. But the War is clearly
permeating the book in terms of the personal disruption that Forster
suffered and underwent following it. *To the Lighthouse* is a third of
these; it came out in 1927, and the War is all but invisible, but it is
nevertheless there, momentarily. I mean it would be a perfectly
respectable critical thing to say, 'So what?' It's not really like *A
Passage to India* or *Women in Love* at all; it's much more personal,
aesthetic, symbolic, and that might be a thing to argue about. But
that momentary presence does fascinate me.

We then come to her last novel, *Between the Acts*, which, as one bit
of homework for this Conference, I re-read, for the first time in

many years, and enjoyed very much. I thought, well this is a book
much more *open* to history. I mean it was written after the Second
World War had started, and it is placed at that particular moment,
very precise in time, June 1939. And though the pageant looks back
in various, I think sometimes rather factitious ways at English
history, there is also the fact that war is impending, and certain stock
properties of the 1930s are actually *there* – like aeroplanes flying
over. And I think that book can be related to other books of the late
thirties and early forties which to my mind focus that particular
moment in history, the period 1938–39: Louis MacNeice's *Autumn
Journal*, Orwell's *Coming Up For Air*, and a rather less well known
book, very good, Patrick Hamilton's *Hangover Square*, which is set
precisely in the period 1938-9, and *ends* on the day when the Second
World War broke out. So this is perhaps a rather unusual
perspective in which to see Virginia Woolf, but maybe it's a way of
taking her, in this particular novel, out of the normal Woolf context,
the modernist context, and placing it into a number of books that do
illuminate from within a very crucial historical moment.

GB: Yes, I'm actually amazed, if I can jump in before everyone else,
. . . to hear you saying that there's just a sort of fleeting reference to
the First World War in *To the Lighthouse*, because it seems to me that
the whole section 'Time Passes' *is* the period of the War, that there is
a very strong sense of cataclysm, of the thing dissolving . . . The
book won't hold together, is shattered apart by this central section
and she's making the effort that Lawrence also made in what was to
be *The Sisters* – to hold a family history in one place, in one piece. He
couldn't do it because of the intervention of the First World War
she just about does it, but she does it by having this extrusion of the
War, with references to it which make quite clear what's going on
what's that boat doing? Why is it going down? The whole of that
section is *full* of references to the War. Certainly I would agree with
you about *Between the Acts*; it's a highly political novel, and one
which, I think, is very properly to be connected strongly to *Three
Guineas* and her feelings about militarism and to the advent of the
Second World War. But in *To the Lighthouse*, I just can't see the War
as absent; I've always seen it as absolutely there.

BB: I'm willing to take correction from you there, Gillian, because I
did not actually look up the passage; I'm just talking off the top of
my head. I thought it was briefer than you tell me it is. But I think it

is still true that most people's memories of *To the Lighthouse* are of other things than that middle section.

IM: I think I agree with Gillian here on this point about *To the Lighthouse*. I thought the device of the square brackets in which terrible events were very briefly recorded was successful, had got a kind of tragic point to it, that one felt that this was going on and somehow these brief things conjured it up very well. This makes me want to say something about *The Voyage Out* which nobody seems to want to put on their list, but which I like very much. I think my two favourites would be *To the Lighthouse* and *The Voyage Out*. I like it because perhaps Virginia Woolf was doing something there which she later decided was improper for her to do, and that is to tell a terribly sad story in great detail. I think that the second part of *The Voyage Out* is a very good novel. And it's something which reminds me of Conrad (who I think, incidentally, is a better writer, but that's by the way). It's something which Conrad might have done . . . the notion of the visit to the village, the mysteriousness, the ambiguity, the fear, and then the tragedy ensuing. I think this is marvellous. And there are little touches in *To the Lighthouse* which seem to me to have that sort of tragic force also. . . .

I'm worried about *Mrs Dalloway* and the business of dispersion and permeation – though you did say that this is in fact a way of doing a plot; the plot doesn't disappear, it is just part of this pattern. I think that one can go too far in the direction of dispersion, through images becoming sort of self-directed pleasures instead of being the servant of some other idea. And the danger of writing this, what one might rather crudely call 'poetic prose', is that invention at this level can sometimes inhibit really *deep* invention. I look for really deep inventions in her work, and I think there are a number of them. But I think that sometimes she, as I said before, deliberately decides that she won't make deep inventions.

GB: Now I think we can throw this open to the floor; there were a couple of people with questions . . .

Teresa Vanneck-Murray: I've got about twenty points now, and I'm going to be in a muddle. But I'd like to go right back to the beginning and, with all due respect to Bernard, whom I know, and to John, whom I don't know, say that I don't know why we haven't got four women novelists up there, because I do believe that

Virginia Woolf is important as a woman writer and to us now. I don't belong to any particular group of feminist thinking, but I really do think she must be approached as a woman. Now when John was talking, he was talking in a very masculine fashion about things, about *negotiation* especially. And it seems to me that what comes out of that book is how the *woman* negotiates this concern with her father – a father for a woman is a quite different person from a father for a man – and it also tells us something about how women negotiate within their society, within the spectrum of things they have to see to, within their families for instance, a point which also comes out in *Mrs Dalloway*. It seems to me that in her work we have got the stream of consciousness done in very feminine terms, without being stupidly or sugarily feminine . . . . The whole approach, it seems to me, is as a woman, and this is why I think Virginia Woolf has been neglected. Yet suddenly we see . . . a great mass of women; I've never been to a Conference with so many women in it. And I think that this is because she *does* say something, she does have perceptions about how a lot of women (one can't possibly say all) perceive experience, deal with experience, and about how women negotiate with the society they are a part of – very often as rather invisible presences. We *are* invisible presences, except for here. . . . Now women are coming to the fore Virginia Woolf is .becoming more and more appreciated, because she is being appreciated by half the population that were invisible before . . . .

GB: Okay. [applause] Before I hand it back to John and Bernard [laughter] is there someone else? Hermione?

Hermione Lee: Yes, it was just to raise a point in pursuit of what Bernard Bergonzi was saying, which actually is in contradistinction to what's just been said. This is to pursue comparison you mentioned between Virginia Woolf and Henry Green. The question is: why should modernism have to be in another bag from realism? We have been talking about her as a modernist, but it is perhaps more interesting to talk about her in this group of 1930s realist writers, leading up to the War. If you put *Between the Acts* with *Party Going* – which is a book which I thought you might mention but didn't – what you've got are two modernist texts, in that they are highly formalist – *Between the Acts* relying heavily on the process of fragmentation, *Party Going* being an extremely mannered, contained, odd narrative – but both about the imminence of the

War as it affects a particular class. They both seem to me to be about something you may call historical, to be historical novels if you like, and also to be modernist texts in the way you've been talking about modernism. As a footnote one might say Henry Green is a male writer, *Virginia Woolf* is a female writer; but I think there is a considerable overlap in what they're doing.

BB: Well I think I would agree with that; I think it's a valuable comparison with *Party Going*. And yes, I suppose there's no real reason why realism and modernism shouldn't go together. I've probably had my mind blown by reading so much criticism which says that now realism is totally finished, that a text is a text is a text, and that word and world have no relation . . . and I'm coming back to find it's not true after all.

JH: I fear I lack the essential qualification to give a proper answer to the questioner before last. I'd have thought, however, that her question would confirm that it is especially male authority, male ego, that gets under women's skin, as it were, and that it does therefore actually seem a fit subject for a novel by a woman. . . . I wouldn't want to try to speak about areas of experience where she may be very good but where I'm in a sense disqualified from speaking. I wonder though, where she is best at that? The novel I've got in my mind as one of the good ones is *Night and Day*, which I re-read recently and which seemed to me very direct and sensitive and strong in its approach to just those questions about feminine experience which you were raising. . . . I really am not clear and would be glad for guidance as to indications of strength in the representation of distinctively feminine experience in the later fiction.

GB: Would you like to come back on that? Or is there another woman who would like to speak to this?

Sandra Lummis: It seems to me interesting that in the two earlier novels Virginia Woolf does particularly talk about women being attracted to men because they see the *woman* in the man; that she refers to them as in fact having feminine sensibilities. Indeed, Rachel and Katherine eventually accept their suitors for this reason. I don't think this comes up particularly in the later novels, but certainly in those two early ones this is very much felt.

Leena Kore: I think it is not so much that one shouldn't be sympathetic to the fact that a woman can respond to a fiction in the way she described herself responding. But the difficulty I have is that Virginia Woolf herself is constantly aiming towards an androgyny. She herself would say that all the greatest novelists were sexless – I think that's a direct quotation. And it's a difficulty that I would have because I think that, ultimately, she would be very unhappy if we remained on the sides of either men or women as regards her fiction. I don't know how you would answer that, but I think it is a problem.

Margaret Bonfiglioli: I'd like to make some links between some of the things which have come up; and to do so, I have to make use of the word *'reality'*, which has a very peculiar relation to the word 'realism' in the way in which Virginia Woolf uses it. And she uses it – I'm afraid I can't tell you exactly where – to talk about the 'reality' behind appearances. I think that in her novels one gets a sort of *surface* realism, but that beneath that she's going for some kind of truth which perfectly ordinary people seem to perceive through mystical experiences. But mystical experiences are not, in our present culture, very easily spoken about – the sort of oceanic feelings of oneness and so on, which, say, the Oxford Religious Experience Unit is able to collect in a way that suggests that forty per cent of the population have them, and that the non-literary, or not specially literary population, have them. Some of the people who have those experiences think that they're mad, because there isn't a way, or because they're out of touch with the traditional ways of talking about them. Now, it seems to me that some of what we might call feminine experience in Virginia Woolf isn't really confined to women at all, but comes into this area of rather 'unspeakable' experience which our present culture isn't very sympathetic to . . . . I'd like to make some connections with the pursuit of truth in Virginia Woolf and the idea of some kind of 'reality', which is I suppose what some people mean by transcendence.

GB: Thank you. . . . Iris, would you like to come back into this discussion?

IM: Well I felt a lot of sympathy with the last speaker. I would see the best of what she does in this kind, the searching for 'reality' behind appearances, which I think describes what all good artists are trying to do. This takes a particular form with her because of the tremendous net of glittering appearances which she spreads out. I would sympathise with your picturing this as a kind of *ordinary* mysticism – not any sort of weird mysticism, but the intensity of present experience thought of as part of the *value* of the person's mode of being, the value of their consciousness. And this question of value coming in is, I think, important and deep, and is to do with truth. I mean is truth here being displayed? I would certainly connect that with a notion of mysticism and truth, and the word 'transcendence' being in place – though all this would have to be explained rather carefully – rather than mixing it in any way *in* with feminine sensibility.

Ian Gregor: I wonder if I could just come back to a point Hermione was making about wanting to get away from notions of modernism and realism being separate. I can see why you would want to do that, but at the same time it does seem to me that to consider Virginia Woolf as a modernist is very helpful in the sense that it seems to me her art is very much an art of allusion and of hint, and that there is behind the novels an unwritten story which is, I think, very much a point about the novelist's art. We've talked about Henry Green, but I think there's a very fruitful comparison with the archetypal figure of modernism, Eliot himself. The comparisons between 'The Waste Land' and *Mrs Dalloway* are extremely interesting; they both seem to me to get their interest through this art of implication and allusion, and the sense of an unwritten story, rather than through any kind of accumulated story, the detailed story which we associate with realism.

Eric Warner: Could I just pick up on that and see if I can piece together a few things in the discussion? Bernard Bergonzi was talking about the a-historical quality in Woolf, her peculiar relation, at any rate, to what we know as history, and I found myself wondering if this isn't because her sense of history is so dominantly *literary*. She is one of the most well read of a well-read generation, after all, and the sense of allusion that Ian Gregor pointed to, which certainly is there, is almost entirely one of literary allusion. *Between the Acts* is surely the novel where one sees that, inasmuch as the images of past history, in the pageant and so on, are all of literary history. Now I wonder if this doesn't connect with what Iris

Murdoch said, that in some ways she was always writing about *art*, which in turn would strengthen the link with Eliot just mentioned, in view of his conception of tradition, where all art is linked to, or has a sense of communion with, other art which has gone before, and all artists, regardless of their particular time, are in this sense reaching toward the same thing. I wonder if you would care to comment on that?

BB: Well, she certainly is a very literary writer, yes indeed; and to some extent sheltered from the most disagreeable historical realities of her time. But only to some extent. She did live through the First World War and its aftermath, and also through a bit of the Second World War. I think, to go back to *Between the Acts*, I mean, yes, of course, it is an extraordinary kind of *literary* work, with its particular kind of English literary-historical consciousness working through the pageant, and all the pastiche and imitation of earlier literary styles. To look at it one way, yes it is overburdened with literary material. And yet, the history is there, the aeroplanes fly over and drown out the sound of the pageant for a while. That, to me, is emblematic of the way in which the harsher aspects of history come in and almost obliterate the sound of literature.

GB: Yes. One of my pupils once pointed out to me that they're collecting money to put new lighting into the church and, of course, the blackout is just about to descend.

Juliet Dusinberre: I think the lady who spoke about feminine experience and about whether there should have been female novelists on the panel, deserves a follow-up. I didn't agree with Dr Harvey about Mrs Ramsay, because as a woman reader I feel Mrs Ramsay is a wonderful portrait of the mothering consciousness, and that the description of her relation with her children is unmatched in literature. The only thing I've read which can compare with it is Tolstoy's portrait of Dolly Oblonsky in *Anna Karenina*. Now when one has said that, one is back at the question of whether one can separate male and female writers, because Tolstoy has evoked marvellously the feelings of a woman about her children, as indeed Virginia Woolf has, even though she herself had no children. I think that while recognising that area as feminine experience one should allow the creative artist, male or female, to explore it.

What is powerful in *To the Lighthouse* is the search of both sexes for permanence. You get this with Mr Ramsay and his books – will they last? And then he goes and reads Scott and thinks: 'If this is lasting, my books will last', for, as he says, it is so alive, so full of vigour. In a sense this is what Mrs Ramsay is doing when she says: 'You *must* marry; Lily, you must marry, Minta, you must marry', because the way you pass on life and permanence is through having children. What unites both sexes is the concern for how to place permanence against the daily evidence which one sees in the book – and particularly in that war passage – of transience in human life. I am anxious for this distinguished panel of creative writers to talk about their own work and about whether they are conscious of a search for permanence, or whether they think this is something specific to Virginia Woolf and writers of that time.

IM: To comment first of all on what you said at the beginning, I don't like the idea of feminine experience . . . . I think there's human experience; and I don't think a woman's mind differs essentially from a man's, except in the sense that women are often less well educated. The women in Virginia Woolf's stories are always emphasising this fact, that they don't know Latin and Greek and the men do. Well, these things change; now nobody knows Latin and Greek [laughter] . . . . But I think that there are very relevant changes in society, relevant to this discussion, since her time and certainly since Tolstoy's time. You very charmingly tell us about Mrs Ramsay as the ideal mother, then you mention Tolstoy who also does it, so one sees it can be done by either. I think, though, that perhaps for very simple reasons it hasn't been done well in the past, because men and women didn't know each other with such freedom as they do now. I mean, women didn't know men, as is often pointed out about various women writers in the past who found it difficult to portray men, and men didn't really know women. Conrad, for example, had difficulty in portraying women, which is one of the blemishes, I think, in his work. But that's all a sort of footnote to my saying that I don't think there's a female intellect as opposed to a male intellect, or a female artistry, though there are obviously all sorts of accidental features about people's lives which enable them to portray one thing better than another.

But to come to this other thing about transience and permanence . . yes, I think that is a deep thing. I certainly feel it in my own work; but there are so many different ways of being concerned with it. I feel concerned with it in relation to the idea of morality. I think it's often a good thing to ask about a philosopher, and maybe about a novelist, what are they afraid of? That's certainly illuminating about philosophers . . . . I think I'm afraid of relativism. I'm afraid of it turning out that it doesn't matter very much how you behave after all, instead of the importance and reality of goodness being something absolute. And I think that great art does convey this; and that Virginia Woolf's novels very often, though not always, can convey it. And in her case, as you say, very beautifully in *To the Lighthouse*, which is concerned with marriage and with permanence under this image.

                                                                    . . .

JH: It's not clear to me that Mrs Ramsay *is* an ideal mother. That is to say, it's not clear to me that the kind of concern she has for her children and for other people too is offered by the novel as an ideal concern. I would have thought that the novel takes pains to show that a lot of the things she tries to force on people are mistakes, that the marriage she is shown forcing is a mistake, that her prescriptions for Lily Briscoe aren't a help. Actually, I'd have thought that feminine experience and its intensities and difficulties are much more interestingly registered in Lily Briscoe, than they are in Mrs Ramsay. I think Virginia Woolf is most telling on these questions, not in the direct writing about what you feel for your children, but in those *contretemps* where Ramsay comes claustrophobically close to Lily, pressing on her all the exorbitant emotional demands which he feels entitled to make because she's a woman, and which it's clear that he would never make of a man.

Lily also registers very fully and very subtly the problems for any woman wanting to be an artist – and for that matter, a writer – when she ponders the statement 'Women can't write, women can't paint'. Moreover, she also, just by the way, takes in the question of realism or modernism. It's not clear how abstract Lily's painting is; it clearly has a real subject in the house in front of which she positions her canvas. And yet the way the painting is discussed makes it sound to quite an extent an abstract or modernist work, when she discusses the balancing of what are, for her, masses or squares or large areas of colour in the painting. These are discussed in an abstract manner, but at the same time they are felt by her and by Virginia Woolf to involve balancing emotional claims and realities and truths. Finally, I think that here the novel really does converge on the suggestion of androgyny mentioned before – I'd have thought that is one of the significances of that single line which, for Lily Briscoe, is the completion of her painting and the epitome of her vision, balancing the truths of Mr and Mrs Ramsay. All in all, therefore, I think that she, Lily, is *the* sensitive and interesting feminine focus in the novel.

. . .

GB: Perhaps we could, because there was applause when Juliet Dusinberre suggested we should hear more about people's own novels, and the idea of permanence and aim towards transcendence, perhaps we could now ask Bernard and John if they would like to comment along these lines on their own work.

BB: I don't want to talk about the one brief novel I've published in the same context as a great novelist like Virginia Woolf; I find it rather embarrassing. In Virginia Woolf clearly I think one has got what I take it a lot of major art does, which is to try to save something from the flux. This is perhaps *the* great thing about literature; life is flux and falling away, and one is trying to make something of it, something that will endure, something that will last. And analogies with marriage, childhood and so on are very common – Shakespeare's Sonnets and other Elizabethan literature, and in many other genres. So if she's doing that, and I think she is in *To the Lighthouse*, yes, 'create' is the word, surely, create form against dissolution, flux and so on, which by analogy is perhaps what human life is all about. I mean I think one is getting rather exalted, into rather vague terms perhaps; but I think we all understand the underlying gesture. I would certainly accept Juliet's analysis and leave it at that.

JH: Likewise I don't feel it's appropriate to start talking about myself here. Virginia Woolf is clearly concerned with permanence, especially with finding right moments which epitomise someone, the moments by which they are to be associated, to be remembered, which represent them at their best. I'd have thought, to refer tiresomely to Mr Ramsay again, that for him it would be that moment where he leaves the boat and jumps onto the rock, as if he were saying (as perhaps he had as a young man) 'There is no God',

but also with his youth seen in his movements. This is the moment
which the novel opts for as its last glimpse of him; this, if anything is
to preserve him for permanence. She seems to have an interest in this
sort of moment and the kind of timelessness it might have.

GB: And that is a moment of high comedy as well as deep feeling, it
seems to me. I was very struck when right at the beginning Iris
Murdoch was commenting on the comedy and the characters and
the plot . . . .

One of the most curious things about Virginia Woolf's work is
that she is a superb comic writer, but that we tend, somehow, not to
talk about that. I think it is partly because on the page the abrasions
and difficulties (the ways in which the shifting scale of comedy
function) are smoothed out by the silence of narrative. If any of her
work is read aloud, people start to laugh. But what *voice* is that aloud
voice that is reading it? Is there a real obliteration of voice in her
text?

In order for the comedy not to become supreme, is there a kind of
silence in her narrative? Or should we sometimes read her aloud
restore the voice? Hear it as a woman's voice speaking, making
comic difficulties in the text? But perhaps, Iris, I could turn to you
and ask you if you could say a bit more about the idea of comedy in
her work.

IM: Well, I think that humour and comedy are very important in
the novel, and it's difficult to think of any great novel which lack
these, whether in the form of irony, or in the form of what one might
call the deep comic, the sort of Shakespearian comic, which is a
great and marvellous form and very much at home in the novel.
would personally restrict the word 'tragedy'. There are no tragedies
in life; tragedy is an idea that belongs to art, and to very few bits of
art; there are very few tragedies really. Comedy is everywhere in
human life, and is also everywhere in art, and of course particularly
in the novel. I was thinking again about Mrs Ramsay, how
characters are *saved* by the funny bits, which, as Gillian was saying
we sometimes tend to forget because of some dominating feeling we
have about a writer. For instance, Dostoevsky is an *extremely* funny
writer, but people think of him always as a terribly intense, quasi
religious, dramatic writer. And thinking of Mrs Ramsay, I like the
bit where the Mannings are mentioned and someone remarks that
they've got a billiard room now, which surprises her; 'the *Mannings*

have got a *billiard* room'! And then she thinks, 'But I haven't thought about them for years', and then she thinks 'Perhaps they haven't thought about me for years either' . . . . [laughter]

Ellman Crasnow: Yes, we might take this idea of comedy a little further, extending it beyond character by going back to what's been said about women's writing. I think most of the interventions from a feminist point of view have been on the lines of feminine critiques of gender behaviour, models of male and female, etc. But there is also a feminist critique that applies to the way in which you can or cannot speak, because certain institutions give you a discourse. Now there's no doubt that Woolf was very aware of this – there's ample evidence to that effect – so that she simply has an adversary relationship to most of her received models of narrative discourse. And among other things, this seems to make for a great deal of comedy: when I think of, say, the ironic narrator of *Orlando*, this is one of the things that always makes me laugh . . . .

Panel Discussion 2

Eric Warner (Chair), Hermione Lee, Frank Kermode, Elaine
Feinstein

EW: I'd like to start off today's Panel Discussion by focussing on two
themes or ideas which have emerged during this Conference. One is
the question of Virginia Woolf's place today – what do we gain from
a centenary perspective? What do we see now looking back at her
one hundred years after her birth? And the second is a more
difficult, perhaps more interesting idea, which is: is there a canon?
Do we have a Virginia Woolf canon? Professor Bayley's paper this
morning made the rather unusual suggestion that *The Voyage Out* is
one of her best novels, which clearly challenges some notions of that
canon which we may have. So I hope we can start off this discussion
by focussing on these two points.

The first question, that of a centenary perspective, clearly has
links with the question of her influence, and Hermione Lee will start
us off with her thoughts about that.

HL: I think one can talk about the question of influence in a lot of
different ways. When you actually come to ask yourself, is there a
Virginia Woolf tradition? it is a very difficult question to answer. It
is quite easy to talk about a Joyce tradition; it's much harder to talk
about the influence of Virginia Woolf – *except*, as John Bayley
mentioned this morning, on the early novels of Elizabeth Bowen
(In *Friends and Relations*, for instance, there is a scene where a mother
puts her child to bed which is obviously influenced by the moment
where Mrs Ramsay is getting Cam to go to sleep in *To the
Lighthouse*.) But if you look at what's being done in the English novel
now, by women writers (I'm purposely narrowing the field), it is
difficult to find any residual influence of Virginia Woolf. (Iris
Murdoch yesterday disclaimed any great influence from Virginia
Woolf.) I'd like to begin, then, by asking why this is.

If I could just make a rough statement about how I see the
women's novel in England at the moment . . . You could perhaps

divide them into two broad groups. There is the group which gives the call to social struggle, producing the big, opaque, political, George Eliot kind of novel that is being written by, say, Antonia Byatt or Margaret Drabble; or, in another way, by Doris Lessing. Those writers seem to me to produce good, powerful examples of a certain kind of English novel, which in a way attempts a documentary, historical work. Then there is another group which produced glittering, little malevolent texts – very polished, dry, quizzical, ironical. I'm thinking of novels by Beryl Bainbridge, of two novels by a wonderful writer called Caroline Blackwood – *Great Granny Webster* and *The Fate of Mary Rose* – also of a novel by Alice Thomas Ellis called *The 27th Kingdom*, and one by Molly Keane called *Good Behaviour*, both of which are fine examples of this 'glittering', precise and finished mode.

There are, of course, other kinds of work being done. There's the fierce, mythic, feminist kind of writing which is being done superbly well by Angela Carter; and there are more polemical, documentary kinds of younger feminist writers, for example Zoe Fairbairns, whose novel, *Benefits*, I was very struck by. I'm just roughing out the sort of divisions which seem to me to come up over and over again, and I don't think that within them you find a Woolfian novel: a novel which is stylistically interested in lyrical, 'poetic' prose. When you do, it's usually not very good. I was disappointed last year by Maggie Gee's novel, called *Dying In Other Words*, which in some ways is very much in the Woolfian tradition; it's written in a sustained, lyrical, impressionistic prose about a writer writing about her own death. I can think of other writers whom you may or may not know – there's a writer called Janice Eliot, a writer called Rose Tremaine – who I think are trying to do some sorts of Woolfian lyric prose. But it seems to me that on the whole, in England, that tradition is no longer alive. (Perhaps it is in America or Canada, in the work of Margaret Atwood, Tillie Olsen, and before them, Eudora Welty; I was reminded this morning that there are perhaps more Woolfian writers on the other side of the Atlantic.) But I'd like to ask *why*, as it seems to me, there is so little stylistic influence? Is it because the 'psychological sentence of the feminine gender' (which is how Virginia Woolf described Dorothy Richardson's work) is no longer a necessary thing for women writers to do? They don't have to do that any more, they don't have to prove, as it were, woman's sentence? Is it part of the reaction against formalism? a reaction back to nineteenth century realism? I raise all these questions hoping they will come back in the discussion, to see if we can come to any conclusion as to why Woolf's influence is not very strong in the English female novel.

I would like to go on from here, very briefly, and suggest three ways in which I think *is* influential. Perhaps talk about *stylistic* influence is misleading. I want to suggest three more indirect means of influence. The first of these is in her polemical methods. I think that the strategy of *A Room of One's Own* is absolutely trail-blazing and lies behind many major feminist documents: for instance, Germaine Greer's *The Female Eunuch* and Kate Millet's *Sexual Politics*. What Virginia Woolf does in *A Room of One's Own* is to say what has so often been said since: the personal *is* the political; that is, to marry personal feelings about her place with a historical literary critique, illustrated with anecdotes about what is happening to her in her own life. That method, I think, has been immensely influential.

The second form of influence is a kind of playfulness with textuality which I think is there, obviously, in *Orlando*. I was struck when I went to a conference on Virginia Woolf in France in 1973, by the fact that the favourite books, the books that everybody wanted to talk about, were *Orlando* and *A Room of One's Own*. This, it seemed to me, tied in with a particularly French interest in playfulness with the text. We're all very used to novels in which a biographer is writing a biography of an artist, such as Nabokov's *Pale Fire*, or novels in which fictional characters rub shoulders with real characters, such as Anthony Burgess's *Earthly Powers*, or novels which play with endings, such as David Lodge's *Changing Places*, or novels which take off from or make use of other fictional works (a good example is a novel by Sue Roe, who is at this Conference, called *Estella, Her Expectations*, which derives from *Great Expectations*). And aspects of Virginia Woolf's work are influential on all these kinds of fictional 'playfulness'. The third way in which she might be thought to be influential, is her interest in the comedy of embarrassment. I was delighted to listen to John Bayley talking this morning about *The Voyage Out* and *Between the Acts* in this way. *Between the Acts* is full of embarrassing conversations which don't get off the ground, in which people can't or won't say what they want to say. I'll just give you a brief example from *Between the Acts*, which is from the discussion about the painting of Bartholomew's ancestor:

'That,' he indicated the man with the horse, 'was my ancestor.

He had a dog. The dog was famous. The dog has his place in history. He left it on record that he wished his dog to be buried with him.'

They looked at the picture.

'I always feel,' Lucy broke the silence, 'he's saying: "Paint my dog".'

'But what about the horse?' said Mrs Manresa.

'The horse,' said Bartholomew, putting on his glasses. He looked at the horse. The hindquarters were not satisfactory.

But William Dodge was still looking at the lady.

'Ah,' said Bartholomew, who had bought that picture because he liked that picture, 'you're an artist.'

Dodge denied it, for the second time in half an hour, or so Isa noted.

What for did a good sort like the woman Manresa bring these half-breeds in her trail? Giles asked himself. And his silence made its contribution to talk – Dodge, that is, shook his head. 'I like that picture.' That was all he could bring himself to say.

'And you're right,' said Bartholomew. 'A man – I forget his name – a man connected with some Institute, a man who goes about giving advice, gratis, to descendents like ourselves, degenerate descendents, said . . . said . . .' He paused. They all looked at the lady. But she looked over their heads, looking at nothing. She led them down green glades into the heart of silence.

'Said it was by Sir Joshua?' Mrs Manresa broke the silence abruptly.

'No, no,' William Dodge said hastily, but under his breath.

And so on . . . That conversation, which I think is very funny and very uncomfortable, and contains what Jane Austen called 'the little zig-zags of embarrassment' between people who are too close in a small group, that conversation I think has its legacy in Pinter. Nobody's mentioned Albee's *Who's Afraid of Virginia Woolf* yet – I thought they would have done by now – but a lot of what goes on in modern domestic drama may owe something, perhaps unconsciously, to Virginia Woolf. The awful, hostile, ominous silences in the plays of Pinter may have something to do with her.

So to sum up what I've said: I think it is surprising that she's not more stylistically influential in England at the moment, particularly among women writers, but I think there are these other rather odd ways in which she is influential.

EW: Thank you Hermione Lee for that extraordinary survey of the present. I'm sure you've sown many seeds for the discussion to come. I'd like to turn now to Frank Kermode and ask him: is there an influence? Is there a tradition?

FK: Well, I was going to say that nobody writes like Virginia Woolf, but I haven't read as many people as Hermione Lee; if she says there are *some* influences, however attenuated, then I suppose we have to accept that. I find that the novelists I know that she mentioned, which are the ones that belong to a particular group, like Beryl Bainbridge, Caroline Blackwood, and possibly Penelope Fitzgerald, . . . don't make me think at all of Virginia Woolf. I have just read this summer forty unpublished novels for a competition, and they're of all sorts and descriptions; but not a single one of them whatsoever owed any debt that I could see to Virginia Woolf.

Now I think that this *negative* result is in its way as important as the positive attenuations that Hermione Lee mentions. I think we've taken our decision against the kind of novel that Virginia Woolf wrote; and this is just a matter of empirical observation: people don't do it any more; they're not likely to do it any more. When they do anything like it, they do it not under the influence of Virginia Woolf but under that of the French New Novel. In other words, I believe – and the Chairman says let's be provocative – I believe that the revival of interest in Virginia Woolf is a sort of epiphenomenon of the revival of feminism, and has very little to do, really, with literary substance. That substance I would describe as being defined by what happens to her as she gets older and, on the whole, better. When you get to *The Waves*, which I find – and I use the word without any kind of emotional charge – an intolerable novel, I mean I find it intolerable in that it makes me sick, in fact, to try and read it, there is one thing that interests me very much, and that is what Bernard has to say about narrative, about stories. You remember he says he is tired of stories: 'Life is not susceptible, perhaps, to the treatment we give it when we try to tell it', he says. And he goes on to say that in order to do anything of that sort we have got to devise what he calls 'a little language, such as lovers use'. Now I think that *unrest* with the boring requirement of narrative and all that goes with it, characters and so on, actually grows very strong in Virginia Woolf, until we get to what I take to be her undoubted masterpiece, *Between the Acts*. There, she actually writes into the story itself the line, 'Don't bother about the plot; the plot's nothing', which, of course, is absolutely true of it.

Now the canon was mentioned, and I think if you have somebody in the canon (there is such a thing and it's very important), if you have a writer in it you can't pick and choose, you've got to have the whole lot. I mean if you have *Hamlet*, you've got to have *The Merry Wives of Windsor* as well; and if you have *Between the Acts* and *To the Lighthouse* (which are the ones I would choose if I were simply picking), you've got to have *Orlando* and, I suppose, *Flush* as well. But the two works that seem to me real peaks, extraordinary achievements, are *To the Lighthouse* and *Between the Acts*. And they are in some ways balanced, because whereas *Between the Acts* is rightly and properly an extremely self-indulgent piece of work, *To the Lighthouse* is actually a very rigorous piece of work. What it's concerned with, I think interestingly in view of the opening topics of this discussion, is partly the relationship between making some kind of formal presentation and the actual stuff of life. You may remember we heard yesterday that *To the Lighthouse* was a way of exorcising, I think the exact word was 'negotiating', rather curiously used, her relationship with her father. But what she thought it was, was an exorcising of her mother; she says so. And I think that fits the book very well, because you have to choose between the mother of a child, sitting at the window, and the triangular purple patch in Lily Briscoe's painting. This is expressly put before you, and while the book is telling you about characters, it is also very much concerned with what is called 'the balance of masses'. It is about getting things together in a picture plane, which has to be two things: it has to represent something, and to be something at the same time. And it is Lily Briscoe and Miss La Trobe who actually get things together while all about them they're falling apart. And they get them together, as Miss La Trobe does, by *removing* what is called reality.

So, to my mind, *To the Lighthouse* is a kind of extraordinary intellectual achievement which is meant to balance these competing requirements of the novel, but which will lead in the end to that 'little language' which dominates *Between the Acts*, and which in fact is much rougher on reality. It is precisely the sense that to get it all in, to produce some kind of impossible *summa*, which Virginia Woolf always said she was trying to do, what you need is this extreme, linguistic self-indulgence (though that's not precisely what I mean; I'll try to define it more clearly later), and on the other hand you need this intense attitude to form and to writing as something that is, to the writer, when writing, actually more important than the world – indeed the most important thing in the world as it's the only way in which the world can be fully represented. It's a sort of formalism which, as I say, we have now pretty well given up. I don't think any of the witty, strange, sometimes bizarre women writers of today have any notion, really, of what Virginia Woolf was trying to do in that last novel. I don't think that the interesting things in modern fiction – and there may be more of them than I suppose; Hermione Lee suggests there are – I don't think they have any connection with her. *This* is the road not taken; this is where we turned away and went perhaps backward, but certainly in a different direction, with a different notion of what the proper relation of novels to the world should be.

EW: Well, Elaine Feinstein, down the road not taken . . . Do you agree?

EF: It certainly is a road I haven't taken myself; I'm not sure whether it is closed forever. There are some reasons I could suggest why I haven't taken it, which aren't scholarly reasons but personal ones. You will have to forgive me since I am not a scholar and I speak more personally than the speakers who went before. I'm not attempting to evaluate Virginia Woolf's work, some of which I admire a great deal – *To the Lighthouse* which has already been mentioned, particularly, and *Mrs Dalloway*. For me . . . I began as a poet, and I felt that the business of language, when it aspired to the lyrical, was to do in some way with song; and that there was another kind of language, which was much more closely related to speech, which was the business of the novel. And Virginia Woolf, it seems to me, sits somewhere between the two, sometimes extremely elegantly, sometimes awkwardly, often (I'm glad to be reminded) with a wonderful sense of the absurd, and the absurdity of the posture. But in my case, since I write both poetry and prose now, I can sort of chart a development in which I've moved away from the early modernist novel.

When I began writing novels, which was rather late, there was a continuity between my first novel's *voice*, and the voice of my poetry. And I know 'voice' is not a very fashionable word to use, and I'm aware that one is supposed to be looking for a text, and that the 'voice' is in some sense a fiction, an imagination. And yet, when I write poetry I try to notate it for the voice; and when I wrote my early novels, they were also aimed to catch, not perhaps my own speech, but a kind of idealised version of its pauses. I think, actually, it may have been Quentin Bell who's here, and who will remember if it is, who speaks of Virginia Woolf's writing for the mind rather than the speaking voice; it is the movement of the thinking mind. But *my* thinking is not as syntactically controlled, I find, as writers who want to reach the lyrical in any kind of Virginia Woolf tradition that I could imagine. So that in my early novels I tried to catch the speaking voice, and I tried to catch the movement of the mind that frequently ends uncomfortably, without finishing its sentence . . . as I may be doing now.

So, in a way I have been influenced by a tradition which Professor Kermode says is dead; that is, I have tried to connect poetry back into prose through *rhythms*, which is what I think she is doing, though they have been very different rhythms from hers. But as I have written more novels I have grown away from feeling that entirely works. I suppose the first four of my novels have that quality; but since then I've aimed at . . . quite modestly I've aimed at lucidity, I've aimed at control, really quite nineteenth century virtues, rather than the earlier ones I was speaking of. If I had to say what I felt about Virginia Woolf, looking back on her over the past week in bits and pieces as I have, I think it would be that that trembling, oscillating, rhapsodic quality is actually *not* what I mean by the lyrical, and is in some sense alien to me as a person. I have a feeling that I would have been found too blunt had Virginia Woolf ever met me, that she would have missed altogether all those moments rising from the earthy, and the ordinary and the everyday, which I actually rather prize in my work. I say that without apology.

I think I don't want to form a canon of her work – I'm altogether unfitted to do so in any case – but in actual fact *To the Lighthouse* was the book I reread most recently which I enjoyed the most. And I forgave the incandescence which runs round Mrs Ramsay altogether. I believed in it – not because I've actually ever met anyone who has that extraordinary quality, but I was persuaded of the possibility of such a kind of beauty. I was particularly persuaded of it at one moment, and that was when she was standing at a window and her husband is rather hoping she will say she loves him (and she never does say that, so I don't know why he goes on hoping to hear it; but people are like that, it's very true), and she doesn't actually say it then and there, but she turns and smiles at him. And that moment, it seems to me, is what Virginia Woolf does best, absolutely better than any writer I know. I had that wonderful glow of feeling that, here was a woman who had great power over those that knew her. . . .

Before I end I should say that one thing I felt I had in common with her was something which has nothing to do with the novels at all, but a way in which I felt her material *rose* in her. She speaks of writing by accretion . . . I know she drafted things many times, but I think that is how things come most truly. She speaks about the line that she drew in *To the Lighthouse* and then how things accreted around it, and that is a magnificent way to write if you can – I identified very strongly with that journal note of hers. What I liked about the idea of accretion as such, is that it did away with the enormously grand-plan novel which is usually dead before it starts, because if you already know what's going to happen in Chapter 10 when you start, I think you easily get a sense of deadness in the writing. I have always admired novelists who gave me the sense they *didn't* know where they were going when they began; they might re-draft it when they found they had got to the wrong place, but they didn't actually know where they were going as they were writing. Thus they let the story and the characters develop or accrete as the writing progressed. I admire Virginia Woolf very much for this sense.

EW: Thank you, Elaine. Well we seem to have some sort of feeling that Virginia Woolf is a value that we look back upon, if not exactly an influence on other writers directly, a point I think we've reached before during these two days. I just want to pose a question here, which maybe the panellists will care to comment on, a question that takes up Frank Kermode's point about her representing a road not taken in contemporary fiction. I myself see Virginia Woolf very much in the tradition of Henry James, whom no one has mentioned, in the sense that she is clearly concerned with a drama of consciousness, a drama of perception, and also that at the core of many of her works we find an epistemological quest, some search for knowledge as it relates to *value*. We spoke yesterday of Mrs Ramsay being a kind of luminous value which arches over the novel, and though this was rather slighted, that's actually one of the things I like about the book. And if we think, for instance, of that very touching moment in *To the Lighthouse* when Lily in her room comes face to face with Mrs Ramsay and says 'what art was there, known to love or cunning, by which one could penetrate behind Mrs Ramsay's beauty?' to find there the *secret*, 'the meaning of life', this phrase that keeps recurring in the novel – that has always reminded me very much of James, particularly late James. Think of Strether and Mme de Vionnet in *The Ambassadors*; there is this surpassing artful beauty behind which lies some secret, some tantalising depth and value, which he is trying to discover and which keeps eluding him.

I think this search for value and meaning, this epistemological quest if you like, *is* a persistent concern in her work. And I think perhaps in that sense one could see it as coming at the end of a tradition rather than at the beginning. Virginia Woolf is usually referred to as this archetypal modernist figure, who liberated fiction from the nineteenth century; yet I sometimes wonder if it isn't richer to see her as the culmination, the climax of the tradition of the late nineteenth century novel. She is really this kind of mediator. We've talked about her in a position of balancing opposites, and opening up different sorts of complexities in that pose. And I think of her very much in that way, as balancing the great literary heritage of the nineteenth century, of which she was *so* conscious, so aware, with the sense of how it could be, not so much extended as brought to a certain perfection, or climax. She does, as many people throughout these two days have testified, retain a subtle but tenacious hold on such things as character, narrative, plot and soforth. Therefore, I don't think it is surprising to see that it's the road not taken, if you look at it in that way; in a sense there was no further to go along that road. Would you like to come back to that Professor Kermode?

FK: Well, I don't know how you decide whether it's the end of the road or not. But I was reminded as you were speaking of some remarks in the Diary about *The Wings of the Dove*, where she's actually rather far from in love with it. She says that in *The Wings of Dove* there's a great flourishing of silk handkerchiefs and Milly disappears behind them. She didn't like that kind of novel, did she? Milly disappears and then we have all this wonderful prose, this splendid syntactic perfection, and then she concludes that it is somehow rather vulgar and American to write like that. Of course there would be some James rubbing off, just as there was some Joyce rubbing off, I suppose. But it seems to me that her direction, as I understand it, was always totally un-Jamesian. I can't think, for example, that she would of greatly admired *What Maisie Knew*, because it seems to me that it is precisely that sort of theorised trickery that she doesn't really go in for.

EW: If I could just defend my point briefly, I think that the sense of making a great deal of what people think of one another, and what they might be imagining of one another, is the sort of Jamesian strain I was thinking of, which I believe she was often picking up on. Hermione, did you want to comment on this?

HL: Yes, I think it is a very good thing to have raised the *ethical* dimension of her aesthetics, which is what, not in a precise but in a more general way, makes her Jamesian. There's that famous sentence in *To the Lighthouse* where Lily is thinking about her picture and says: 'It was an exacting form of intercourse anyhow. Other worshipful objects were content with worship; men, women, God, all let one kneel prostrate; but this form, were it only the shape of a white lampshade looming on a wicker table, roused one to perpetual combat, challenged one to a fight in which one was bound to be worsted'. The terms in which the artist's task are put there are ethical terms. It's a battle for the right, as it were; you've got to get it right. It's more important than religion, it's more important than relationships. And in that sense I would say that she's in a Jamesian tradition.

Margaret Bonfiglioli: May I interrupt? . . . I was very struck and fascinated by the fact that when *The Golden Bowl* appeared Lytton Strachey said that: 'He's got Bloomsbury. How extraordinary! How did he do it? How did he know?' This made me think about James, not in relation to Strachey, but in relation to Virginia Woolf. And I think that some of her technical methods, of actually putting into the sentence the unspoken, are very close to the ways that James works in *The Golden Bowl* – those 'its' which don't have very clear references, for example. . . . Although she sometimes speaks of James unadmiringly, I can't help but feel that there is some sort of underground, less conscious, connection going on in the prose techniques at least. I feel she learned a lot from him, so I was glad that you brought up James.

Ellman Crasnow: That attitude to James is mixed, isn't it? Because she very much admires some of the ghost stories, she very much admires the autobiographical writing. But your point about this nineteenth century search for what lies *behind*, in relation to Woolf – perhaps one needs to distinguish between a kind of transcendental tic, always asking the question with the expectation of finding an essence, and the realisation in some writers that you might be caught up in that habit but that there isn't anything there. I suppose both of those are present in Mallarmé, and one might see in Woolf a shift from a concentration on the first to a concentration on the second, with the emptiness of *Between the Acts* very much part of the second. That might be one way of looking at it which perhaps doesn't place her so firmly in the nineteenth century tradition you were speaking of.

EW: Elaine Feinstein, did you want to comment on this?

EF: Well, there doesn't really seem to be much more room in that area. I mean, we're agreeing that she perfected things in the novel, and that Lytton Strachey observed a resemblance to James. I think all this must be true. But it still doesn't answer the question, which for the first time actually intrigues me, as to *why* it feels so alien to writers now, when clearly to all of you it doesn't feel alien at all.

FK: I think that's probably an unfair inference. I think it does feel strange to lots of people here.

EF: *Does* it?

FK: Yes, because it's unfamiliar, it's something that has no real connection, if I can repeat myself, with what you do, or what most writers now do . . . .

EW: But I think Elaine's point is that, on the part of the reading public it *isn't* so strange a tradition, that the late nineteenth – early twentieth century novel, coming through Henry James and so forth, doesn't feel alien, feels quite comfortable in fact. Wasn't that what you were saying?

EF: Yes, I think that is what I was trying to say. In a curious kind of way, what has happened is that people are much more at ease with that tradition – not that they don't read contemporary novels, but that people are very comfortable and at home with work which in Virginia Woolf's time didn't, after all, reach an enormous audience. . . .

Roger Poole: May I make some comments? I think this is perhaps the moment to make an objection to the last two days' proceedings as a whole. I have felt, and I think others have felt, that we are more concerned to bury Caesar than to praise him! This has now arisen in an acute form when Virginia Woolf is virtually being written off.

I would have thought that everyone here had come to this Conference because they were interested either in the life or in the writing of Virginia Woolf. So I think I must in a mild way protest on behalf of us all at the present train of events. Today's speakers seem to be inviting us to close shop; Virginia Woolf is now being presented as a writer of the past. So why did all we others, here on the floor, come at all?

Coupled with this invitation to close shop is another worrying thing. There has been a tremendous ambiguity maintained here about the relation of a writer's life to what he or she actually writes. In the last essays of the fourth volume of her *Collected Essays*, Virginia Woolf was quite prepared to talk about the incompatibility of 'the truth of fact and the truth of fiction', and to claim that what she calls 'the creative fact, the fertile fact, the fact that suggests and engenders' is in some sense more real, for a biographer, than what she calls 'the facts of science'. She would always have regarded her own characters as derived from the reality of her own life. And the greatest character that she creates, of course, is her own. That was touched on this morning, when her work was described as a *bildungsroman*. There is a sense in which all Woolf's novels accrete into one huge novel, some vast composite novel, in which what the characters do and say is, to some extent, a self-education.

So, it seems to me a pity, to write Virginia Woolf off as someone who has come to the end of her pitch and relevance. In the face of current American criticism, which has quite dissolved the authorial subject, the writer, it seems to me a precious resource to have a novelist who can create and maintain in being a vast and complex subjectivity, which embraces not only her age but the Victorian age which lay behind it. In other words, she can be viewed as a kind of reservoir, as well as a debt. I will not use a word like 'transcendence', because words like that have a tendency to turn the discourse into a religious one. But our speakers today are imposing a very narrow context on Virginia Woolf. Freud and Marx, for instance, have hardly been mentioned, and it seems to me incredible that we can talk about Virginia Woolf for two days without noting, even in passing, that she belonged to a distinct social group and that she represents a very special class consciousness. Whether one is Marxist or not (and I am not) the question of what significance a writer has for his or her writing community must surely be a central one? And yet this question has been avoided, I think deliberately, for two days, which is why our speakers have progressively led us into this odd position where we are being asked to believe that Virginia Woolf no longer has any relevance for us.

Well, if you avoid all the contexts, you come to no interesting conclusions. We still live in that society which she described, inhabited, and made real. She indicated some of its values; others she maintained. It seems to me that she created in her novels enormous possibilities for fiction which have hardly yet been absorbed, let alone made obsolete – particularly those open to the subject in a largely hostile, menacing world, which is actually something of increasing relevance as we talk. With the book virtually disappearing through the floor and the 39-channel TV just around the corner, what is going to happen to us as individuals, as subjects and as readers, is a very critical problem. It will perhaps not be long before Virginia Woolf is bought and sold on the black market, as something virtually too rare, or too expensive, or too forbidden to have around. Moreover, her depiction of the two sexes, locked in a conflict of interests, bitterly hostile to each others' sexual roles and identities is also relevant today. One only has to look at the Virago Modern Classics catalogue to see this, with nearly one hundred titles by and about women.

So I would like to oppose the view of nearly everyone on the panel, if I may, and insist that Virginia Woolf is only just at the beginning of her career as an influence upon writers. Even if she has reached the end of one kind of narrowly-defined technical prominence, her work points forward to all sorts of other relevances that we are only just discovering. She may well have been thrown into artifical relief by the feminist movement, as Professor Kermode has said, but that cannot disguise the fact that her actual achievement as a novelist is second to none in this century. Professor Bayley proposed this morning that her novels were 'amateur' or in some sense less than professional. This too, I think, must be strongly opposed. If ever a writer *worked*, at draft after draft, it was Virginia

Woolf. The characters in some of her early novels may be too clearly cut from life, some of the late novels may be queried as too experimental, yet all this seems to me a kind of special pleading, a refusal to acknowledge her achievement as a whole. We have also been ignoring the importance of the Diary and of the Letters. As the successive volumes have appeared, these two posthumous works of the novelist have had an enormous literary influence. Indeed only the comparison that occurs to me is that of Kierkegaard, whose *Journals* and *Papers* combine, in a similarly complex way, with the books he actually published, books which were themselves 'indirect communications'.

And all of Woolf's work is in the service of the protection, I think, of some intensely valuable concept of the self, which we stand in great danger of losing. So since the ethical and political judgements one has to make seem to me urgent and necessary, I think I have to oppose the idea that we have ceased to have any use for Virginia Woolf . . . .

EW: I think I'd like to come back to you, Dr Poole, on two points. The first is that the question we were considering was has Virginia Woolf had any influence specifically on *writers*, in the way in which Hermione Lee pointed out that Joyce has. That was an open question; *has* she been influential in that way? I don't think this is avoiding anything so much as focussing the discussion, though indeed we haven't broadened to the issues you raise. So I would like first to ask you how you would answer this question we were considering. Secondly, your remarks were broadening to the whole corpus of Virginia Woolf's work, her letters and diaries, which I thought was an interesting point. Lyndall Gordon touched on it this morning, I think – that in fact she is extremely well documented, perhaps more so than any other writer we have. Would you like to comment further on this?

Roger Poole: Well there's a simple answer to the first point. I haven't read all the novels that were cited before but surely Virginia Woolf has had an influence on *writers* second to none. There is her sheer bravery, for instance. She has transmitted that to two generations of women writers. To write a novel is in itself an act of considerable bravery, I think, since you're working from weakness, you're materialising the immaterial, you're proposing the out-rageous, you're daring things . . . . In that sense I think Virginia

Woolf underwrites a vast complex of authorial dares, just as Joyce does, and makes possible the writing of others in a vast and complex sense. I don't think it is a question of pointing to particular tricks of the trade here. But I very much doubt whether without Joyce and Woolf between them (and Proust; we must add that name), there would be twentieth century fiction in the way we know it, whatever name you name. . . . Woolf's a terrific act of underwriting, I think.

As for the second point, I'm really trying to suggest (although I know this is going to be outrageous) that the Diary as constituted is very near to being a fictional work. It might even be her most interesting novel. If that is so, and if the Diary relates to the novels in some such way as Kierkegaard's *Journal* relates to his 'indirect communications', then we stand before an enormous, complex structure which belongs almost entirely to the future. It seems to me that it's a good thing to have; I'd rather have it than not, and it will be useful in the future I think.

EW: Would you care to comment on this, Professor Kermode?

FK: Well, I can only say that we were in fact talking about practitioners in a rather restricted way. I don't find much to disagree with what Roger said at all. I think the fact that a great many people here read and presumably also teach Virginia Woolf, some or all of her, is absolutely as it ought to be – that the justification of our trade, very largely, is after all to keep alive in the consciousness of our contemporaries the sense of books which nobody voluntarily reads any more. So it would not be strange if a modern writer like Virginia Woolf joined that group. . . . It is our institutional duty to make sure that things of this kind happen.

Incidentally, we have at various moments heard that nobody read Virginia Woolf in the 1950s. I think this is untrue; I think Virginia Woolf was quite widely read in the fifties. My point about the present outburst of celebration for Virginia Woolf, the centenary apart, is partly dependent upon this, to my mind, adventitious element of her association with feminism. But at any rate, that does not seem to me an argument about the quality of Virginia Woolf at all – that's not the point I'm making. And I'm perfectly happy to accept as a historical possibility, or even a probability, that she will, given the sort of phenomenological approach you're advocating, come to seem very much more important and in a very much more restricted way. I was merely commenting upon, as requested, the state of affairs with regard to writing now, insofar as I know that, which, as I said, is not all that much compared with Hermione Lee.

HL: I just want to say two things. One is that I think it would be misrepresentation of what I was trying to say, to claim that I was writing her off. I don't think I was saying that; rather I was saying that I was surprised that she was so little *imitated* stylistically, and I think that that is a very interesting literary fact. Otherwise, I was actually trying to say that I thought she *was* influential. The other thing, just as one way of replying to Roger Poole, is that I myself feel that one of the ways in which she *is* likely to be written off is by the kind of critique which explains her fiction in terms of her childhood sexual traumas. That is likely, it seems to me, to make her seem a less important rather than a more important figure.

                                                                    . . .

Roger Poole: Before we go on, may I reply to the *ad hominem* point, which I suppose must be replied to *ad feminam*? My study of Virginia Woolf's so-called 'madness', to which Hermione Lee referred, is in no sense reductive. On the contrary, I have made an enormous claim for the dignity and rightness of Virginia Woolf in the face of positivist reductive medicine. But may I just add this: it seems to me that *any* writer is writing from his life, from his own self, his own vision. So far as you try to understand that, whether it's a philosopher, a poet or a novelist, you're engaging with the man himself. Whether it's Michel de Montaigne, or Marcel Proust, or Virginia Woolf, you're going behind, as it were, the filigree to find the person who is emitting this fantastically interesting message. Consequently, necessarily, you must know about the life. But the reason why a work like mine is not reductive is that it pays an enormous respect to the concept of the subjective, or to the subject – shall we say, to the subjective experience? – without which no writer could write.

HL: If I were to reply it would be to embark on a long dialogue, so I think we should leave it for now.

                                                                    . . .

Allen McLaurin: I wonder whether, when we are talking about Virginia Woolf's significance for us as writers and critics and readers, we shouldn't be talking about what is, in a way, prophetic in her works. I mean, I would agree with Roger Poole, but in a narrower sense, looking at what is prophetic in terms of literature. And I think we can make the link by taking up Hermione's point about Pinter, which is a very interesting one. Pinter can form a sort of way into placing Virginia Woolf in relation to an earlier tradition, whilst at the same time pointing forward towards what's to come later. If we take, for example, Chekhov's *Seagull*, which has its play within a play, which uses the actual, or supposedly actual, scene as the background of the play, we can see a similarity with the inset pageant and *its* use of the 'real' scene in *Between the Acts*. Chekhov might well have influenced Virginia Woolf's writing. But Virginia Woolf's use of Chekhov in *Between the Acts* points forward to Pinter, particularly his *Landscape* play, where you get a kind of interior monologue, two characters unable to communicate with each other, but their thoughts evoking landscapes. So you can make a sort of continuity. And one final point, if we think about what is prophetic in Virginia Woolf's work, and the sketches and stories were mentioned, we might see a similarity between what she is doing in something like 'The Mark on the Wall', and some of Beckett's later writing. *Ill Seen Ill Said* seems to me in many ways comparable to what Virginia Woolf is doing, even to the extent of its reliance on or influence by painting. So there seem to be things in Virginia Woolf's work which point forward to the future, which we don't have to call 'influence'.

Gillian Beer: Yes, I think perhaps the question of influence itself is bedevilling the discussion, in that clearly influence is not a matter of creating a simulacrum of yourself, but rather of being a resource or a permitting way. Even though Elaine sees no connection between her work and Virginia Woolf's, I think *others* reading it might see connections, particularly in the imagistic force of Elaine's work – which is not in any way identical with Virginia Woolf's – or Fay Weldon, with her use of gossip, of interruption, this extraordinary, wonderful, high skeining of speech. These seems to me to be writers who are not, as it were, cumbersomely indebted to Virginia Woolf, but who have skeined out possibilities that were presented by her.

EF: Well, actually, it's very difficult if you want to make a general point, and you are also standing here, representing part of yourself. I tried to do it by suggesting that in the first four books there were clearly fragments – the use of fragments, in itself, is actually a Woolfian device. Yes, I'd accept that of course. . . . But could I just say something about this question of Pinter? It seems to me really to be a misleading point, and perhaps my debt is misleading too, because clearly Pinter had Beckett intervening, and the use of the pause was there, intervening already, and I don't feel that Beckett got that from Virginia Woolf. So is one really to look for an influence, is it to mean anything to talk about influence? I'm beginning to wonder if it does mean anything. . . . I mean, I knew Pinter at the time of *The Birthday Party*, and I doubt if he had read a *word* of Virginia Woolf; but he certainly had read Beckett. Now if that's an influence, is it in the air you breathe? Is it somehow something you get as part of the culture? Do you have to read the books?

HL: It's like the question about Virginia Woolf and Bergson, isn't it? I actually don't know whether she did read Bergson or not; but presumably she knew about him, and was with people who were talking about him, and so it is a kind of influence, I suppose.

                                                                        . . .

Ian Gregor: Just to remark on this complexity of influence, a name that hasn't been mentioned but that Virginia Woolf herself talks about is Lawrence. And I think her remarks about Lawrence show the sort of switchback nature of influence – where she says, I think from having read *Sons and Lovers*,: 'I read Lawrence again with the same sense of irritation. We have too much in common – the same pressure to be ourselves'. I think that curious mixture of acceptance and rejection suggests the difficulty of the whole business.

I wonder, though, if I could just pick up on a point Professor Kermode was making about *Between the Acts*. I admire the novel too, but I'm a little worried about it in the sense of its being so *knowing*. Professor Bayley this morning put a good deal of stress on *potential* in fiction, undeveloped potential, and these are the kinds of things we tend to respond to. It seems to me that in *Between the Acts* everything has been weighed, and calculated, and designed, and I don't feel out of that novel other novels burgeoning, in the way in which one feels out of a great fiction. I wondered if you feel that built into the very brilliance of interrogation of the art, there is a kind of scepticism which seems to forbid further advance. So that it might be her last novel in more ways than one. . .

FK: Yes, I think this is why I called it self-indulgent. It is, I think, gloriously and perfectly justifiably so; and if anybody was going to develop undeveloped potential in Virginia Woolf, they probably wouldn't start from *Between the Acts*. It has a sort of finality; it is the last chapter of the long autobiography that Roger Poole speaks of, in a way, and it's full of wanton . . . jokes, really. Someone, I think it was Gillian Beer, actually mentioned yesterday the forbidden subject of Virginia Woolf's humour; well I think there's a good deal of it in *Between the Acts*. But it is of a sort that derives from or depends upon, her own dialectic to an extraordinary degree, and I don't think anyone would dream of trying to mimic that dialectic. So, no, it hasn't got potential in that sense.

Index